ON THE BRO

James MacManus graduated from St Andrews University in Scotland in 1966 and has worked as a reporter and foreign correspondent for a number of national newspapers in the UK. He was the Paris correspondent, Africa Correspondent and then Middle East correspondent for the *Guardian* between 1974 and 1986. He joined *The Times* in November 1992 as Assistant Editor and took over as Managing Editor in September 1996. He is now Managing Director of the *Times Literary Supplement*. His first book, *Ocean Devil, The Life and Legend of George Hogg*, has been made into a feature film called *The Children of Huang Shi*, directed by Roger Spottiswoode. *On the Broken Shore* is his first novel.

Also by James MacManus

Ocean Devil, The Life and Legend of George Hogg

JAMES MACMANUS

On the Broken Shore

HARPER

Harper
An Imprint of HarperCollins*Publishers*
77–85 Fulham Palace Road,
Hammersmith, London W6 8JB

www.harpercollins.co.uk

This paperback edition 2010
1

First published in Great Britain by
HarperCollins 2010

A catalogue record for this book is
available from the British Library

ISBN: 978 0 00 733860 3

Set in Sabon by Palimpsest Book Production Limited,
Grangemouth, Stirlingshire

Printed and bound in Great Britain by
Clays Ltd, St Ives plc

In memory of my parents,
Niall and Fiona.

Don't give your heart
On the broken shore
Where seals and sea dreams
Sing love's song

For wind and wave
Will take your heart
And drown your dreams
On the broken shore

Anon. translated from the Gaelic by Leo Kemp

PROLOGUE

The teak tree had been 25 metres in height and weighed four tonnes when it fell to a chainsaw somewhere in the deep south of Brazil. It had been stripped of its branches, hauled from the rainforest and trucked to the port of São Paulo in a shipment of 400 similar sized hardwood trunks.

He knew this because in the madness of his grief he had spent hours researching the three month journey of that single tree from the rainforest to the coastal waters of Cape Cod.

He worked out how old the tree had been, how many years of rain and sunlight had nurtured it, and how and when it had been logged.

Most hardwood from the rainforest was trucked over-land to Central and North America. He knew that just as he knew this consignment from the south of the country was sent to São Paulo to take the cheaper sea route to North America. At the port it had been loaded into a container which had been hoisted on to the deck of a cargo vessel.

Ninety miles out in the Atlantic off the New England coast en route to Boston the ballast had shifted in a storm. One, just one, container had broken its deck moorings and gone overboard. The end-gate locking mechanism had snapped and.ten prime teak trunks spilt into the sea. Four days later one, just one, had found its way into the path of his Zodiac boat. He was left only with the mystery of the cruel fate that had chosen it to be the instrument of his son's death.

Cruellest of all it was his fault. Well, that's what she thought anyway.

He'd taken Julian on his first seal-watching trip to Monomoy Island, a couple of miles off the Cape Cod coast, although the distance from shore kept shifting, and the latest storms had almost turned the eight miles of sand and scrub into a peninsula.

It was September three years ago, a calm day after the holiday crowds had gone. The Cape was winding down. Julian had been on at him to go for months. His mother said the Atlantic was the Atlantic whether you were twenty yards from shore or twenty miles. And it was no place for a boy. But Julian was his father's son, and alongside all the passions of a 10-year-old – the Boston Red Sox, the endless planning that he and his friends put into catapult attacks on the seagull population of Falmouth Heights Beach, – was a desire to see what Dad really did on his research trips.

'Lowering microphones into the water, Dad? Why? What for?'

'Good question,' said his mother.

It was a calm day, but the swell had strengthened as they passed Gansett Point and headed north-west up the coast past the villages and beaches that carry Native American and pilgrim history in their names: Washburn, Maushop, Popponesset, Mashpee, Cotuit, Wianno.

About a mile off Point Gammon, with Hyannis point in clear view, their boat had struck a semi-submerged object almost invisible in the water. The Zodiac had been moving fast, maybe 15 knots, and had slid over it, but the propeller shaft of the outboard motor had caught the trunk and flipped them over. They had both gone into the water.

Julian's lifejacket had been on, and he should have been fine, but his head had struck something hard, maybe the outboard motor, maybe the teak trunk, as he hit the water. He never recovered consciousness. He died in the Boston general hospital three days later. Double cranial fracture and brain haemorrhage, said the doctors. He hadn't stood a chance.

Julian's school, like probably every other one in the United States, had campaigned on all the great environmental issues of the day: Save the Rainforest, Stop the Whale Culling, Recycle your Household Waste. Posters had been made, letters written to Congressmen and company executives, and plays performed on the school stage. It was what schools do so well. And Julian had helped create the rainforest poster, a 36-square-foot laminated work that had been given pride of place in the entry hall. Monkeys and parrots had been drawn into a rich green canopy, below which the trunk of every tree in the forest was carefully named. Teak, Rosewood and Tropical Oak were the mighty giants of the forest. And below that was a chart counting down the years, with 2049 as year zero. No more trees in the rainforest, unless the world stops the logging. Then the world will pay a terrible price.

And I've already paid the price, he thought. Here was death delivered to my son from the endangered rainforest in a sequence of events and with astronomical odds that no computer could ever calculate.

MAY

ONE

This was the best time, the time before the tourists arrived in their hundreds of thousands, the time when the winter gales had stopped battering this bent arm of land thrust into the Atlantic, a time when Cape Cod allowed you to look back on the harpooners, sailors and fishermen who shaped its past while urging you to put your dollars down and book a whitewashed shingle house for the summer.

May was always a good month on the Cape: buds breaking on the beech, birch, hemlock and maple trees, the old elms throwing a green tracery of young leaves against a spring sky, beach rose plants showing the first pink blooms; young birds on the wing along every stretch of shore – dunlin, sandpiper, yellow legs, oystercatchers, egrets; seal pups wearing big eyes and grey whiskers flopping on the sandbanks; and prices half what you were going to pay after Memorial Weekend at the end of the month.

Leo Kemp dropped in on the Foodworks café in Falmouth for a breakfast of free-range scrambled eggs and a mug of fair-trade Colombian coffee: Foodworks was run by a bottle-tanned Californian princess who wore bright green eye shadow and a T-shirt that said *Overnight Sensation* on the back and *You Are What You Eat* on the front. Leo paid $12.35 including tip for breakfast. It would be a third more in ten days' time, he thought.

He had left Margot asleep in bed, lying on her back with Sam's head nestling in the crook of her outstretched arm. Sam who at 16, half-woman, half-child, still burrowed into their bed at unreasonable hours of the morning. Two careless, sleeping faces framed by a tangle of fair hair.

The old Saab 900 pretty much drove itself the four miles to the Coldharbor Institute for Marine Studies while Leo let his mind drift to his nine o'clock lecture with the new class. They were second-year marine biology post-graduate students. For those who persevered – and the dropout rate was high – their Ph.D. would lead to more postgrad studies, a year or two of fieldwork, a series of papers in academic journals, maybe a book, and then on to the lower rungs of academia, where they would begin their scramble up the ladder towards tenure.

If you sat them down and asked them why they wanted to study oceanography, the answers would be variants on a single theme: climate change. Fair enough, thought Kemp: the oceans and the weather are inextricably linked; but the answer missed the real point.

And if you asked them what they really, really wanted

8

to do with their careers, the honest ones would admit that they would prefer to stay and work here at the Institute.

And why not?

Coldharbor, as Leo had tried to convince himself far too many times, was a great and beautiful place in which to learn and teach; a place in which to enjoy a comfortable lifestyle, raise a family and grow old gracefully.

And it was true. The Institute dominated what had once been a little fishing village and was now the main terminal for the ferries that ploughed to and from Martha's Vineyard, fourteen times a day in winter, eighteen times in the summer. Apart from a handful of restaurants, bars and tourist souvenir shops clustered around the terminal, and several hundred holiday homes for the yachting crowd, the Institute pretty much *was* Coldharbor.

When the pilgrims first came to the Cape in the 1620s they found to their amazement that the local Wampanoag Indians were already expert whalers. Canoes made from birch branches and animal hide carried those fearless fishermen on hunting expeditions into the Atlantic armed only with stone-headed arrows and crude spears attached to short lines with wooden floats.

The Coldharbor Institute saw its researchers and scientists as the intellectual equivalent of those daring early fishermen: seekers after the secrets of the seven great oceans of the world, rather than the oil and blubber of the mighty cetaceans that swam in them.

Here the world's leading marine biologists and scientists from every discipline of oceanography gathered to study the salinity and density of the oceans, the currents that swirled within their uncharted depths, the topography of the seabed, the effects of wind on the sea and wave on the shoreline.

Coldharbor also concerned itself with the behaviour of sea mammals: whales, dolphins and seals, the warm-blooded, oxygen-breathing creatures that inhabit our oceans. But the stars of the Institute's repertoire were the deep-sea submersibles, known more prosaically as autonomous underwater vehicles, which could descend to depths of 17,000 feet and which, with the ocean-going vessels that supported and launched them, all operated from this small harbour on the Cape.

Leo Kemp was a part of this family of scientists with a solid body of published research to prove it. A family – that was how the Institute thought of itself: a community of researchers, educators and explorers, bound together by loyalty and a common cause – unravelling the secrets of the oceans and of the fish and the mammals that live in them.

It had been a long, blustery winter, followed by an unusually warm spring. Crossing the quad, Leo felt the warmth of early summer on his back. He looked at the line of modern buildings, all steel, chrome and glass, functional but not inelegant, that stretched along the ridge overlooking Vineyard Sound. Research centres, laboratories, aquaria, offices, libraries, lecture rooms; all the academic infrastructure to drive the institute forward on its mission.

And there was plenty of money to make it happen. The Institute's president and chief executive, Tallulah Bonner,

55 years old and with a treacly Southern drawl that stretched all the way back to her home town of Atlanta, made sure of that. 'Bonner's bounty', they called it.

Chief Executive Bonner understood big money. She knew that for every big private donation there was always a payback.

Every year at the annual financial review with the Board of Governors she made the same speech. Coldharbor was a private institute that received funds from government departments, especially the US Navy, she reminded them. But it relied mostly on private endowments from the wealthy.

'Big donors are not putting a down payment on eternity when they give to us. Sure, they get their name up somewhere carved in wood or stone. And they're not looking for gratitude, because the rich can buy that any day of the week. No, what they're looking for is *fulfilment*. They want the assurance they're making a contribution to the development of scientific knowledge on which the future of the human race depends. And, gentlemen, I make damn sure they understand that their generosity is critical to our mission.'

And she did. She knew exactly how to make the super-wealthy feel good about giving.

'The rich are like you and me when it comes to dying. They want to look back and feel they've done something with their life.'

At elegant fundraisers in New York and Boston, Tallulah Bonner knew better than to waffle on about the strategic importance of oceanography. Donors would always give for a good cause, and she gave them that cause through

11

the simple but persuasive argument that the dawn of the space age should never detract from the study of marine science.

Let NASA spend trillions proving that there was no life on Mars, but spare a few hundred million for the study of what really mattered, the oceans that covered four-fifths of the earth's surface.

Luckily the Pentagon had supported this thesis, or at least accepted that oceanography had an important if secondary role in mapping out future war scenarios. Submarines had proved themselves in the cold war era, and their territory – the canyons and valleys that shape the landscape of the ocean floor – was exactly where Coldharbor devoted the bulk of its research.

So while Houston and the space cowboys took the lion's share of the money – and the glory – Coldharbor quietly took in enough funds to get on with what really mattered.

Trouble was, thought Leo, what really mattered on a warm morning, when the beaches were empty and the sea clean and fresh, was getting even a handful of students to listen to him.

He took the stairs to the second-floor lecture hall two at a time. His father, a retired doctor from Melbourne, had always told him that lifts were a greater health hazard than nicotine: 'The elevator has contributed more to the high rate of heart attacks in America than cigarettes, alcohol and fatty foods put together.' This oft-stated paternal thesis translated into equally frequent advice that not only should his son never take a lift, but that he should always eat porridge for breakfast.

His father was a living proof of the validity of his own advice, having reached the age of 92 without ever having taken a lift, or so he claimed. The fact that he continued to smoke and drink well in excess of the most liberal health guidelines merely confirmed the aged parent's view about Mr Otis and the invention that had transformed urban skylines around the world.

There were thirty postgraduate students in the class but, as Leo had guessed, just twelve faces looked up from their iPods, BlackBerries, magazines and even a few copies of the *Boston Globe* as he walked in.

The tiered ranks of empty seating that rose before the podium seemed a perfect comment on the lecture subject: language and communication among mature pinnipeds.

Leo placed a sheaf of papers on the lecture stand. There was a reluctant rustle as the students stashed their papers, detached themselves from their earplugs and swung their attention to him.

He began with the traditional welcome, wishing them well in their studies. He then left the podium and walked up the staircase that divided the seating, speaking without notes. It was an old trick, but it always worked.

'At the beginning of this course, I just want to say two things. First, we humans are defined not by what we know, but by what we do not know. The science that has brought you here, like all scientific disciplines, has no final frontiers, and it never will have.'

He explained that this world of theirs was a water planet. Their forebears had crawled from the oceans millions of years ago and begun to climb the evolutionary ladder.

Many millions of years later, when man first emerged from the African rain forest on to the savannah and was forced to stand upright – some five million years ago – the marine mammals, the seals, dolphins and whales he had left behind in the sea, were fully formed and living in a complex ecosystem that had sustained them and us ever since.

'Yet throughout human history we have slaughtered those mammals, and today we have gone a step further. We have begun to destroy the environment on which this planet depends – its oceans. We are urbanising and industrialising the great seas of the world.

'So as you progress through your studies, I want you to remember that our future on this planet depends not on the exploration of space – important though that is – but on understanding the oceans that surround us and first gave us life, and still do today.'

Leo paused at the top of the staircase. Twelve heads had now turned, necks craned to keep him in sight. Was that a flicker of interest down there? Had his words triggered the smallest thought processes in those heads? Probably not.

He walked back to the podium.

'What I want to talk about today is the language of sea mammals, and especially seals. Until recently we did not know that they communicated at all. Now we do know that whales, dolphins and seals all have their language, but we don't know how they use that language. These are highly intelligent creatures – we know that – but how are we to decode the intelligence in those remarkable brains?'

A few pens were moving across the big spiral-bound notepads. It was always the girls first. Then the boys would follow suit. Pretty girls, too. Mostly American, but some from Finland, Norway and Japan, where they took marine science seriously. So seriously in Norway that they slaughtered seals as vermin and even ate them.

Leo decided to wake the class up.

'We're going to take a break,' he said, and pressed a switch.

They all stirred, even the boys.

The room darkened. The students sat up, suddenly interested; a screen came down at the touch of a button.

'You are here to study marine biology. Why? Because the oceans around us hold the key to our survival on earth?

'Maybe.

'Because the seas cover four-fifths of the earth's surface, and we know so little about how they work?

'Definitely.

'And perhaps because we need to get hold of this fact: twenty-first-century science, science that can take a man to the moon and land a machine on Mars, cannot answer some fundamental questions posed by our oceans. Why not? Take a look at this.'

Leo pressed a switch. He loved and hated the Institute in almost equal measure, but on the love side came a real respect for the technology bought by all those endowments. Things really worked. Back at St Andrews University in Scotland where he had begun his career some eighteen years earlier, you were lucky to find a slide rule that worked.

The screen glowed into life, showing a snowy landscape. The camera tracked to the foreshore of a broad,

15

tree-lined estuary, with a soundtrack of running water and wind in the leaves. It then zoomed in on a group of wading birds the size of small seagulls. The birds had brown-flecked plumage, long legs and curved beaks. They walked slowly along the water's edge, pausing to stab their beaks into the soft mud and then throwing their heads back to swallow whatever morsel they had found below the surface. Suddenly alarmed, the flock wheeled as one into the air, their outsize wings lifting them rapidly away from whatever danger they had perceived.

A voice-over said: 'The bar-tailed godwit has been tracked by the Pacific Shorebird Migration Project via satellite tagging, and has been proved to be the world's avian migratory champion, flying further non-stop than any other migrating bird. The godwit flies 10,200 miles south from its breeding ground in Alaska without stopping in flight. It can make the flight in seven days with the benefit of a tailwind, and can return north in nine days. Incredibly, godwit chicks can make the southbound flight when only two months old. These are amazing journeys, which the latest technology has allowed us to track and feed into our ongoing research into migration patterns.'

Kemp flipped a switch, and the lights came back on. 'OK, what's missing there?'

A hand went up. It would be him. That studious boy from Michigan, Jacob Sylvester, a state scholar. Leo had met his new students at an induction class. He always tried to spot the ones that were going to make something of the subject but it was difficult. Sometimes the shy, silent types produced original thinking in their coursework while the pushy talkers simply regurgitated everything they had read.

Sylvester was a talker; he asked all the right questions and took notes in laborious longhand. He had a Ph.D. and academic career stamped all over him. Rachel Ginsberg wasn't really shy but she pretended to be and looked at the floor while asking complex questions about the marking of grades. She would flash him quick looks from under long eyelashes to see if he was listening and smile slightly when he nodded her to go on. He sensed she was very ambitious and he knew her foxy-faced good looks would take her up the corporate ladder in some big company.

Then there was Gunbrit Nielsen, very serious, very pretty, with slate-grey eyes and a long plaited pigtail. She was far too beautiful to be sitting in anyone's class studying marine biology. She should be on a movie set on the west coast. But here she was in his class working for a Ph.D. that would take her back home to a teaching job in Sweden, marriage to a man with a thick red beard and four children.

He would get to know them well over the course of the year and would watch to see how, just as in the wild, a natural leader emerged from the group. Already they seemed to take their lead from Sylvester, letting him ask the questions.

'Sea mammals, sir. This isn't our subject,' said Sylvester.

Leo snapped out of his reverie.

'Well, clearly a godwit is not a seal, Mr Sylvester. Let me repeat the question: what is missing from that commentary? Something important, really important, that has been left unsaid?'

Silence, heads lowered, sidelong glances: What's he talking about? When's the break?

'OK, here goes. What that commentary did not tell you is that those birds, the godwits, make their migrations without food or water, flying huge distance for seven days southbound and nine days northbound. It didn't tell you that because we don't know how they do it. No one knows.

'Scientists', he continued, 'cannot explain the godwit's ability to lift and transport its body weight of eight to ten ounces for that distance without in-flight refuelling. And science does not like the irrational. The flight of the godwit is incomprehensible to science, because science tells us, and the naturalists tell us, and the nutritionists tell us, that a small bird like that cannot fly such a distance without sustenance.

'We know that swifts and swallows make similar journeys, but they eat their natural food – flying insects – on the wing. Godwits do not. Their food – worms and molluscs – lies beneath the sand on the shoreline. And there are no shorelines at ten thousand feet. They should not be able to survive their annual migration. But they do.

'Mr Sylvester.' Leo pointed to him, arm outstretched, finger extended.

'Yes, sir?'

Leo had the class now; he loved it when he made a breakthrough and grabbed the attention of those media-choked minds, brains buzzing with electronic music, video games, sex, sport and fast food. Cut through the media

18

dazzle with some original godwit-thinking and you find that there is life in the interior of their minds; thin soil maybe, but enough to plant the seed of thought.

'Your point is that a godwit is not a seal?'

'Right on.'

'Absolutely correct, but my original principle applies. It's what we don't know that should interest and excite us, not what we do know. Seals have always had their own language, but we do not know what they are saying.'

The Swedish girl had put up her hand.

'Yes, Miss Nielsen?'

'Why are we only interested in the language of these seals? Surely there is much more to learn about the seas in which they live?'

She spoke in slightly guttural English that Kemp, whose own accent was a mixture of his native Australian layered with lowland Scottish, found hard to follow.

'Well, we have only begun to understand how these mammals communicate. But you are right. Our oceans are all around us – we swim in them, travel on them, feed from them and prepare to make war beneath their waves. Yet we have little understanding of them, or of the creatures that live in them.'

He had said too much. This was very much the way he always kicked off the first lecture, but perhaps he had overreached himself this time.

Time for a surprise, he thought.

'All right. What I am saying is this. Once we understand that the oceans remain the greatest mystery on earth, once we hold that thought in our heads and hearts – yes, in our hearts – then we can move forward. Acknowledge your ignorance. Take nothing for granted. Any questions?'

'But who says we know it all anyway?'

That boy again. Jacob Sylvester.

'Never underestimate the arrogance of the science establishment, Mr Sylvester. Big money goes into science in order to produce answers. Scientists have to play the game and pretend that there are answers. My point to you today is that sometimes there are no answers, at least not ones that conventional science can uncover.'

Then he surprised them: there would be an unscheduled field trip the next day, on the tug *Antoine*. Since only twelve students had turned up he would take them all. Tomorrow was a Friday, and a sea trip would be a great way to start the weekend. They were to meet at the Institute's own landing dock at 10 a.m., he told them. 'Bring wet-weather clothing. Packed lunches and lifejackets provided. See you tomorrow.' He picked up his notes.

'Where are we are going?' It was Gunbrit Nielsen again.

He told her that, weather permitting, they would run up to Monomoy Island – a favoured hauling-up place for grey and harbour seals. They would take hydrophones and recorders and spend the day on the water. Field trips were not picnics, he said, they were hard work.

'And if anyone who didn't make it here today wants to come, please tell them they'll have to wait for another time – the boat has a full complement.'

There was a buzz as the class left. Field trips were popular. As Leo liked to say, what better place for marine biology students than out on the ocean?

He picked up the rest of his papers and walked back
to the car. The 15-year-old Saab 900 had doubled its resale
price thanks to the film *Sideways* a few years previously,
in which the same model had a key supporting role. It
was probably his most successful investment. His cell
chirped: two text messages.

The first was from Sandy Rowan, local journalist and
Leo's occasional drinking companion. Sandy's passions in
life were second-hand books, his cat (called Shakespeare),
Cleo the waitress at his favourite bar in town and the
Orleans wine company, a local vineyard in which he had
made a modest investment some years ago and whose
Viognier-Syrah blend he had pioneered, proclaiming the
result to be better than anything out of California.

*Hoover story really got them going. Watch your back
– and your front.*

The second message was from Margot. An official letter
from the Institute had been delivered at home by courier.
It was from the chief executive's office.

Margot Kemp held the mug of coffee tight in her hands
– no shakes today – and looked out over the roofs of
Falmouth down to the harbour. She was hungry and needed
breakfast. She checked her watch. It was 11 a.m. Call it
brunch then. Betsy's Diner with its large neon sign saying
'Eat Heavy' would do; eggs, bacon, waffles, more coffee,
anything but a drink.

She turned the letter over in her hand: 'From the office
of the President, Coldharbor Institute for Marine Studies'
was engraved on the envelope.

She knew what it would say. Leo had blown it. All that stuff about Hoover the talking seal, the coded attack on the science establishment and the abuse of the big money that flowed into Coldharbor. Add in her husband's obsession with the lobby behind the fishing industry and his unfashionable view that seals had nothing to do with depleted fishing stocks and you had layer upon layer of controversy: press reports, angry letters to the papers, the snide, back-stabbing comments of his colleagues.

He had been warned, of course. The Institute had told him a year ago to stay out of the media, stop giving interviews, stick to his work. It was in his contract, for God's sake. She could recite the wording because she had read it out to him – well, shouted it at him – during one of their many rows.

'In no circumstances must you bring the Institute or its officers into disrepute, nor damage in any way its reputation for academic excellence . . . approval for all media interviews must be sought from the director of communications . . .'

And now it had come to this. She fanned herself with the letter. A warm spring was turning into a hot summer, and it was not even Memorial Day yet.

Well, good. They could get out of this place, she thought.

'Mrs Kemp?'

She turned. Tilda had finished in the kitchen.

'Can I do the bedroom now?'

'No, let's leave it for this morning.'

'You want another coffee?'

'No thanks, Tilda.'

She went into the kitchen to check. It was spotless, as ever.

Tilda even rearranged the fridge letters which said sweet, silly things like *I love you Mum* and *No 1 Dad*, and made sure they also said *We need milk*.

She opened the fridge door. Tilda's attention to detail extended to making sure that every level of the fridge had its own produce: dairy, fruit and meat, with eggs, wine and milk neatly slotted into the side section. Maybe she would have that drink. She took out a bottle of Pinot Grigio. There was enough for a decent glass left in the bottom. She poured it into a tumbler and slung the bottle into the recycling bin.

They had been married sixteen years, nine of them spent here in Coldharbor, where she had watched her husband vanish into a world of his own, a world in which the language of seals seemed to mean more to him than anything she had to offer.

That was what men did, of course, she thought: they displaced you, diminished you and then deserted you. What had happened to her interior-design business? It didn't take a lot of money with it when it went bust, but it took away her pride, her sense of self-confidence. Leo had tried to help, but typically did so in the most hurtful way. 'You're a wonderful teacher. That's where your talents lie, and that's what you should stick to,' he would say. 'Do what you do best.'

She had told him over and over that teaching qualifications gained in the UK did not allow her to teach in America, and that she would have to retrain. But he didn't listen. He just told her to face the facts: she was not good enough to be an interior designer, exterior designer, any kind of designer, at least not here on the Cape; she didn't have the talent. It might have worked in Scotland, where they think haggis is haute cuisine, but it wouldn't here. Cape Cod was stiff with designers, artists, interior decorators and every kind of smart-ass, trendy, boutique-owning fashionista.

The business collapse didn't finish them, nor her drinking, nor his endless belittling of Scotland (why did he hate the place so much?).

What lay between them would always lie between them. It looked down from the mantelpiece, from the painting in the sitting room and from her bedside: Julian with the uncertain look of a 9-year-old in his first school uniform; Julian on the beach, tousled hair and head poking out from a sand burial; Julian aged 10, the last picture, on his bike outside the bookshop on Main Street. He had gone on the research trip in the Zodiac rubber dinghy the next morning with his father.

Margot took the wine into the bedroom and placed it on the bedside table beside the framed portrait of her son. She kissed the tips of her fingers and laid them gently on his forehead. She turned the frame to the wall, drank some wine and lay back on the bed. There were only ever two painkillers that worked for her and drink was one of them. The postman had been, the housekeeper had gone, and Leo was God knew where. She pulled up her skirt and let her hand drift between her legs, fluttering her fingers like butterfly wings.

She thought of the last time at the Squire bar in Chatham, the fisherman with salt tang on his body, the dragon's head tattoo entwined around his thighs with long tongues pointing to his crotch, and whisky on his breath. It was quick, sordid, car-park sex. And why not? It was great. It made her feel good just thinking about it; not because it was any kind of revenge against Leo, far from it. But because, as she told herself, it was my choice, my pleasure, my sex, my lust, and I'll have it how and when I want. I am a mother of two – well, one now – and with a husband lost to the sea just as all those widowed women on the Cape lost their husbands to the sea.

The sea is made of women's tears, they say on the Cape, and they're right. I know how those widows feel. I don't have affairs; too bloody complicated, and anyway, you always wind up with a needy, whining man telling you he loves you more than anything in the world, when all he really wants is guiltless, risk-free, zero-cost sex. I will take my pleasures as and when I want to. She raised herself on to an elbow, drained the glass of wine, took the phone off the hook and reached into the bedside drawer. It was always there, her ever-dependable friend, none too discreetly covered by a clothing catalogue. She wondered if Tilda knew. She didn't care if Leo knew or not. She lay back on the bed thinking of the fisherman with salt on his skin and whisky on his breath.

TWO

The Dark Side was a steakhouse on the main street of Coldharbor with a long teak bar that stretched the length of the building to a small conservatory overlooking the inner harbour, called Eel Pond, at the back. The place was unlit except for candles which cast their flickering light over every table. Summer or winter, day or night, the Dark Side was always the same.

Kemp sometimes used the place for meetings with colleagues and overseas visitors when he felt such occasions would go better with a drink: they always did. But he and Sandy mostly used it as an unofficial headquarters for emergency lunches or drinks when one of them had something interesting to report, gossip to discuss, grumbles to share. Today was definitely an emergency meeting. Kemp bought a copy of the *Herald* and pushed open the swing doors of the Dark Side, standing on the threshold for a moment to allow his eyes to accustom themselves to the gloom.

The *Cape Herald* was a local daily paper packed with the news the locals really wanted: court reports, road works, sewage spills, the latest inane decision of the Barnstaple county municipal authorities. After twenty years on the paper Sandy Rowan was senior enough to leave the small stuff to the trainees who (amazingly) still came in every year from college media courses wanting to learn how to be journalists. Sandy never understood it. Every kid you saw these days was glued to a laptop, mobile or iPod, yet here they were, queuing up, year in year out to work in an industry that created its main product by squirting ink on to pulp made from dead trees.

Sandy specialised in the big stories: the Kennedys in their Hyannis compound (the paper made sure it was very respectful to them); tracking the tourist dollars to check that at least some of local tax-take went back into the sewage-treatment plants, the roads and the schools; and of course Cape Cod's most famous institution: the Coldharbor Institute for Marine Studies.

What had made Sandy something of a Cape celebrity was his weekly column, a collection of controversial news, views and reviews about life on the Cape. The column appeared on Tuesdays, with a photograph that made him look a lot younger than his forty-six years, under the rubric 'Rowan's Ride'.

Sandy did not set out to be controversial, and intensely disliked over-opinionated columnists who peddled fake moral outrage from the dubious vantage point of their own shallow lives. But he took pride in exposing cosy consensual opinions held to be self-evident because they had been repeated for so long. This did not always make him popular.

When a touring theatrical company put on one of the more celebrated plays of the twentieth-century American canon, Sandy had caused outrage with his review, which began:

Eugene O'Neill tried to drink himself to death on the Cape, at his house in Provincetown to be precise. Pity he didn't succeed. Have you ever sat through five hours of *Long Day's Journey into Night*? Try it. It will make the rest of your life feel like you made it to heaven early.

The editor stood by his star columnist, up to a point. But Sandy was never asked to review a play again.

He was already at their table when Kemp arrived.

'The usual, please, Cleo,' said Kemp, smiling at the tall, pale waitress, who had already mixed his favourite drink.

He sat down, checked his BlackBerry, and then pocketed it as Cleo emerged from the gloom with a long glass of chilled green tea, cut with lime juice and ginger ale and served with crushed ice, a slice of lemon and a sprig of mint. Leo called it 'green dawn', a name he had dreamt up along with the recipe. One day he would get round to taking out a patent and would market it as one of the world's best-tasting health drinks – one day. In the evening he added a double shot of vodka, to put a little kick into the health habit.

'Trouble?' said Leo.

'That Hoover piece we did.'

'You mean the interview you begged me to do after that lecture I gave?'

'I didn't beg you.'

'Of course not: you just rang me every day for a week pleading.'

'It was a good story. It was picked up a lot.'

'I know. I did all the interviews, remember?'

'Yeah. Well, I hear that some people are not best pleased.'

'Some people never are.'

'Your people, Leo.'

'Like who?'

Sandy took a gulp of his white wine. 'This is just what I hear. There are people in Boston and here on the Cape who think you brought the Institute into disrepute.'

'Oh, come on,' said Leo. 'That seal died years ago. He picked up a few English phrases and I used that as a metaphor for how useless we are at understanding these animals. I mean, if one seal can learn English, how do we know there isn't a whole ensemble of them out there playing Hamlet three hundred feet below the waves every night?'

'Very funny,' said Sandy. 'But they didn't get the joke. If you'd left it like that, then OK. But it's all the other stuff you threw in: calling the science establishment arrogant, all-knowing, all-powerful – that sort of thing. And then there was all that conspiracy stuff about seal culls and fish stocks.'

'So what?'

'So what? They don't like it, that's so what. The way they see it, a seal that can talk a few words of English is just a joke. What isn't a joke is you telling the world that hundreds of millions of dollars of investment in marine research isn't being spent properly, that it isn't being used to find out the big things we don't know. I mean, that doesn't sit well with the management. It's not good for business.'

'You sound like the chief executive.'

Sandy drank deeply, and then put his almost empty glass on the table.

'Maybe she's got a point. I'm just trying to tell you what they're saying out there. Don't shoot the messenger. You want another drink?'

'No thanks. How do you know about this?'

Sandy turned in his chair to signal for another drink. He's playing for time, thought Kemp.

'We got a call asking for the notes of the interview.'

'From?

'Bonner's office.'

'When?'

'Last week.'

'And you didn't tell me?'

'I was told not to. Sorry.'

'I thought journos were supposed to protect their sources.'

'Everyone knew it was you – your name was on the piece.'

'That's not what I meant. You could have warned me. Thanks a lot.'

Leo stood up, drained his glass and looked down at the unhappy face of his friend. He put a hand on Sandy's shoulder and squeezed it slightly.

'Don't worry. I'll deal with it. I've got a field trip tomorrow. Let's have a real drink tomorrow night.'

Sandy nodded. 'How's the book going by the way?'

Leo shook his head. *The Full and Final Circle of Evolution: Man's Return to the Sea* was long overdue at the publishers, but they weren't exactly biting his hand off for it.

'Don't ask,' he said and walked out, blinking in the bright sunlight.

So that was the letter Margot had mentioned. He should have known Hoover would get him into trouble. The famous talking seal had been dead for twenty-three years, and his story had been all but forgotten until Kemp had reignited interest in the phenomenon and the controversy around it.

He used Hoover in his off-campus sessions with the students. He would take them to the aquarium café in Coldharbor, buy them all coffee and promise to answer any question they chose. One question always came up. How do you know seals are so intelligent; how can you be sure they really communicate with each other; animal noises are just animal noises, aren't they?

So he would tell them the story of Hoover, a seal that not only spoke English but did so in a Maine accent: 'Good morning,' 'How are ya?' 'Whaddya doing?' 'Gedd over here,' and so forth were standard greetings to visitors to the Boston aquarium where Hoover lived most of his adult life.

An orphaned pup, Hoover had been picked up shortly after birth by a Maine fisherman. He had been taken home, put in the bathtub and bought up as the family pet. He was given the name Hoover because of the huge quantity of fish he ate. Even for a fisherman, the expense of feeding a seal soon became too much, and Hoover was given to the New England Aquarium in Boston. And that was where he started talking to anyone who cared to listen.

The jaw structure and vocal cords of a seal are very much like those of a human, Leo explained to his students. The scientific explanation for what Hoover could do was clear. He had simply heard the fisherman and his family talking, and had learnt to mimic their speech. It was still a pretty remarkable achievement for a seal. Hoover remained the only non-human mammal ever to vocalise in this way. The media loved him, and he became the subject of many newspaper and magazine articles, and appeared on TV and radio shows. But marine scientists did not appreciate Hoover. To them he was just a freak, a distraction. When Hoover died in 1985, he was paid the tribute of an obituary in the *Boston Globe*.

And then, years later, when Hoover had been almost forgotten, along came Leo Kemp, with his argument that to dismiss a talking seal as a freak of nature demonstrated exactly the kind of arrogance that Galileo had encountered when he argued that the sun did not revolve around the earth. That may have been stretching it a bit, but the marine science establishment got the point, and they hated him for making it. Leo didn't mind. The important thing was that some of his students got the point too. An animal that can learn to mimic English is a highly intelligent creature.

That wasn't good enough for Jacob Sylvester and Rachel Ginsberg, who seemed to have become his girlfriend. They were regulars at the Q. and A. sessions, along with a quiet red-haired Brit, Duncan Dudman, who spoke with a deep West Country accent, which the American students could not get enough of. It came from Somerset, where the cider apples grow, he explained.

'A seal that can talk is just serendipity,' said Sylvester, straight from the shoulder as usual. 'Parrots can talk. Doesn't prove they're intelligent. I can't see you proved your point, sir.'

Leo rolled out the heavy artillery.

'Consider these facts,' he said, looking at Sylvester, 'and then tell me how you rate the intelligence of a seal. There are two types of killer whale – those that feed only on salmon, and those that seek out seals, dolphins and other whales. The behaviour of these two separate populations of killer whales is so different that they are essentially different species. But they all look exactly alike to the untrained eye – black, with a white belly patch extending up the flanks, a white patch behind the eyes and another behind the dorsal fin. Only small variations in the skin patterns and the shape of the dorsal fin distinguish the two varieties of orca.

'So here is the question: If the difference between the two species of orca is that minute, how is it that seals can differentiate between a deadly foe and its harmless cousin? How do the seals know that there are killer whales within threateningly close range of their pod? A seal's whiskers are like underwater radar, and can pick up minute vibrations or changes of water pressure, converting those signals into data about the presence of food or foe, or a sudden change in the weather.

'Could it be that the seals' acute hearing or its radar whiskers can pick up the whales' own echo-locating communications and decode them?

'Either way,' said Leo, 'the seals always seek shelter in the tumbling surf close to shore when killer whales are nearby. That way they block the whales' locating signals.'

'That's definitely not serendipity,' said Duncan.

Leo looked at Jacob Sylvester. God, the arrogance of the boy. He could never admit there might be another viewpoint than his own.

'OK, I take your point,' he said finally.

Joe Buckland, known to everyone for as long as he could remember as Buck, was a mile off South Chatham on his gillnet boat with nets out for flounder, bass, maybe squid, when the call came to get the tug ready for a field trip the next morning. Buck turned his boat towards shore, grumbling to himself. He liked the money – the Institute paid $400 for a four-hour trip, exclusive of fuel – but why the short notice? He had other things to do.

When his father had bought the *Antoine* from the docks at Boston after the Second World War, everyone had laughed. It wasn't a proper tug, because the builders had gone broke in the Depression and had left the superstructure half finished, with a two-storey plywood box cabin and a bow that reared up like a wounded stag. The *Antoine* was now 80 years old, an ocean workhorse that for years had shipped out of Boston to salvage and assist wrecked or disabled ships in rough seas off the east coast. Locals joked that she should have been in a museum, but Buck said she was as much an American classic as the 1948 Chevrolet, and just as able to do the job.

His father had died in 1952 when Buck was 18. The *Antoine* was all he left his son. Once it became clear that the tug was going to make him some money Buck had torn down the old plywood cabin and built a proper superstructure, fitting for a standard seagoing tug of its day: a two-level deckhouse with the second level split between the open Texas deck and the pilothouse, the highest point on the tug. Here, polished to perfection, was the equipment he had bought second-hand from the breakers' yards: a large manual wooden wheel, the smaller brass power wheel, the polished oak binnacle for the compass. Only the ship-to-shore radio was new.

'What are you going to do with it?' his father's friends had asked. He had his answer when the Institute chartered the tug to take research students up the coast, and occasionally far out into the Atlantic. That was in the early fifties, when the first postgrad students were arriving at Coldharbor. The *Antoine* had paid for herself many times over since then. Now she was on permanent charter to the Institute, and Buck had a regular income, unlike some fishermen, who were reduced to scrabbling for clams at low tide in the off season.

He still fished from March to October, and had his own line of lobster pots out in the season; lobsters were good business, but the money was not regular because the bureaucrats in the Fisheries Department kept changing the weight and size of permitted take. Worse still, they were now charging up to $100,000 a year for a general fishing licence.

Buck had been lucky. He had spent his best years in a business he loved. Now the fish stocks were declining – and Buck well knew whose fault that was – and the industry was dying. Young men still came into the business, but he wondered what for.

His passion for fishing had begun at the age of 8, when his grandfather let him use a small rowing boat on a lake near his home in Massachusetts. It was when Buck was allowed out night fishing on his own that his young world changed.

The *Cape Herald* had interviewed him some years before as the oldest working fisherman on the Cape. Sandy Rowan was a rare journalist, in that he reported exactly what people said in interviews. 'That way you get the truth, and get a feel for the person behind the words even if you do lose the grammar,' he said. So Buck's words were laid out on a centre spread between two huge quotation marks, alongside pictures showing him from boy to man with rods and reels, and finally as an old-timer pointing to the nets on his 43-foot fibreglass day boat.

'Out there on the lake at night the bug bit; I was just a kid but I got this amazing sense of freedom and I suppose responsibility. I mean, I was alone, in charge of the boat, the rods, everything. I could have fallen in or anything, but Grandpa let me go off. I spent as much time with him as I could, and fished whenever I could. When I got older and went out on dates, after I dropped the girl off – yeah, this was a long time ago, and we did that in those days – I'd get the boat out and go fishing on the lake. It didn't pay, so I became an electrical engineer and began going to the Cape at weekends. Salt-water fishing was different. You had to know everything about that damned bitch the sea – currents, tides, weather, and the habits of the fish. I learnt it all. Out there on the ocean you're always thinking – you have to. It was like going to a school you loved.'

The article was headlined 'The Happy Hunter'. Both Leo and Sandy reckoned Buck was the happiest man they were ever likely to know.

Buck had no illusions about the future of the fishing industry. It was almost finished and he wasn't going to spend his last years competing with the other boats for the last fish in the sea. His final destination was a small cashew-nut farm in Hawaii that he had bought back in the fifties, when land was cheap. He had managed to hold on to the farm when he and his wife divorced, and had married second time around to a Filipina called Renee.

Leo had met Buck on his first research trip after arriving at Coldharbor, and long before it became fashionable the two would take Buck's boat and some beer and spend all day on the Stellwagen Bank watching whales. That was when Leo began to understand what was happening to one of America's greatest marine sanctuaries.

Leo drove home the four miles to Falmouth, taking care to keep the needle on thirty. In the off season the Cape police had nothing to do but hand out speeding tickets. That was mostly all they did in the high season, come to that. He killed time over a coffee at Betsy's Diner thinking about the letter; a summons to a meeting, most likely. Tallulah Bonner was a pain, but he had to admit that she did a great job on the money side. The tax-efficient endowments rolled in. Trouble was, he had more than once expressed his doubts to her about how it was being spent.

'Tell me exactly what you mean,' she had demanded. 'Give me an example of what we should be doing that we are not.' When she was angry the treacle in her voice hardened and the Southern drawl tightened.

So Leo tried to tell her. It was difficult, he said, because he was talking about a culture here: a Big Science culture. Hubris, arrogance, the overwhelming view that we know most of what there is to know about planet earth and that we just need to fill in a few gaps.

'Examples,' she had snapped at him. 'Give me examples.'

So he told her how some years back an eminent physicist had dropped a deep-water recording probe into the

Southern Ocean, and at 12,000 feet below the surface, well beyond the diving depth of a whale, it detected something enormous, really enormous, passing beneath it.

'So? What was it?'

'We don't know, Tallulah.'

He told her that there were hydrophones throughout the seven seas, mostly operated by the big-power navies, that could pick up the whisper of a distant submarine and from the sound of its propeller identify its class, direction and speed. Sometimes the operators listening in heard a roaring noise from the ocean depths, a roar that was clearly biological in origin. The wavelength of the sound told them it was not that of the blue whale, the largest creature on the planet. It was something much bigger. Something unknown to science.

'And what conclusion are you asking me to draw from that?' The treacle was back in her voice now.

'I'm honestly not trying to be awkward. I'm just saying that we should be a little more honest about what we don't know, and less arrogant about what we do know.'

Maybe he had told her that once too often. Still, beneath those starched linen suits, the endless talk of budgets and quarter-one forecasts there was a real human being, a management caterpillar who briefly took wing as a butterfly on the annual staff picnic outing to Nantucket. Kids buried her in the sand; she drank a little too much beer, let the salt water ruin her hair and wore a diaphanous Indian garment that billowed up showing long, shapely legs.

Kemp parked his car in the driveway, noticed the needle in the fuel gauge was once more on empty, and yet again made a mental note to sell the gas guzzler. Sixteen miles to the gallon. With the way gas prices were going, that was crazy.

The Kemps had bought their house in Falmouth Heights when they arrived nine years before, a modest storey-and-a-half clapboard-clad four-bedroom home with a steep roof to break the buffeting winter winds and shed rain and snow. It was warm when the autumn gales blew, and cool in the summer when the wooden shingle roof let the house breathe. It was exactly what an $80,000-a-year (plus a decent housing allowance of $20,000) academic at the Institute could afford. As the housing bubble pushed up prices in the nineties, Margot had tried to persuade him to sell up and move inland, maybe even off the Cape, to a bigger, cheaper place. His refusal led to one row after another.

Margot loathed the discipline of the household budget, the weekly payments into the joint account and Leo's oh-so-casual questions about this payment and that cheque. Her plan had always been to make the money to help pay for a bigger place, but one project after another had failed. Still, the house was big enough now that Julian was gone. Dead. Her son was dead. She still didn't believe it. She understood now the painful truth behind that old cliché that the bereaved always came out with, the one about expecting to see the lost loved one walk through the door just the same as before. That's what she felt so often. The wind banged a door shut or the dog made a noise in the next room and her heart would jump and she would turn to see him, to hear him and to hold him in her arms. But he was never there.

One look at his wife and Leo could tell whether she'd been drinking, whether she was angry, whether there was going to be a scene.

'Hi.' He leant forward to give her a kiss and she averted her face to receive it on the cheek, as she always did these days. 'Where's Sam?'

'She's gone straight from school to a friend's. She's got a sleepover tonight. Here's your letter.'

They sat down in the sitting room, facing each other in the same chairs they always used. It was a nice room, with some really good paintings by a Scottish artist, Ethel Walker, who was inspired by the play of sun and moonlight on ruffled loch waters; and there was a clutter of marine art – the sort of stuff the local artists did with driftwood, the residue of one of her failed businesses.

Sixteen years of marriage. It had been good enough, but not for long enough. They married in 1992 in the Anglican Church in Queens Gardens, St Andrews. They were both too young and they knew it, but at that age who cares? She was 20 and heavily pregnant, he 23 and a rising young academic star in an area of science that was just beginning to become fashionable. She daringly wore a tight ivory-coloured dress at the service that emphasised rather than concealed her swelling. Her parents wore their Sunday best suits, Dad with an amazing pink carnation.

Leo's father had flown over from Melbourne and

surprised everyone by wearing a morning suit and making a speech which brilliantly evoked his son's early expeditions on the scallop boats working out of Mornington harbour north of Melbourne, shunning team sports with his school friends and instead spending every Saturday free-diving for molluscs in the warm coastal waters. Then he surprised everyone again by asking them to kneel and say a prayer in memory of his late wife, Dulcie, Leo's mother. The congregation obediently got to their knees, wondering at the strange direction the wedding service seemed to have taken.

Dulcie Kemp had died some years before, although Leo refused to talk about it. When he finally did, after their wedding, Margot understood the reason for his reluctance. His mother had suffered from high blood pressure all her life, and a series of strokes had transformed an intelligent and loving woman into a human husk, recognising nothing and no one. She had spent years in that condition until released by a final stroke.

They didn't marry because of Margot's pregnancy. They married because they were the glamorous couple, the green-eyed gorgeous primary-school teacher and her smitten Australian academic, who gave interviews to *The Scientist* and *The Scotsman* and the *Glasgow Herald*. They called him 'the man from SMRU', playing on the popular TV series from the sixties that was being repeated at the time, *The Man from U.N.C.L.E.* Leo had even managed to invest some glamour into the ugly and unpronounceable acronym that stood for the Sea Mammal Research Unit.

They were in love with being loved; the celebrity couple

who bridged the social divide between town and gown in St Andrews and went to parties hosted by the social elite of both communities.

If the truth be told, their summer wedding with a double-decker bus to take the guests to a marquee on the West Sands was just a way to keep the party going. The wedding celebrations seemed to go on for days.

But there was so much more to their relationship than that – at least for Margot. Leo became her life, lifting her from domestic drudgery at home and the boredom of teaching at school and taking her, quite literally, over the horizon to the far side of the sea. That's where he told her they were going on their second night out as they walked down to the harbour on a calm midsummer's night in June.

He took her miles out into the North Sea in a borrowed 14-foot boat with an outboard motor. He cut the engine halfway to Norway – at least that's where he said they were – and they lay under an old blanket on the damp planking watching the moon and the stars. Then he stood up, stripped off and dived overboard. Margot screamed, first at the sight of her date stark naked and then again because he had swum away in the moonlight laughing. Then he vanished completely and silence fell on the sea. Margot began to panic when the boat rocked violently and he came sprawling aboard. He was shaking with cold but started the engine, lashed the tiller on course for the coast and hugged her tightly – for warmth he said – all the way back.

After that she gave him her love with an exquisite sense

of surrender. Of course she liked the glamour of being first the girlfriend, and then the wife, of a rising academic star at a fashionable university. But he meant so much more to her, much more than she to him, she felt. He had given her belief in herself, a feeling of real belonging in his world. And his world was crazy; he was always doing something new, always on the move, always testing new ideas, reading new books that no one had ever heard of. When a girlfriend asked what it was like going out with Leo she had said just one word: 'Exciting.'

'I'll bet,' said the friend. 'In bed? Do tell.'

'Not that,' said Margot. 'Well, yes, that as well.'

He was a wonderful lover; gentle and oh, so slow. That was new too, after her few rough-and-tumble experiences at the calloused hands of inept boyfriends.

Now it had all gone. And the loss of Julian had compounded the pain. That is what made her so bitter. The death of her son would have been so much less agonising if Leo had been at her side; the old Leo, the mad, fun-loving Leo, the man who had read somewhere that seven winds met on a hilltop near Forgan in Fife and that if you climbed that hill when the winds were blowing you would be cured of all illnesses; so naturally they spent every weekend for months trekking up wet and windy hills all over the county.

Then there was the trip to the Aran Islands off the Atlantic coast of Ireland to count seals in colonies scattered around the archipelago. There were no research funds for the trip and they had lived in a tent for two weeks. Drinking with some fishermen one night Leo had heard of the blind poet and musician Raftery who had sought sanctuary on the islands some 200 years earlier when fleeing an angry landlord. Raftery was a wandering minstrel who wrote in Gaelic and Leo had dug up a copy of his verses in translation in a bookshop in Westport, Co Mayo.

One poem in particular he recited to her again and again:

> I'm Raftery the poet
> Full of hope and love,
> My eyes without sight,
> My mind without torment.
>
> Going west on my journey
> By the light of my heart,
> Weary and tired
> To the end of my road.
>
> Behold me now
> With my back to the wall
> Playing music
> To empty pockets.

He said it was their love song and he glued matchsticks to a thick piece of cardboard to make the words 'By the light of your heart' and gave it to her on her twenty-first birthday. She still had it somewhere although the glue had dried and some of the letters were missing.

He was her Paladin then and could do no wrong. Now

it was as if a stranger had walked into her life and shared her food and her bed. Leo had been drawn into a world that he refused to share with her. That wonderful, mad, funny man had become cold, aloof, an alien.

And every minute of the day she longed to escape, to go back home where she could start again with Sam, and leave Leo to probe the secrets of the talking seals.

Leo knew she longed to be back there, close to her family in Scotland – the Kingdom of Fife to be precise. That's what she called it. He knew too that she hated the Cape, with its suffocating traffic and crowds in the summer, and the emptiness of the long Atlantic winters.

He also knew that wasn't the real problem.

Margot poured them both a glass of wine and watched him open the letter. It was brutally direct. He had been dismissed under the terms of his contract, paragraph four of which stated that any behaviour liable to bring the Institute or its officers into disrepute was cause for dismissal without compensation. Not only had he not been given management clearance to conduct a series of media interviews, but those interviews were damaging to the reputation of the Institute. This was not the first such occasion. He had been warned before, both verbally and in writing. The Dean and Board felt there was no recourse but to sever their relationship with him.

There was an appeal process to which Kemp could apply. In any case, Chief Executive Bonner wished to see him to discuss his options the following Monday.

Should he wish to appeal he would be within his rights to continue teaching class. However, he should communicate directly with the chief executive's office to let them know his decision. The Board would understand if he wished to stop working while the appeal process was under way. If he did not wish to appeal he should stop teaching immediately, and leave the campus within two weeks.

Kemp looked up from the letter. Margot was watching him with a strange Mona Lisa smile. His wife never smirked, muttered or signalled her displeasure with an eyebrow. She always told you straight out. Now she was smirking. Christ, I've finally made her happy, he thought.

'I told you those interviews would get you into trouble.'

'This isn't trouble, Margot. This is the end of my career. Over and out. Finito.'

He had hoped for tenure, for a life in the comfort zone. Or had he really? How many times had he told himself that tenure was just another stage on the academic conveyor belt, that it would turn him into just another template lecturer, machine-moulded to produce the same thoughts, the same arguments, the same mindless posturing at the same conferences around the world as every other conveyor-belt professor.

Why should universities seek to shape young minds with a predetermined set of intellectual verities? Why not produce unicorns, mermaids, fairies, centaurs? Myth-making, rule-breaking creatures that challenged the way we think, the way we are taught to think? Intellectual anarchy, that's what we need. Maybe he had made that view known a little too often.

'You've blown it, haven't you?' said Margot. 'No tenure – no life on academic easy street. Well, I'll tell you something. I'm pleased. Know something else? You're halfway pleased too. Now let's get out of here. Leave this dammed place.'

He looked at her, wondering, as always, how people once so close could have grown so far apart. People who had once laughed at each other's inane jokes. People who could sit in the ornate splendour of the Number One restaurant in Edinburgh's Balmoral Hotel and lean across a starched white linen tablecloth to mix a mouthful of Château Margaux 1961 (hers) with his Chablis 1985 in a passionate kiss that knocked the water jug off the table and sent a cocktail of wine sluicing from their mouths down her white linen suit top, his dinner jacket and on to the tablecloth.

Margot claimed she was so named because she was conceived after her parents had drunk a bottle of Château Margaux they had won in a raffle at a Christmas dinner in the Station Hotel in Perth. Her parents had led the blameless but threadbare lives of teachers in the Scottish state-school system, and her mother had been shocked to be told the bottle they had won was worth £20. That was in 1972, a year when £20 went a very long way for a Scottish primary-school teacher.

Twenty years later Margot and Leo, celebrating their decision to marry, had paid £95 for a bottle of Margaux in the Balmoral, and had shocked the wine waiter as much by their choice of fish cakes with the wine as by splashing the stuff over themselves and the table.

Before daybreak the next morning they had climbed Arthur's Seat, the hill on the outskirts of Edinburgh rich in ancient tales of witchcraft. It was the site of an Iron Age fort which was supposedly where Celtic tribal chiefs had raised the flag of rebellion against the great King Arthur. Dawn was breaking as they staggered breathlessly to the summit. They made love on the cold, damp grass behind a screen of gorse as the sun struggled out of the North Sea. Suddenly Margot stiffened, her nails digging into his back and her whole body going rigid as her gaze fixed on something over his shoulder.

A small boy with a runny nose and Coke-bottle glasses was peering down at them.

'Why don' ye git a room like other folk?' he demanded and ran off.

Kemp looked at the letter, and back to his wife. He suddenly felt an irrational urge to reach out to her, to hold her, to hug her, to tell her that he was sorry, that he was a stupid arrogant idiot, that everything was going to be all right, that he would get his job back. But he didn't. He couldn't. Too much troubled water under too many broken bridges, he told himself, too much scar tissue layered over old wounds. They had both gone too far down different roads to turn back. This is what they call 'the doorway moment' in films, he thought. The main character stands framed briefly in the doorway, walks through it, and everything changes.

'There are too many ghosts here,' she said suddenly.

'Ghosts? Is that who they are?' He smiled at her.

She ignored that challenge, turned and poured a glass of wine. 'Want one?'

'Sure.'

They paused, both of them avoiding the row that lay between them like a puddle of petrol waiting for a match.

'I've got a field trip tomorrow.'

'A field trip? You've just been fired.'

'I'm still going. I've booked Buck. If it's the last time, at least it will be with him.'

'You'd better believe it's the last time, Leo. I'm over Coldharbor. You've been fired. It's finished.'

'I'm going to appeal. I'm seeing Bonner on Monday. And the field trip is on.'

Ego trip more likely, she thought. Another chance to impose upon those kids his theories about animal communication: seal talk, whale songs, dolphin poetry. Who cared if seals talked or whales wrote novels?

'It might be interesting, don't you think?' he said gently.

'It bloody well might not, Leo. It's bullshit. It's everything you criticise in the eggheads up at the Institute: self-indulgent, up-your-arse research into stuff that interests nobody, matters to nobody and will be forgotten by everybody. Those are your words, not mine.'

This was where it always went. She couldn't stand his work; he couldn't take her drinking; and the only way either of them could deal with Julian's death was to inflict their pain on each other.

'Living with the death of a child is not living if you have a shred of responsibility for that death, and I do!' she had screamed at him during one of their frequent rows. 'I let you take him in that fucking rubber boat out on the Atlantic, for God's sake!'

He had tried to put an arm around her, this woman

51

who had crushed his hand and looked at him with eyes pleading for the pain to stop during Sam's long and bloody delivery, who had clung to him in bed like a baby when Julian had died and the tears and the whisky and the dope had done nothing to dull the pain; this woman who had cooked his favourite linguine di mare for him every Friday, ironed his sea-island cotton shirts with care and made love to him for seventeen years.

She pushed him away.

He poured another drink and took it upstairs to the small deck they had built alongside the children's bedrooms on the first floor. You could just see the sea and the distant shoreline of Martha's Vineyard across the sound.

Plenty of marriages survived the death of a child thought Leo Kemp. It happened to other people, didn't it? So how come theirs hadn't?

The saddest thing of all was that he and Margot could not comfort each other. They tried, but it just made things worse. At first Margot simply vanished for hours at a time, and then occasionally for whole nights. Only Sam kept them sane, kept them together.

Shy, quiet, funny, wounded Sam. Her mother's beak of a nose on her father's oval face revealed a confident and thoughtful character, well able to ride out the storms of the teenage years; but she was much quieter now that her brother was gone. Julian's death had brought father and daughter closer together. That was what made Leo feel guilty. He had missed so much of her growing up: the first sleepover; the first clumsy attempts at make-up; the first time she had come back from a school dance aged twelve and said that a boy had tried to kiss her.

Now she was almost a young woman, who looked at him with reproachful eyes, remembering all their earlier arguments.

'Why are you always with Julian, Dad? You spoil him, you know you do.'

'No,' he would say. 'I love you just as much as Julian, but he's a boy so maybe I do more stuff with him. It's a different relationship. But I love you just as much—'

'There you are, you've said it. See? I was right.'

'Darling, your mum spent more time with you than she did with Julian. Maybe that's the way parental love works. But we still love you both the same.'

'Don't care.' And she would leave the room, banging the door.

Then he would bring her back and make her laugh by telling the story of her reaction to Julian's birth. After a week of observing the new addition to the family, Sam, then aged 4, had asked, 'When is he going home?'

'He is home, darling,' said Margot. 'He's your brother and I'm his mummy.' Sam had fled the room in tears.

After her brother's death Sam tried to become the family peacemaker, patrolling the frontiers of their marriage, anxiously assessing threats from outside and signs of discord within.

'Dad, why don't you spend more time with Mum? You're always working, always at the Institute, always away for weekends.'

And she would tell Margot to be kinder, nicer, more

gentle; bury the anger that burns in your soul, Mum, she wanted to say, but she could never find the right words.

Yet, against the odds, she held them together.

Leo heard the front door close and a car engine start. Margot was not one for scenes any more. No slamming doors, no wheel-spin on the drive, no transparent excuses about going to the gym. Their marriage had sunk into that quiet and desperate place where there was no need to alarm the neighbours or traumatise their child. The china-smashing rows broadcast to the whole street had stopped. She did what she wanted to, and went where she wanted to go. And so did he.

He knew she went drinking with the fishermen. She'd begun to go down to the harbour bars in Falmouth and Chatham after Julian died. She said she liked the company, and that for all their bravado and tribal loyalties the men were so vulnerable, always at the mercy of the weather, regulations, the volatile market price for their products and the fickle nature of their chosen workplace, the North Atlantic. They were just like little boys really.

She listened sympathetically to their doom-laden stories about a dying industry being slowly throttled by state and federal regulators. She knew all about the Marine Mammal Protection Act of 1972, brought in to stop the killing of seals but which was now killing their industry – or so the fishermen said. It was the same at home in the UK, she told them. There were more lawnmower repairmen in Britain than fishermen, a statistic she had once heard somewhere.

On the Broken Shore

Leo looked across Vineyard Sound. A light south-westerly ruffled the waves; the sky was clear, with high cirrus cloud forming mares' tales four or five miles up. The weather should be good for the field trip tomorrow – his last, unless the appeal was successful.

THREE

The twelve students were waiting for Leo on the Institute's pier. Jacob Sylvester and Rachel Ginsberg helped him carry on board the large tape deck containing the recording equipment. They lowered the machine, which was waterproofed with a crude plastic cover, on to the deck using Leo's lifejacket to provide some padding.

He ran through a checklist of names, carefully ticked them off on his clipboard and handed out packed lunches and a bottle of water each. There was nobody missing, and Leo was gratified that for once they seemed pleased to see him. He corrected himself. That was too harsh. On the whole his students were usually pleased to see him. He had had coffee with Gunbrit once in the commissary, and had asked her what the students thought of him. She smiled at the question, looked into her coffee mug and said shyly, 'They think you are a little unusual.' He took that as a compliment.

Most of the students were carrying smart digital cameras with pop-out lenses that took brilliant pictures even at a distance. There were seasick pills for those who wanted them. Only two did.

On board he assembled the group on the rear of the transom deck and handed out lifejackets and oilskins. This was to be a six-hour trip, he told them, during which they would be listening to, and recording, underwater communications among seal rookeries up the coast, but mainly at Monomoy Island. Lifejackets were to be worn at all times, there was to be no smoking, no use of mobile phones, and in an emergency they were to do exactly what the captain told them. They all knew Buck, who waved from the upper deck.

Leo had already asked the group to read the *Herald* profile of Buck, and he wanted them to spend some time with him. 'If you want to understand the ecology of the sea,' he had told them, 'you need to know what's happening to fish stocks, and for that Buck is your man. Talk to him. Take him out for a coffee, a drink maybe.'

The weather was fine, as the sky had promised the previous evening. Leo checked his watch and steadied himself as the tug rocked in the swell of a departing Martha's Vineyard ferry. The big 1,000-ton ferries were still running off-season schedules, and thankfully the whale-watching, dolphin-spotting tourist boats had yet to begin operating. In *The Great Gatsby* F. Scott Fitzgerald described Long Island Sound as the busiest body of water in the western hemisphere. He had obviously not seen the stretch of sea between the Cape and Martha's Vineyard in the summer. But today they would mostly have the sea to themselves.

The tug nosed out of the harbour, passing Penzance Point to the west with its $10-million homes. That was where Tallulah Bonner lived, and Leo swung his binoculars along the shoreline, searching for her house. But they all looked the same, big two-storey houses with swimming pools, green carpet lawns and white flagpoles, all built after the First World War when the big money came down from Boston to find weekend retreats to rival the Hamptons.

Several of the students gathered at the stern watching as the boat rode a gentle swell, trailing a white wake of foam and a flock of seagulls that fell upon the small fish churned to the surface. The *Antoine* headed out to sea for half a mile, and then turned north-east, leaving Martha's Vineyard to the south-west to run up the coast.

Leo looked at the horizon. A ridge of grey nimbus was building where the sky met the ocean. He climbed the steps to the top deck where Buck was fiddling with the radio. Buck had been the first person Leo had met outside his colleagues at the campus when he arrived all those years ago, and they had worked together on these research trips ever since.

It was Buck who had opened his eyes to the power of the fishing lobby when they took his boat out to the Stellwagen sanctuary, 842 square miles of federally protected ocean between Cape Ann and Cape Cod, ten miles north of Provincetown at the mouth of Massachusetts Bay. They had made the first of several trips to Stellwagen a month after Leo had arrived on the Cape. The point about Stellwagen was that it wasn't a sanctuary and it wasn't protected, as Buck showed him. On calm days Buck would turn the engines off over the bank, a kidney-shaped shelf that rose to within 100 feet of the surface, and let the boat drift. Around them were the whale-watching boats, and as the day drew on the fishing boats working out of Gloucester, Portland and Portsmouth up the coast.

They would open their beers, unwrap cold steak sandwiches, and Buck would tell his story. The shallow waters of the bank were the heart of the sanctuary, but beyond lay deeper water, dropping at some places to a depth of 600 feet. The steep sides of the bank created rising currents which brought nutrients into the shallows. In turn the fish followed, and they brought the whales.

The fish brought the fishermen, and the whales brought the tourist boats. And both were killing Stellwagen. But the main culprits were the fishermen.

'That's me,' said Buck. 'Well, people like me. We've fished this place to hell and back. Know what? They should have no-take zones in every marine sanctuary, especially here. No fishing. Full stop. But the politicians daren't do it. Gutless cowards.'

As Leo discovered, it was all true. The fishing industry along the coasts of Maine and Massachusetts could easily withstand the creation of a fully protected reserve over Stellwagen, but all that happened was a seemingly endless series of studies commissioned by the National Oceanographic and Atmospheric Administration – and the continuation of bottom-trawling over the bank.

So 80 species of fish and 22 species of marine mammals were being studied to death by Federal bureaucrats, fished to extinction by the local boats, and all the while gawped at by the 300,000 tourists who cruised these waters in the summer months.

That was the way Leo put it in his lectures, and in a guest column for the *Herald*.

Leo watched Buck at the wheel, his deeply lined face jutting out from an old captain's cap, his rough hands almost stroking the polished wooden casing of the compass. He wanted to tell Buck that he had been fired. This would be the last trip they would make together on the *Antoine*, and Buck needed to know. Now seemed as good a moment as any. He watched the older man's face as he registered the news. Like most Cape Codders, Buck was intensely proud of the Institute, the work it did and the jobs it created. He had lived in its shadow most of his life.

Buck peered ahead, rubbing a cloth on the windscreen. 'How come?'

Leo explained about his interview with the *Herald* and how the *Boston Globe* had picked it up and how in the age of the 24-hour news cycle his words were soon out on the wires on radio and television.

'What did you say in the interview?' Buck kept his eyes on the sea and a hand on the wheel.

Leo told him he had used the example of Hoover the talking seal, long dead but still the subject of some controversy, as a metaphor to expose the arrogant mindset of the marine science establishment in general. And he had thrown in the fishing lobby and Stellwagen and all that stuff.

When he had finished, Buck slapped him on the back.

'Congratulations! No more students, no more getting up for nine o'clock lectures. Now you can get a real life. You never could stand all that hassle up there, could you?'

'I like teaching, Buck.'

'You can teach anywhere,' said Buck, spinning the wheel and bringing the bow of the boat around so that it pointed shoreward. 'We'll be there in twenty minutes.'

Monomoy Island appeared out of the haze, a low-lying smudge on the horizon that gained shape and colour as the boat drew closer to it. As Leo scanned the white, yellow and pink of the island's sand and rock, covered in the grey-green of coarse sea grass and gorse, he made a mental note to sign up for a week's watercolour course with Gloria Gulliver.

She was a Cape divorcee in her mid-fifties who wore startling low-cut one-piece swimsuits in the summer, revealing a heart-shaped strawberry birthmark on her right breast. Leo focused on the image of her breasts, holding them in his head as he had in his hands. Her breasts in his hands, his mouth on her lips, the unforgettable Mrs Gloria Gulliver.

He looked back at the strangely unfamiliar shoreline. Wind, tide and the autumnal Atlantic gales had reshaped the island since he had last seen it. It happened to the whole Cape coastline almost every year, rendering charts outdated almost as soon as they were published. Navigation depended on local knowledge and every spring, fishermen working out of Chatham, Coldharbor and Hyannis had to plot the new shoals, skerries and channels carved out by tide, current, and wind.

Back in 1942 a whole island had vanished. It was called Billingsgate, after the old fish market in London, and had a school, a lighthouse and a small fishing community. The sea took them all, as it will the whole Cape in time. Occasionally winter storms would excavate an old wreck from the depths, bringing it perilously close to the surface.

Buck had lost his last fishing boat that way. The nets snagged on the funnel of a tramp steamer that had gone down in a sudden autumn storm in 1917. In the heavy sea the stern of Buck's boat had been pulled under. It went down in seconds as the sea flooded the rear deck. Buck and his three crew had got off in their liferaft, and had been picked up two hours later. He bought another boat, of course. He always had a fishing boat but it was the tug that brought in the steady money.

Kemp had already decided that he would ask Buck to help him with his appeal. He was the only fisherman he knew who would stand up and tell the truth about the fishing lobby. Fish stocks were in freefall because of overfishing. Seals were being culled in their hundreds of thousands because they were blamed for the declining stocks. The fishing industry and the powerful politicians behind them were slaughtering seals for no purpose.

If there was going to be an argument, Buck was a good guy to have on your side. He had done it before at a conference in San Diego that Leo had persuaded him to attend as a guest speaker: the raw voice of the sea telling a gathering of marine biologists what was really happening to fish stocks and why.

That was how Joe Buckland, nervously clasping and unclasping his hands, desperate for the large rum that Leo had refused him and wishing himself rather in the eye of a hurricane at sea than in that place, came to stand in front of 300 delegates at the Scripps Institution of Oceanography in San Diego, California. Leo had told him that Scripps was the oldest, biggest and most important centre for marine research science in the world. Looking at the large, oak-panelled auditorium with its motto inscribed in Latin on the proscenium arch, he believed it.

Buck had wowed them from the start.

'I have been asked to talk to you about why fish stocks are falling, why the cod has gone, why other fish are going too. Halibut, marlin, you name 'em, they're going. The problem is simple. You're looking at it right here in front of you. I'm a fisherman. But I'm only half of the problem. You ladies and gentlemen are the other half. You eat too much fish,' he said.

'I've been told to get to the point early, and here it is. Hands up who knows what a steaker is.'

Not a hand in the hall went up

'Steakers are what fishing people call the best cuts of fish, the ones with real big steaks on them. And you know what? Fishermen throw back dead into the sea any fish that doesn't look like a steaker. Every fishing boat does it. They'll deny it, but they do. Fishermen throw more fish back into the sea dead than they land for market.

Not just us here in the US. They do it everywhere. That's why the stocks have collapsed.'

Buck was applauded as he left the stage, and afterwards some very charming women smiled sweetly at him and pressed drinks into his hand. He told Leo he reckoned he made a wrong career choice all those years ago. He should have become an academic. The money was easy. They paid you to stand up and talk sense, and they even gave you a drink afterwards.

Kemp turned towards the stern and looked down at his students, all of them working towards a degree that would lead to the further study of the minutiae of the ocean rather than of the warm-blooded mammals that lived in it. Endless papers circulated within the academic community – and then what? Maybe Margot was right. It was all nothing but chatter on the academic networks. But maybe all the research, the lengthy dissertations and those closed conferences so beloved by academics might lead to a new way of thinking about the seas from which we all crawled so many millions of years ago.

Some hope, thought Kemp. And he wasn't putting much faith in his own book setting the scientific world to rights either.

Buck turned the boat, slowed the engine and moved towards a series of sandbanks that had risen above the water-line on the back of a falling tide. Already grey seals and harbour seals were hauled up on them, dozing under a darkening sky. One or two of the females were still pregnant, but most had already pupped, and the young were nervously flopping towards the water, having caught sight of the intruder.

In the channels between the sandbanks grey-whiskered heads turned as the *Antoine* approached, then vanished beneath the waves, reappearing a few feet away, ducking, diving and resurfacing. It was too early in the year for the young seals to have got used to boats, and many had not seen or heard one before. The older ones paid less attention.

In their identical black oilskins and yellow lifejackets the students looked like outsize penguins as they trained their binoculars on the seals. Kemp knelt down and pushed the tape deck firmly under the slight overhang of the enclosed deck rail that ran around the transom. He plugged in the leads to four headsets and attached four other leads to a set of hydrophones: large cigar-shaped microphones encased in thick transparent plastic casing.

The technology was a big improvement on what he had been used to in those early days at St Andrews, but it was still petty crude compared to the latest equipment being used by the military. In the 1960s the US Navy laid a grid of underwater listening posts around the world to track Soviet submarines. The fixed hydrophones were linked to onshore listening stations by cable, and the Navy called the whole thing the Sound Surveillance System (SOSUS). When the cold war ended the system was made available to marine scientists studying whale communication. But the more rarefied area of seal communication did not get a look-in, and Leo had to make do with an off-the-shelf version. It was expensive enough, as the treasurer at Coldharbor had pointed out when he signed it off.

'A ten-thousand-dollar recording outfit just to listen to seals – right?'

'Right,' replied Kemp, and that was that.

Kemp paused as a larger swell than usual lifted the boat, causing his students to stumble and clutch each other. Gunbrit Nielsen seemed to have more than her fair share of helping hands.

A casual glance towards shore brought one of those surprises that could lift these trips from the routine to the extraordinary. There, on the furthest sandbank, was a small pod of hooded seals. Normally found only in Arctic waters, they were rarely seen at this time of year on the Cape. The inflatable hoods on top of the heads of the adult males made them look comical, like circus creatures.

When excited or nervous the seals closed their noses and pumped air into these hoods, which swelled up to the size of footballs. That was what they had done now, and Kemp shouted to his group to take a look and to get some photographs. He handed his binoculars to Jacob Sylvester, who took a quick look before passing them back and joining the others in taking photographs that would be uploaded on to computers and winged around the world to friends and family, showing inhabitants of a cold Arctic world sunning themselves within sight of some of the Cape's most popular summer beaches.

Kemp raised his glasses and swung them seaward; the cloud base had darkened and thickened. Over Chatham harbour a mile away the skies were still clear, and he pointed out to the students the old Marconi radio masts moved there from Wellfleet up the coast, where in January 1903

President Theodore Roosevelt had sent the first radio message across the Atlantic, to King Edward VII in the village of Poldhu in Cornwall. A king emperor conversing with an American president who liked to talk softly and carry a big stick. Leo always wondered what they had talked about in that first brief transatlantic conversation: probably that great British default topic of conversation, the weather.

The masts had now been adapted with wooden platforms on which ospreys built their stick nests. The birds had almost been wiped out by DDT poisoning in the 1960s, but were now increasing in numbers; an example of old technology infrastructure being used to repair the damage done by what had once been hailed as the new wonder chemical herbicide.

'See what I mean,' Leo told his students, although more accurately he told Gunbrit and let the others listen in. 'Take nothing for granted. DDT wasn't a modern miracle, it was poison. But everyone fell for it, like asbestos.'

No sooner had he said this than he wished he had kept quiet and let them work it out for themselves. Maybe he was banging on too much; becoming a bore, a one-track mind with a message that had lost all its potency through endless repetition. Maybe he should just shut up.

He shook himself out of these thoughts and turned his mind to the task at hand. 'All right, everyone, gather round. Bring your mikes and pair off.'

He helped the students lower the hydrophones into the water. They needed to be positioned carefully so that the sensors were facing the source of the sound. There was one headset for every two people.

'What's the depth?' he yelled to Buck.

'Thirty feet.'

'OK, lower the hydros to twenty feet and turn the sensors to face the sandbanks. And get your headphones on,' he shouted to the students.

Seal talk, Kemp called it. Down there in the waters around the sandbanks the seals would be sending their rumbling signals to each other, warning of dangerous intruders. It was a language he knew well, and there were times when he felt he could half guess the meaning of these long underwater conversations. But the real code he had yet to crack.

He had made his name at St Andrews, where an unusually generous subsidy from a government determined to prove it cared about its maritime heritage had led to the establishment of the Sea Mammal Research Unit. Out of curiosity, on a field trip to the north of Scotland he had lowered his hydrophones into 100 feet of water below the mile-long Cromarty Firth Bridge that carries the A9 road north from the Black Isle. The waters there were rich in fish and heavily populated with seals. With Loch Ness only a few miles to the west it was no surprise that the coast was also rich in marine mythology.

The fishermen working out of the deep-water ports of Inverness and Aberdeen had plenty of stories about seals and how they could talk and sing. Even today the older generation who crew the deep-sea trawlers out of Scotland recount the Celtic myths about the selkies, the seals who come ashore, shedding their skin to take human shape as beautiful women. The stories vary little among the fishing communities around the Celtic rim of Britain – the Orkneys, the Hebrides and the Aran Islands off the Irish coast: a seal in human form bewitches and marries a local fisherman only to flee back to the sea, sometimes years later, leaving behind motherless children, broken hearts and empty beds.

Science paid no attention to such fantasies, of course, and at first Kemp thought his own discoveries would be treated in the same light. No one had ever identified and recorded the language of seals until that day in 1992 when his hydrophones had picked up low rumbling noises. At other times he picked up a crescendo of noise, like a bowling ball and the crash of skittles. At first he thought that it was trucks passing over the Cromarty Bridge above him. But the strange rumbling noise continued after the trucks had gone. There, 100 feet down in the darkness of the estuary, harbour seals were making sounds no one had heard before – or if they had heard them, they certainly had not been identified as seal talk.

Kemp had taken his tapes back to the university and played them to his boss at the research unit. Professor Melrose Stubbs had listened, eyes fastened on the revolving spools of tape, smoke from a clenched pipe drifting out of the window.

'No one's heard this before?'

'If they have, they didn't know what it was.'

'And you do?'

'Harbour seals. There was nothing else down there.'

'And if I said, "So what?"'

Typical Stubbs. He was as impressed as hell, but hated

showing it. He delighted in the counter-intuitive challenge, and always insisted on making his students work hard for the answer that he already knew.

So Leo told him what they both knew: that identifying the language of creatures that had been on the planet longer than humans was the start of a scientific journey to unlock the minds of those with whom we share this earth.

They had had a celebratory drink that night, first at the small bar next to the old Cross Keys Hotel, and then back at Stubbs's flat in Hope Street. It was four o'clock in the morning and light when he and a few collegues straggled down to the West Sands and fell down on the dunes to watch the sun come up over the bay. Freezing cold, of course, but with that much whisky inside them it didn't matter.

And then, their darkened heads just visible over the waves, a pod of grey seals appeared with the sun, slipping through the water, hunting for sand eels and flat fish that had come in with the tide.

It was a magical moment. And Margot had been somewhere in the crowd that had collected as the party gathered pace throughout the evening; a young primary-school teacher who hung out with the junior academics looking for a little intellectual stimulation and a break from the boredom of cramming maths into the minds of 9-year-olds.

After the publication of his paper 'Underwater Vocalisation of the North Sea Harbour and Grey Seal', Kemp's reputation in the small and cloistered world of sea-mammal research was born. Invitations to speak came from the most prestigious institutions, the ocean sciences department at the University of California Santa Cruz and the Australian Institute of Marine Science among them

But as Stubbs had said after a final few puffs on his pipe: 'Finding a new language is one thing – now you've got to decode it, laddie, and tell us what it means.'

Mating signals, flirtation, the language of sexual desire and long-distance communications between pods of seals as much as fifty or sixty miles apart – that was what it meant. Using mikes attached to old lobster pots, Kemp had been able to plot the position of the seals below water by listening to the rumbling exchanges that would continue for thirty to forty minutes at a time.

As he eavesdropped on three or four seals talking to each other over an area of two square miles, Kemp did not know who else was listening in on this amorous chit-chat. But he was certain that others were joining in the conversation. Sound travels long distances underwater. Far out in the North Sea, female harbour seals would hear – and, who knows, respond to – the love calls from the Scottish coast.

The vision had stayed with him. There in the Cromarty Firth, seals swimming 100 feet below the surface had been talking to each other, singing love songs and what else? He knew seals had developed acoustic predator recognition. Their sensitive whiskers were like radar scanners and could detect the presence, even miles away, of killer whales. So amid the love talk there would also be warning signals sent rumbling over the seabed: a pod of whales had been detected heading north two miles offshore, maybe mammal-eaters, maybe not.

Later, diving off the Isle of May off the Fife coast, Kemp had seen harbour seals sitting on rocky outcrops fifty to eighty feet underwater. He could not see any facial signs of conversation, or hear their signals, but he knew they would be sending out those extraordinary sounds to alert other seals in the area to his presence. The sight of a diver in their own territory evoked a playful response from the seals, which swam up and peered through his face mask, gently nudging him with their snouts, pushing him back out of their kingdom.

Leo switched his attention back to the exercise. The students were now absorbed in their work, squatting on the deck, heads bowed as they listened to the sounds below the surface. On the Sony recording deck needles flickered on the dials, showing that recording was in progress.

Leo loved this part of the field trips. He wanted his students to feel the same thrill he had when he first dropped his probes into the peaty waters of the Cromarty Firth. He wanted them to experience the fascination of a world below the waves where seals, whales and dolphins communicated in the languages of their species. Once you had heard that submarine conversational chatter, exchanging information about mating, eating and danger – and who knows what else – the questions never ceased.

Buck was having a cigarette behind the cabin and sipping a mug of wozza – his little joke: it wozza cup of coffee before I put some rum into it. But the rum was no joke. Good 40 per cent proof with a kick that came all the way from the Caribbean. Old sea dogs only drink rum, Buck said, although he did sometimes use Diet

Coke as a mixer, proving that even old dogs can learn new tricks.

The sea was choppier now, and the sky had darkened. The students were intent on their task, and Leo could see from their faces and the furious notes they were scribbling that they too were coming under the spell of the underwater world they were listening into.

There were sixty or seventy seals hauled up on three sandbars; as many again would be in the water around the banks. Kemp checked his watch. It was three o'clock. They had been out almost four hours.

On the sandbanks, one or two of the older seals had stiffened and raised their heads, looking seaward. The sky was darkening fast. The horizon was closing in. Where cloud and water met in a palette of grey and black, a thin white line had formed.

A sudden swell, six feet or so from trough to peak, lifted the boat, sending students sprawling and sliding across the deck.

As the wave struck, Buck was already moving quickly towards the cabin.

'Haul up the mikes!' Kemp yelled, lurching across the transom deck as another swell lifted the boat.

'Get in the cabin – now!' shouted Buck. 'Leave the mikes!'

The tug's engines kicked into life. Kemp reached the cabin as Buck was spinning the wheel, bringing the bow round to face seaward.

'What the fuck are you doing?' said Kemp. 'Those mikes cost money!'

Buck tossed him the binoculars.

'Small-bore tsunami. It happens now and then. Get everyone into the cabin, and dump the mikes.'

Kemp didn't need binoculars to see the thin white line of surf moving fast a mile or less away. A flash of lightning lit the foam-flecked waves. It began raining hard, grey stair rods falling from the lowering cloud base.

Kemp saw the last of the seals, a mother heavy with pup, waddling urgently into the water.

'In here!' Kemp shouted at the students. The Norwegian girl was bent over the transom being sick. One of the British students tried to put his arm around her, but she shrugged it off.

Kemp ran down to the deck and pulled the girl round. Her face was white, and she doubled up and retched over his shoes. The deck surged below them as he half dragged her up the steps into the cabin, where the rest of the students were now jammed in behind Buck.

'What's happening?' asked Jacob Sylvester, a faint trace of alarm in his voice.

'Nothing. It's OK, just weather,' said Buck, his voice thick and heavy.

Christ, he's drunk, Kemp thought.

The tug was still swinging round to seaward when the sandbanks suddenly emerged from the water as if propelled upwards by a hidden hand.

Kemp and Buck exchanged a glance: the tidal pull of a tsunami gathering the sea to strengthen the wave that would break over them.

Kemp had heard of freak waves rolling out of the Atlantic and overwhelming fishing boats. He had heard old men's tales of small-bores when the tide, wind, waves and maybe the marginal movement of the seabed in the deeps between Greenland and Newfoundland combined to start a ripple 1,000 miles off the coast that quickly became a fast-moving wave. Very rare, he told himself, and nothing like the great tsunami in the Far East that crashed into the headlines in the last days of 2004, leaving thousands of dead washed up on the evening news.

Down on the transom the $10,000 tape deck lay with its mikes and headphones still plugged in, getting wet, very wet. Leo pushed through his students and took a look out of the cabin window. Dump the mikes? What was Buck talking about? He wanted his job back. He needed that tape deck. Insurance? My tape deck got soaked in a sudden storm. Forget it.

He could make it. He had thirty seconds maybe. The wave was still about 400 yards away, its foaming crest gleaming bright in the gloaming that had descended. He had time.

Above the engine noise he heard Buck shouting as he leapt down the stairs to the deck. He slipped as he ran across rain-slicked decking. At the exact moment that he reached the far end of the transom and raised the $10,000-worth of recording equipment to his chest the bow lifted, the wave broke over the foredeck and surged the length of the vessel. The last thing he saw was white, frightened faces peering at him through the rear windows of the cabin.

Everything went dark and he felt himself being sucked down, pushed sideways and tumbled head over heels. The tape deck was torn from his grasp.

Hold your breath, he told himself. Don't panic. Don't flail around. Kick off your boots. The old lessons drilled into him on research trips to the Hebrides in his Scottish days. Someone had scrawled some helpful advice on the first page of the marine safety book they had to take with them: 'What do you do if you're washed overboard? Answer: Never let yourself get into that situation.'

Kemp broke the surface and breathed a lungful of salty air and spray; the sky and sea seemed to have merged into watery darkness. He couldn't see the *Antoine* in the murk. The sandbanks had vanished into a mist of spume and spindrift, whipped off the wave tops by the wind.

He kicked off his boots, feeling a ridiculous pang of regret that his recently bought expensive footwear should be abandoned to the ocean. Then he thought of the $10,000 recording machine that even now was heading for the ocean bed, and his boots didn't seem so important after all. A flash of deeper, darker pain came with the realisation that he was never going to see Sam again, never going to watch her grow up and get married, have children, his grandchildren. He wriggled out of his jacket, fingers tearing at the buttons. Freed up, he began to swim towards where he reckoned the sandbanks had been. Hard rain was calming the sea, smoothing the waves down to three to four feet between trough and foamy crest.

Beside him in the water the head of a seal appeared briefly, and then vanished. Its long, elongated snout gave it an equine appearance and made it easily recognisable as one of the grey species. Seals can ride out any rough weather, but usually in these circumstances they will make for land and haul up.

Ahead in a trough between the waves two more seal heads appeared. Kemp kicked into a looping crawl, throwing his head right back to avoid swallowing too much water. He remembered being told that people drown at sea long before exhaustion sets in followed by the easy slide beneath the waves. They swallow sea water, panic and choke to death.

He was tired, but he felt no cold, probably because the shock had anaesthetised him. The sea was calmer now, and he could see the island shoreline about 800 yards away. The waves weren't so high now, and a pod of seals broke the surface in a circle around him. Grey seals again, with well-whiskered roman noses, their heads bobbing up and down on the waves. Their two inches of blubber and their waterproof coat of short thick hair made them impervious to cold; they had also made them an attractive prey to man through the millennia. Early man used the oily blubber as fuel for crude lamps, fashioned seal skins into clothing and ate the red, musky flesh. The lamps of Europe and America had been lit with seal and whale blubber for centuries.

No blubber on me, thought Kemp. But he didn't feel cold as he swam more slowly, conserving energy. The seals' circle widened until they were about two or three yards distant on either side. They slipped through the water with sinuous, graceful ease. Occasionally surfers had told stories about being bitten by seals, but such cases were very rare, and only when pups had been directly threatened.

Kemp kicked hard to bring his head above the wave line, but there was no sign of the *Antoine*. He guessed that Buck would have kept heading straight out to sea, to keep his bow into a second wave. The first rule of tsunamis and earthquakes is that there is usually a second one. The rain had eased off and the seals were now close, as close as Kemp had ever been to them in the wild. Long whiskers, sleek skins that looked like wet leather, and those big eyes.

They were making no sounds that were audible to him, but he knew they were communicating with each other, signalling somehow on an agreed destination, or maybe commenting on this strange addition to their pod.

Kemp kicked down, and touched something soft and yielding. He found the bottom with one foot, and then the other. He was on the sandbank. He stood chest deep in the water and took a step forward. Another step, bringing him waist deep now. A few yards ahead the waves were breaking over a bar of sand. The sea was calming; the rain had eased off.

'I've made it,' he told himself. 'I've survived.'

Kemp dropped to his knees and breathed in deep lungfuls of air. He looked at his watch. He had been in the water ten minutes. But he felt no cold. The shock will soon wear off, and then I'll die of exposure, he thought. Where was the *Antoine*?

About fifteen square yards of sandbar had been uncovered as the waves subsided. He looked shoreward. A fast-flowing channel 300 yards wide lay between him and land. He'd never make it in sodden clothing. He unzipped his trousers and pulled them off.

On the seaward side of the sandbank a dozen seal heads rose and fell in the swell. The seals were now in a semi-circle around the sandbar, paying no attention to the stranger in their midst. Kemp was surrounded by creatures that his species had slaughtered throughout the millennia, yet their presence seemed reassuring, almost welcoming.

He shivered suddenly. The wind was cold, the water warmer. He would be better off in the ocean, maybe. He crawled forward on all fours and slipped into the water, beginning a slow breaststroke towards the ring of grey-whiskered heads that turned as he approached and began to move away from the sandbanks. No longer tired, he swam with ease as the seals around him began to arch and slide through the water like their distant cousins the dolphins. They moved easily though the waves towards their apparent destination, a rocky outcrop on the shoreline about half a mile distant.

Kemp swam with them. He seemed to have no difficulty keeping up, using half breaststroke, half sidestroke. What was happening to him was inexplicable, magical even, but it felt quite natural. Logic deserted him as he accepted the reality that he was at sea, swimming among a pod of seals who seemed to regard him as one of their own.

He had no wish to turn shoreward, or towards the island. Why question something that seemed so natural? If this was the afterlife, or a mad dream world that was a prelude to it, why not accept it?

Or maybe, he thought, this is the dream sequence before

death. Maybe this is what happens: the body shuts down, the brain goes into cold storage, leaving a flicker of life, leading to phantasm and madness; like those tanker crews torpedoed in the Atlantic during the war and left lying for days on liferafts, badly burnt and delirious with pain and dehydration. Most of them were mad when they were picked up, and spent the rest of the war, indeed the rest of their lives, in mental homes.

When Buck was safely a mile out to sea, he turned the tug. He had put out a mayday call moments after Kemp had gone overboard. He knew – and he knew that Kemp knew – that he had no option but to seek the safety of the open sea. That was thirty minutes ago, and the response of the rescue services had been slowed by weather. Now he saw the 44-foot lifeboats butting through the waves about a mile to starboard. These were the workhorses of the coast-guard fleet and as always they worked to a grid pattern, boxing off the ocean into squares and assigning boats to each square. A helicopter from Hyannis airport would soon join the search. A radio message had alerted the Institute. Kemp had been in the water almost half an hour, and the water temperature at this time of year meant that he could still be alive.

Buck radioed the coastguard his position and informed them that he would take the tug as close inshore as possible and work up the coast from a point just north of the sand-banks. He manoeuvred the *Antoine* to within fifty yards of the shore, as close as her nine-foot draft allowed on a falling tide.

The students all seemed to be in shock, but he had little time to worry about them. Two or three of the girls were crying. He gave them his binoculars and told them to scan the shoreline, because that was most likely where Kemp would be. He would probably have swum ashore by now, but the currents around the sandbanks meant that he could have been taken a mile or so up the coast.

This was reassuring news for the students, but Buck didn't actually believe it. If Kemp had survived being swept overboard, if he had not been knocked unconscious and drowned straightaway, he would surely have made for the sandbanks. And there was no sign of him either there or on the shore beyond them.

A coastguard boat found Kemp's sea boots and jacket. But it was Gunbrit Nielsen who spotted his trousers floating in the water. Buck fished them out with a billhook. The students stared dumbly as he went through the pockets and then squeezed out the water, balled up the trousers and threw them in the back of the boat. 'Keep looking,' he growled, and climbed the stairs to the top deck. Gunbrit began to cry, brushing the tears away with the back of her hand. The rest of them pretended to look at the shore, but their eyes kept sliding back to the sodden pair of trousers – a graphic reminder that something terrible had happened to their teacher.

Tallulah Bonner was in her office when the head of the coastguard station at Coldharbor phoned with the news that Leo Kemp had been lost at sea. There was a small but rapidly diminishing chance that he would be found alive if he hadn't managed to swim ashore. The coastguard had deployed both their older boats and their latest rigid-hull fast-moving 42-foot craft and a helicopter. The search was now concentrating on the shoreline. The best hope was that he had been washed up on the island. Three fishing vessels from Chatham harbour had been called to make the short trip to Monomoy to join the *Antoine* in searching the foreshore. Everything possible was being done.

'And his family?' asked Bonner.

There was a pause at the other end of the line.

'We thought it appropriate for you to call . . .'

'OK, I'll call his wife. Keep me in touch,' she said.

Damn. This was going to be horrible. How on earth was she going to break the news to Mrs Kemp? From time to time she had to tell senior colleagues that they were no longer wanted at the Institute. She always praised their work, thanked them for their contribution and then worked around to the 'new challenges' ahead, i.e. the challenge of getting another job. That was bad enough; this was awful. She rehearsed her opening remarks. 'Your husband is missing, but we're sure we'll find him. I can't tell you how sorry we are, Mrs Kemp, but I want you and your family to know you are in our prayers. Can we offer you any help?' That was the best she could do, and at least it had the advantage of being honest.

She had met Margot Kemp at the usual functions, and had spent some time with her at the last annual staff picnic. A nice, bright woman, good-looking in a way that men probably thought sexy. But she had been very guarded and quiet since the death of her son. How on earth was she going to take this?

Then there was the press to think about. There would have to be some sort of statement. The papers would make a fuss. Kemp had media friends, newspaper friends. That man Sandy Rowan. They would make a meal of it. But did they know about the decision to remove him from the staff? She hoped not.

She got up and walked to the wall of her office, which was lined with framed citations of the Institute's great achievements. Pride of place went to a UNESCO award for building the deep-sea submersibles that were the first to examine the hydrothermal vent fields in the mid-Atlantic ridge. She remembered Kemp's excitement when they showed staff a film of the black mineral-rich fluid spewing from the ocean floor.

'Damn. What a waste,' she said out loud, surprising herself.

She didn't dislike Kemp. It was just that he wouldn't play by the rules. A paid-up member of the awkward club, as one of the Board directors had told her. Great institutions can tolerate anything but damage to their reputation, because it is on the integrity of their reputation that fund-raising programmes are based and talented staff attracted. And she had built that reputation. In so doing she had raised the whole profile of oceanography at a time when the White House was betting the ranch on manned flights to Mars.

She had made sure that the Coldharbor story was out there, a story of teamwork, intellectual endeavour and innovative research. How many times had she hammered home those themes to her management team? How many times had she told them to impress on all their colleagues that the golden rule of any media campaign is that everyone has to sing from the same hymn sheet?

Nothing, she knew, nothing devalues a brand more than confusion over a great corporation's vision and values. Vision and values, that's what people like Kemp never understood. That's why he had to go. And now it appeared that he had gone.

For good.

She calmed down, and wished she hadn't stopped smoking. Nine months, three weeks and four days. She really could use a cigarette now.

This was going to be a horrible call to make. She would telephone the Board after she had spoken to Mrs Kemp.

Why, oh why, had she given up smoking?

She phoned the janitor at the front lodge. Yes, he did have a pack – would Marlboro be all right? He would bring them up.

Margot was on the road north out of Falmouth, and had just passed Betsy's Diner, with its 'Eat Heavy' sign set to flashing red, when her cell phone chirped. Jamming it to her ear, she checked her rear-view mirror. When they weren't issuing tickets for parking or speeding, the Cape police loved nothing better than to catch a driver using a cell phone behind the wheel; that and busting the young for smoking dope.

'Mrs Kemp, it's Tallulah Bonner from the Institute. Can you talk?'

'Sure,' said Margot, with that sick feeling you get in your stomach when the wrong person phones at the wrong time and asks if you have time to talk.

Bonner was commendably clear in describing what she had been told had happened, and very encouraging about what she thought would happen. But it didn't make sense. Margot found herself shouting down the phone.

'Overboard? But what happened? This was a field trip, for God's sake! They were only going to Monomoy Island, a couple of miles offshore. What do you mean, "small tsunami?" We don't have tsunamis here. This is Cape Cod, not Sumatra or wherever they have tsunamis.'

Bonner inhaled deeply and blew out a cloud of smoke, thanking God for the janitor and making a note to look upon his salary kindly at the next pay review.

'I'm sorry, I don't know what caused it, but I'm told it was the combination of wind and wave, maybe something way out under the sea. But the important thing, Mrs Kemp, is that there's every chance he'll be found alive. He's a strong swimmer. He should have made it to the shore.'

Margot turned the car round and headed home. No point worrying Sam just now. Of course Leo was all right. But she would call Jenny Hathaway, their family doctor and her best friend on the Cape, and a fellow founder member of the WALL club, membership of which Margot regarded as an essential antidote to the long Cape winters. There were only two members, because Margot had never found anyone else suitable to join. WALL stood for Wine And Laughter Lunches, which was a misnomer, because they usually met in the evenings, since, as Jenny pointed out, doctors could not really drink at lunchtime. Not that Jenny drank much anyway. She supplied the laughter, and Margot did the drinking.

Leo would probably have turned up by the time she got home, wouldn't he? But suppose he hadn't? Suppose he had drowned? She held the thought in her mind, turned it over, polished it like the apples that Grandma had shone for her with an old kitchen cloth when she was a child. They always tasted better that way, Grandma said. Suddenly the thought of Leo's death gave her the same pleasure as had that first bite into a polished apple; but the pleasure came gift-wrapped with guilt. By all means lead me into temptation, but deliver me please from the troubled conscience that comes with it. She could go back to Scotland. With the insurance money, she and Sam could be free of this place. A warm, welcoming thought, freighted with guilt.

She bundled the thought away. She must tell Sam, but not now. Wait until she had news. Of course he's not dead.

At home she ignored the welcoming barks of Beano, Sam's dog, and went straight to the kitchen, feeling as if she had stepped into a new and unreal world. She poured a drink, just the one, a decent-sized glass of Chardonnay. She had to pick Sam up from school, and it might be a long night. Her husband was not dead, she told herself.

FOUR

Leo reckoned he had been swimming up the coast with his pod of seals for about half an hour. They could swim at great speed – up to 15 m.p.h. – but this group was slipping easily but much more slowly through the water. Once he ducked his head beneath the surface and forced himself to open his eyes. There was the silver flash of a fish quite clear in the swirling, dim grey-green water. A herring, perhaps, or a striped bass. In the past week the wind had backed from north-east to a south-westerly, bringing warm air from the tropics. As the water warmed, so the fish began their annual migration to northern waters. The herring, squid and bass came first, and the larger predator fish followed, trailing behind them the sharks. Whales were also part of this migration, moving north to feed on sand eels and squid. In October the winds would change and the whole migration reverses itself.

Kemp ducked his head below the waves once again,

89

and sighted a shoal of fish a few yards away. Seals have bifocal vision, which allows them to see and hunt beneath the surface of the water as well as on land. Human beings do not. Further evidence that this is my death dream, he thought. This must be what happens when you drown. Death just becomes a dream, ghostly imaginings on the way from one world to the next.

He had always taken life as it came; now he would take death as it came.

The pod of seals turned shoreward as it reached the point, and headed for a small group of seaweed-covered rocks. Leo turned with them, swimming strongly until his feet found the rising seabed. The seals hauled themselves up on to the rocks, paying no attention to Leo as he crawled ashore.

He lay back on a bed of seaweed and looked up at the blue-grey gloaming. He felt his pulse. I am not dead. I have survived. So this is the ultimate research trip. Why shouldn't I swim with seals? See the fish they see? Watch them as they swim, feed and rest?

Because the human body cannot do that, came the small voice of logic and reason. You're not a seal, so how can you hang out with them?

The seals shifted uneasily as the noise of boat engines became audible. Leo lifted himself on to one elbow. A hundred yards away he saw the *Antoine*, his students leaning over the port side and scanning the shoreline with binoculars. He could hear the chatter of the radio over the water. Up in the cabin, Buck would be looking at the chart and judging the depth. He could imagine the old sailor drinking a very stiff wozza indeed right now. He lay back down, shielded from their view by a jagged line of rocks.

Leo looked around him at the seals scattered over the rocks. Whatever has happened to me, he thought, I am feeling no pain. He tried to explain himself but he could not. He understood how he had survived. That was easy. He'd been lucky. Even without a lifejacket he'd made it through that sea to the sandbanks in minutes. But he could not explain what followed, why he was lying here among the rocks surrounded by seals. Why didn't he stand up and shout to those on the *Antoine*? He just couldn't. That's all he knew. The power of logic and reason had left him.

Sandy Rowan was in his small glass office ('I like to see how hard my staff are working,' said the *Herald*'s editor), leaning back on his swivel chair with his feet on his desk. He was reading that morning's edition when the news editor poked his head around the door: local radio hams had picked up coastguard short-wave traffic about a small-bore wave, five feet high in places, that had washed ashore from Hyannis up to the north end of Nauset Beach.

Coastguards were calling it a little tsunami, and said it had boiled up out of a sudden storm in the Atlantic. A few boats had been bumped in the harbour, beach properties flooded, but there had been no material damage.

Sandy looked out of the window. Cocooned in his office he had not noticed that it was almost dark outside, and a hard rain was falling.

'Thanks,' he said.

The news editor had not finished. There were unconfirmed

reports of a man missing from a boat off the coast. Coastguard lifeboats and a chopper had been deployed. Damn, thought Sandy, a good story and just too late for tomorrow's edition.

'OK, get someone out there,' he said, and went back to that day's paper.

It was a good edition. The golden rule of local papers is to keep the news local. The Aberdeen paper that reported the sinking of the *Titanic* in 1912 by headlining the loss of a local man knew what it was doing.

The front-page lead was a story about local conservationists in yet another campaign against planning applications for new housing. It was a perennial Cape story, but it made good copy. It went to the heart of the old debate about development, heritage and the environment on the Cape. Most importantly, readers really reacted to these stories, firing off volleys of letters and emails in response.

The *Herald*'s new owner had invested heavily in websites for all seven of his titles, but so far it was the classified ads that drew traffic to them, not the news. So the business of squirting ink on to dead trees had a few years left to go, thought Sandy, swinging his legs off the desk as his office door swung open again.

The news editor reappeared, with the self-important look of a man bearing bad news.

'It's Kemp, Sandy, your friend from the Institute. He's the one who went overboard. He was on a seal trip on the *Antoine* with his students.'

Sandy looked at him, his mind racing as he tried to make sense of what he had just heard. How on earth had his friend fallen overboard? It just wasn't possible. He did these trips all the time. OK, anything was possible at sea but Kemp was a strong swimmer. He would have had a lifejacket on. Did Margot know? Where and when did this happen? Do we have a picture of him? Yes, we do: taken when he did that guest column.

'We have a snap of him on the *Antoine*,' he said to the news editor. 'It's on file. Get it up on the web with whatever you've got now. Make the headline "Senior Institute Staffer Missing at Sea".'

Kemp tried Buck's cell as he raced down the stairs to the car park. No reply. He knew they would have been somewhere around Monomoy Island. They always went there, plenty of seals and only a ninety-minute run from Coldharbor. He needed a boat. This time of the season he would have a problem getting someone in Hyannis Port to take him out. He checked his watch. It was 7.30 p.m. When the hell did this happen?

Margery Vickers at the Hyannis family charter boat company had known Sandy's mother well, and had been one of the few to visit her in her last months at the Orleans hospice. She had not seen much of Sandy since his mother died, but she always looked out for him. So when he appeared in her office, clearly in a state, she listened carefully.

She would do her best, she said, but look at the weather. The sky was lightening but there was still a strong after-swell in the harbour. A boat would get out all right, but at this time of the evening it was going to be hard to find someone to take him. Where did he want to go, and did he mind if she asked why?

Mrs Vickers had heard about the search for the missing man, and when Sandy explained the connection she expressed her sympathy but pointed out that there was nothing he could do.

Sandy knew she was right. He got back in his car and took Route 28 down to Falmouth and Coldharbor. When Buck got back, Sandy knew where he would find him.

By the time the *Antoine* arrived back at the Coldharbor pier it was a warm, clear evening that gave little evidence of the brief but violent storm a few hours earlier. Only a strong wind from the east chasing high nimbus inland and a bigger swell than normal suggested that there had been unusual conditions further up the coast that day.

On the slatted wooden pier Margot, Sam and Tallulah Bonner stood watching the tug tie up. Sam clung to her mother, her pale, tear-stained face making her look much younger than her years. A curious crowd who had heard the news were standing at a respectful distance across the road.

On the tug's transom deck the twelve students began to file over the gangplank to the pier with teary, washed-out faces. Tallulah turned, and to Margot's surprise briefly embraced her.

'If I know anything about your husband he's out there somewhere, and very much alive.'

Margot turned away, embarrassed, and muttered a thank you. Tallulah gave Sam a kiss on the cheek and took her hand. The student group trailed past them, shepherded by two Institute staff members towards a bus waiting at the pier head.

Buck was the last person off the tug. He came down the pier with the slightly rolling gait of a man who has been at sea all his life. He briefly shook Tallulah's outstretched hand, and walked past her to Margot.

'Mr Buckland. We need to know what happened,' said Tallulah Bonner.

Buck turned briefly. 'I'll tell you what happened. We lost a good man today, and it was my fault. Now, if you will excuse me.'

Bonner said quietly, 'You're drunk, Mr Buckland. Go home.'

Buck ignored her and gently put his arms around Margot, enveloping her in the warm smell of rum. She eased out of his embrace.

'Tell me what happened, Buck.'

'Sure. Come with me.'

The three of them sat self-consciously in the candlelit Dark Side waiting for their drinks. A Coke for Sam, white wine for Margot and rum and Diet Coke for Buck. He told the story briefly, because, as he said, it all happened very quickly. One minute Leo was safe in the cabin, the next he had run to the transom for the tape recorder, the wave had hit, and over he'd gone.

As wife and daughter sat with their arms around each other, the pent-up tension burst into a flood of questions. Why had he gone back for the recorder? Why couldn't the tug turn around faster, and where had this wave come from? He could still be alive, couldn't he? He was a good swimmer, the water wasn't too cold, and they hadn't been far offshore.

Buck answered as best he could. He didn't stop Leo going back down to the deck because he hadn't seen him until it was too late. He couldn't turn the boat in that sea, there might have been a second wave, and he didn't want to risk getting the tug stern on to a small-bore wave. He might have lost more people. As for the wave, if you look back at the records from the old whaling days you will find occasional reports of killer waves that moved with huge speed out of the ocean, triggered by something hundreds of miles away, on or below the seabed. They could be very local and small, as this one was, or monsters that reared up out of the ocean for no known reason.

'Bigger boats than mine have vanished in the Atlantic just like that,' said Buck, snapping his fingers to make the point. Mistaking the gesture, Cleo started making him another rum and Diet Coke behind the bar.

'Take me out tomorrow,' said Margot. 'I want to see where it happened – just me and Sam.'

Buck nodded, and grunted an 'OK'.

'Do you mind if I come too?'

Startled, they turned and looked up to see Sandy standing beside them, his figure half hidden in the dim light.

'Sorry,' he said. 'I didn't mean to break in. And I'm very sorry, Mrs Kemp, about what happened, but I would really like to . . .'

'No way,' snapped Buck, getting to his feet. 'No journalists. Just us.'

Sandy began to say something, then thought better of it, turned on his heel and walked towards the door.

Sam began crying, and buried her face in her mother's

lap. Margot put her arms around her and rocked her gently to and fro, listening to the sobs from the tear-stained face of her child, no longer a teenager but her baby again.

In the trauma of the last few hours she had forgotten how brave and grown up Sam had been. Now it had all become too much. This was the second great shock in her young life, thought Margot, and I haven't really helped. When Julian had died Sam had been just 13 and she and Leo had spent hours explaining to her how Julian had gone to heaven and was happy with his toys and his friends. Sam had spent days in her room writing him letters, telling her brother what had happened since he left. Leo and Margot took the letters to the church where Sam was a chorister. The three of them lit a candle, said a prayer and left the envelopes on the altar. Then the vicar insisted on coming round and sat, smelling slightly of sherry, talking about the inevitability of the afterlife, and Sam had kept asking him when Julian was going to reply to her letters. There was no answer to that and Sam had quickly seen through the vicar's waffled reply.

And now it was happening all over again. Except, as she kept telling Sam, her daddy was not dead, just missing.

Margot and Sam arrived home to find a note in the hall from the next-door neighbours saying how sorry they were and asking if they could be of any help.

Margot made them both hot chocolate and they sat down to watch the evening news. There was a nice photo of Leo released by the Institute, and an interview with Sandy Rowan at the pier in Coldharbor, with the *Antoine* in the background.

Sandy was upbeat, saying how well Leo knew these waters, and how likely it was that he had swum ashore at some remote beach and decided to bed down for the night in the dunes. 'The guy is fit, he's a strong swimmer and he's a fighter, so he's out there for sure.'

He really cares for my husband, thought Margot. More than I do, perhaps. She regretted not stepping in when Buck had snapped out his refusal to take Sandy with them the next day. Sam started to cry again, and Margot took her in her arms, stroking her hair and telling her that Daddy would be home tomorrow.

The doorbell rang, and a small group of neighbours came in hesitantly. The women hugged Margot, and the men shook her hand, and everyone said how sorry they were and was there anything they could do to help. They brought small gifts of food: a flask of soup, a freshly baked loaf of bread, some home-made chocolate cake.

Leo would have been amazed at this kindness, thought Margot. He hardly knew these people. She thanked them profusely and saw them to the door, assuring them that everything would be all right, although she and they knew that it probably wouldn't.

Sam was half asleep on the sofa with Beano snoozing at her feet. Margot got her upright and sleepwalked her up to bed. She tucked her up and sat watching as she fell into a troubled sleep. For that night Margot allowed Beano, against all the house rules, to sleep in Sam's bedroom. She would get a friend of Sam's around tomorrow to stay over for a night.

*　　*　　*

Leo spent his first night in the wild asleep amid seaweed and rocks. He scraped a hollow out of the sand above the tideline and lay in the damp bed with his head resting on a tangle of dry seaweed. It was a warm night and he felt neither cold nor discomfort. Around him, but some yards distant, the seals also slept. In the starlight he could make out the silhouettes of their slug-like, tubular forms against the rocks.

He awoke the next morning to be reminded that he was very much alive and not imprisoned in a dream after death. He was very hungry. He hadn't eaten for twenty-four hours. The rocks below the tideline were covered in mussels and limpets. The mussels came away easily from the rocks and he picked handfuls and then smashed them open with a small stone, gulping the white flesh and salty liquor from the boat-shaped shells.

The limpets were more difficult, tightening their grip on the base rock with the strong muscular foot housed within a conical shell almost before he had touched them. A quick blow with the stone dislodged all but the largest. Their flesh was meaty and chewier with a stronger flavour than the mussels and, he persuaded himself, no more difficult to digest than sushi.

Around him the pod of a dozen seals was awakening; they were raising their heads and using their front flippers to shift from side to side as if to rouse themselves with early-morning exercise. Leo had never seen or heard of such behaviour and looked on wondrously as the group rocked gently from side to side and then stopped to swing their heads seaward. One seal, the oldest and a survivor of a shark attack, judging by long scars that ran from tail to head, positioned himself on the landward side of the pod and scanned the dune belt and low cliffs beyond.

The seals paid no attention to Leo and as the light brightened with the rising sun they began to shuffle through the rocks towards a sea that had calmed into a gentle swell after the storm the day before. A young male led the pod, followed by the females, and within minutes the whole group had slipped into the water where they waited patiently for the old watchdog to join them. Leo stood up and walked slowly to the shoreline. He entered the water close to the pod, feeling totally at ease as he swam away from the shore. Again the seals appeared to pay him no attention. The pod headed out to sea some 100 yards before turning and swimming slowly up the coast.

Leo found no difficulty in keeping up and was elated at the way he was able to stay with the pod and that they seemed to accept this strange addition to their number.

After twenty minutes the seals turned shoreward towards a long stretch of open beach overlooked by a deserted lighthouse. They hauled up some thirty yards from the water's edge and settled down to face the sea and the sun. Leo walked beyond them into the dunes and sat down. He knew they would stay here for the morning, sunning themselves, snoozing, occasionally sliding into the water when a fish broke surface to indicate the presence of a shoal.

There was no sign of life on a beach that stretched away for miles on either side. Leo worked out that the seals had hauled up on the far end of the island, one that rarely attracted visitors, especially this early in the day. He was pleased with this thought. He did not want to be seen. He was content where and as he was. He had pushed all thoughts of Margot and Sam to the back of his mind. He was an actor on his own stage, with his own role to play. Somewhere backstage there was an old life, old loves, old friends. But they had no meaning for him now.

The shellfish had left him thirsty and hoping to find a dew pond he walked through the dune grass to the old lighthouse. On one side a roofless wooden shed tilted crazily on its base, ready to be reclaimed by the surrounding sand. On the other a water tank had been raised some thirty feet from the ground on iron stilts. Leo climbed the rusting scaffolding and found that at the top a wooden cover had been pulled back and broken, probably by vandals. The water was dark green and looked slimy. He raised some in his hands and smelt it. There was a faint odour of urine and it tasted sharp and metallic, but he told himself it was just brackish rainwater. He scooped out handfuls again and again, drinking deeply.

From his vantage point he could look along miles of empty beach. The seal pod, his pod, had been joined by several others. There were now scores of seals scattered along the sand, resting on front flippers that were tucked out of sight beneath their bodies, gazing seawards. The first of the fishing boats, some carrying camera-laden tourists, were moving up the coast. As he drank from the tank Leo wondered how seals quenched their thirst. It was not a question that had ever occurred to him in his years of studying marine mammals. He could speak for forty-five minutes without notes on the seals' diet and the different fish they sought with the changing seasons but never had he asked himself – or been asked by his students – what they drank. Maybe they simply absorbed the liquid content of the fish they ate. He didn't know and he smiled to think that in years of academic work such a simple question had never arisen. He found nothing strange about looking back on his academic past because whatever life he was leading now, whether as man or seal, whether dead or alive, felt quite natural. It was as if he had shed one skin and slipped into another, as seals did in Celtic mythology.

The *Antoine* left after breakfast the next day. Buck, Margot and Sam stayed in the cabin, scanning the shoreline with binoculars as they made their way up the coast towards Monomoy. Buck had sunk into a silent gloom, and said nothing as he sipped his coffee. Margot and Sam had heard about his favourite drink.

'Is that a wozza?' asked Sam.

'No,' Buck said curtly, cutting off further conversation.

There were few seals to be seen on Monomoy, but two coastguard boats had returned to their search at first light, and a helicopter was making low runs up the shoreline. Margot knew they were looking for a body now.

Beyond Monomoy they kept in close to the shore on the high tide. The beaches were almost empty after yesterday's sudden storm, with just the odd camper and shore fisherman to be seen. There was no way that Leo could have come ashore here and not been found – dead or alive – thought Margot. They passed the long and lonely stretch of Nauset, then the small town-managed beaches, with their eggshell-coloured sand backed by dunes – Orleans, Coast Guard Beach, Marconi.

This is crazy, thought Margot. 'Let's go back,' she said. 'We're not going to find him here, not this way.'

Buck said nothing, and began to turn the wheel. But Sam sprang to her feet and shouted, 'No!' The words came tumbling out as she stood there, white-faced, hands on her hips, suddenly angry and older than her years. How could they turn back now? What right had anyone to decide that her father was not lying half drowned, waiting to be rescued from a shallow shoal, some spit of sand, some lonely beach?

She turned her back on them both and returned to scanning the coast through her binoculars, listening to the occasional crackle of radio traffic and hoping for a sudden burst of sound that would tell them her father had been found alive and well.

They chugged up the coast until the tide turned and pushed them away from the shore. No one said anything when Buck spun the wheel and turned for home. On the way back to Coldharbor he brewed up coffee in the tiny galley and handed round the steaming mugs with a generous slug of rum in each. Sam tried hers and wrinkled her face in disgust.

That night Margot left Sam ensconced in front of the TV with her best friend from school, two takeaway pizzas and large bottles of Coke. She needed time to think, she said. She took the car and drove towards Chatham harbour.

She hadn't had a drink that day apart from the wozza.

103

God knows she had needed one during her long and difficult conversation that evening with her parents back in
Perth. They had wanted to come over, but she had politely
and then probably a little too firmly refused. Too much
emotional hassle, and anyway they could not really afford
the airfares. 'And hey, Mum, he's going to be home tomorrow
anyway, right?'

She called Tom on his cell the moment she cleared
Falmouth Main Street. For some reason phoning him as
she drove past Betsy's and the picture windows of the
bookshop where an arty crowd had gathered for a wine
and poetry evening didn't feel right.

'I can't do it tonight,' he said.

'I must see you.'

'Not possible,' he mumbled.

'TOM, PLEASE! BE THERE! I NEED YOU TONIGHT!'
she shouted, and dropped the cell into the well of the car.

And he would be there, she thought. He would leave
that wife of his, make an excuse about fixing something
on the boat, and he would be there.

The car park behind the Squire is big enough to allow the
summer sailors to park their trailers and boats while they
have a drink after a day on the water. Margot parked in
her usual spot as far away from the rear entrance as
possible, lit a cigarette and listened to an FM news station.
The second item was about the continuing search for a
marine scientist from Coldharbor who had been missing
at sea for over twenty-four hours.

A dented, rusting camper van pulled up alongside and
Margot got in. They drove down to an old car park in

the dunes that the coastguard had placed out of bounds in order to protect nesting plovers in the area. A padlocked gate barred access, but like most local fisherman Tom was allowed a key.

He parked up with the sea just visible through the dunes.

She told herself she was using this as an anaesthetic, that she was in shock, that she was trying to blot out the reality that her husband was a bloated corpse washing around the coast somewhere.

But it was a lie. Her enduring memory of her school days in St Andrews was of her headmistress, Mrs Pomeroy, giving the sixth-form leavers farewell tea and cakes along with her advice for life: the needle on the compass that would point them in the right direction, as she put it.

'Always tell yourself the truth, girls,' she said, 'because if you can't be honest with yourself, you won't be with anyone else.'

And the truth was that Margot was here for a pleasure fix, a high-voltage sex jolt, nothing more, nothing less. Her son had died three years ago, and now her husband had gone. She needed something to remind herself that she was still alive, still had something to live for. Tom was ideal. A decent, dumb, good-looking fisherman who worked the day boats out of Chatham and was on call whenever she needed him. Stop being a bitch, she thought, he's a nice guy. Married, so no hassle, no worries about clingy involvement.

She had told him this would work if they both recognised it for what it was, just a sanity break. He kept saying he wanted to see her for a meal, for a drink somewhere discreet, but she always said no. Stick to what works, and here in the car park, backed up among the dunes, is what works. You come when I call, and I'll come when you call. 'I don't even want to know your last name,' she said. 'You're Tom to me, just Tom.'

But he told her anyway, because he was proud of who he was: Ballantyne, Tom Ballantyne, 28 year-old father of two. Handsome in a baby-faced sort of way, her very own human rabbit.

She was damned if she was going to sit at home in her widow's weeds.

But she would be damned anyway, she thought. Someone would see them and the poisonous gossip would start flowing at the coffee mornings and the drinks parties. If Leo was dead she and Sam would go back to Scotland and start again making a new life with new friends where it all began.

Her first memories were of family picnics on the West Sands at St Andrews. Years later it was on that same beach that she had first seen Leo when she was a primary teacher. She had tagged on to a drinking party of students and their lecturers, and everyone had finished up in the dunes at three-o'freezing-clock in the morning. People were draining quarter-bottles of whisky, falling asleep, or quietly being sick. One adventurous couple was making an effort to have sex, a coupling doomed by the cold and the spiky dune grass. Then, as the sun came up, this tall Australian with a mop of fair hair falling over his forehead walked down to the water's edge to gaze at a pod of seals.

St Andrews was a small place, one road in from Cupar to the north, one road out over the cliffs and along the coast to Crail and Anstruther to the south. If you wanted any fun it was a ninety-minute drive to Edinburgh. For a young teacher the university town had little to offer apart from hanging out with the students and the younger lecturers.

Once she had seen Leo, she found out where his crowd drank. It was on her twentieth birthday, a few days after the beach party, that she saw him for the second time, in the Cross Keys, where the marine biology crew gathered on Friday and Saturday nights. The Keys had a bar, a darts board, two tables, eight chairs and a linoleum floor mottled by cigarette burns. The young teaching staff used it because it had the cheapest pint of 'heavy' in town – on their skinflint wages, that mattered – and because the students avoided it after four of them had been thrown out for vomiting in the lavatories.

And that's where he'd seen her, across a smoke-fugged pub. She'd worn a tight sweater with Marks and Spencer's best push-up bra, and had positioned herself in his line of sight, to make sure he saw her.

He'd seen her all right, and she laughed out loud at the memory. He managed to stare at her and at the same time drink his bitter without spilling it, a well-known Australian technique, he told her later. He'd always said she had great boobs. She breathed in and pushed her chest out. Not as good as they used to be, after two children, but still not bad.

They began going out. He was fresh out of Melbourne

University and had just started his first job at the Sea Mammal Research Unit at St Andrews, partly teaching, partly research. He didn't have much of an Australian accent, it seemed to have got lost on the flight over, but he was passionate about his homeland, and spent hours telling her of his childhood in Mornington, his trips on the scallop boats and free diving in the warm coastal waters.

Then of course on their second date he took her out at night miles into the North Sea to look at the stars far from the mainland light pollution. It was madness, of course, but the night out became the talk of the university and Leo was summoned by the Dean to explain himself.

In those days Leo never stopped talking. They would sit in the smoky bar of the Cross Keys eating soggy sausage rolls with the rain rattling on the windows while he told her of the endless sunshine, the weekend barbecues, the late-night skinny-dipping parties in somebody's pool. Margot was enthralled. She had only ever been on holiday outside Scotland once, to an aunt's house in Cornwall, and a dismally sodden experience that was.

What made it even better was the envy of her girl-friends. The mere fact that Leo was Australian gave him a glamorous appeal in a granite-grey Scottish university town where the chief excitement on offer was a ferry trip across the Tay to Dundee. Standing just over six feet, with fair hair and lightly tanned skin, he was deemed a rare and exciting catch; and Margot had caught him. She found herself in love with a country she had never been to and a young man she hardly knew. There had been boyfriends before, mostly third- and fourth-year students and that man from the oil company in Aberdeen, but nothing like her handsome Australian.

Then suddenly Leo became well known. His papers and lectures on pinniped communication went around the world. When he had first told her what he was working on she was too embarrassed to ask what a pinniped was, and had to look it up in the dictionary. 'A: *adj.*: having feet resembling fins, fin-footed; species belonging to a suborder which have fin-like limbs or flippers. B: *n.*: a pinniped mammal; a seal or walrus.'

Margot was desperate to shed her humdrum life and share the exciting world in which Leo lived. Whenever possible she travelled with him to conferences, first in Britain and then, when they could persuade the organisers to provide an extra ticket for a research assistant, abroad.

They spent the beginning of their married life in Norway, because Leo had been offered a one-year secondment with better pay and a decent flat at the Norwegian Institute of Marine Research in Tromsø. Describing itself as the northernmost city in the world, Tromsø lies 217 miles inside the Arctic Circle. Leo assured Margot that the climate was not that bad: only minus four in winter and an all-day average of twelve in summer. That wasn't the point, however. Summer was bearable, although like a lot of non-natives she found it hard to sleep when daylight stretched around the clock, with a few hours of twilight masquerading as the night. But in the winter, from what she understood, Tromsø made Scotland seem like paradise.

At that time of year daylight amounted to an hour or so of bluish watery twilight. The long hours of darkness during the polar night, Margot read, were alleviated by the Aurora Borealis, which appeared to be the work of some mad artist painting broad brushstrokes of pink and green across the canvas of the night sky. Otherwise visitors and locals seemed to divide their time between the twin national passions of talking about, or playing, football, and drinking. With 65 licensed clubs, pubs and bars for a population of 65,000 people – the highest ratio in any Western city – Tromsø appeared to take civic pride in enabling its inhabitants to drink their way through the winter.

It was a strange place for a newly married couple, but at first they loved it. For a marine biologist whose reputation and career were being built around the study of seals' behaviour, the posting to the Tromsø marine institute seemed like an extraordinary stroke of good fortune. There were huge seal populations scattered over the Arctic wastes that stretched all the way from northern Norway across the seasonally frozen waters of the Barents Sea to the ice-capped archipelagos of Spitzbergen and Franz Joseph Land. The seal territories were only a few hours' flying time from Tromsø, and dog-sledging expeditions took Leo and his colleagues deep into the Arctic Circle for two weeks at a time, camping out at night and tracking seal populations and recording their communications by day.

But it was the long plane trips aboard the flying laboratories crewed by Russians and carrying Norwegian and visiting scientists that alerted Leo to the fact that the research programme in Norway was not entirely what it seemed. The Russians supplied the twin-engined Antonov 26 transport planes and crew, and flew regular aerial surveys along the edge of the ice fields of the northern and central Barents Sea studying seal populations, especially those of the harp seal. In the official language of the Norwegian Ministry of Fisheries, the aim of these flights was 'to gather data to help understand the interaction between marine predators and commercial fish species, including capelin'.

Leo soon realised this was official speak for gathering evidence to convict seals of eating commercial fish species, including capelin – which of course they did – in order to justify their slaughter – which of course the Norwegian government zealously carried out.

After six months of his contract Leo took Margot out to Tromsø's finest restaurant, where they ordered reindeer steaks and he told her they were going home. He had been deceived, he told her. The entire programme as far as he could see was predicated on an unofficial policy that seals and other sea mammals were vermin and should be killed. There was no genuine interest in researching the mysteries of their lives. As for the flights, they were not about the welfare of the seal population. The Russians on board were definitely not interested in seals. With their dark glasses and small cigars they looked more like secret-service operatives, which was what Leo supposed they were. As for the Norwegians, they just wanted to prove that their harp seal population was large enough to justify their slaughter.

In the restaurant that night Leo read out a long letter he had written to Professor Stubbs in St Andrews. He was drunk, and spoke loudly, ignoring Margot's efforts to shush him.

'I find myself in Kafka country. The man I work for in the sea-mammal unit believes in the mass murder of sea mammals, especially seals, but also whales. All the Norwegians want to do is prove the seals are marine pests. Norwegians eat fish, trade in fish and use fish products in a thousand different ways. They take the simple view that if the seals were wiped out there would be more fish for everyone. Here are animals that eat the source of their wealth, health and happiness, so the logical conclusion is kill them.'

And as he had discovered, Norwegians ate seals as well. He had had a seal dinner with some colleagues from the North Polar Institute at a weekend camp. The meat had been sliced into steaks and grilled over a wood fire. The dark black flesh tasted very gamey. Minke whale was on the menu too. It tasted like beef dipped in fish oil.

Looking back, Margot realised that sometime during those months in Tromsø their relationship changed; the balance of need, love and lust had shifted. Leo found in himself a wellspring of anger that quickly turned to hatred. He had found a cause, an enemy to confront, a battle to win. More than a battle, this was a war. Norway, Japan, Iceland, the whale-hunting, seal-slaughtering nations justified their actions in the name of business, pure and simple. They were the enemy. They had to be confronted, to be fought through the media at one end of the spectrum and through direct action at the other. That was the world that began to consume him. He loved her, cherished her, and wanted above all for her to be the mother of his children. But he didn't need her as he had done at St Andrews. What he needed was a cause, a mission in life, a reason for getting out of bed in the morning, and in Norway he found it.

When they got back from Tromsø in February of 1993 Leo resumed his old job at the Sea Mammal Unit, but they both quickly wearied of St Andrews. Sam had been born in Norway, and they settled with their new baby into a one-bedroom first-floor flat over a café in North Street. It was just across from the university library, and beyond that, past the 400-year-old oak tree, lay the new buildings that housed Leo's department. That was very convenient for him, but without a job to do, and no longer being able to travel with him because of the baby, Margot became bored and restless. She felt like a prisoner in the tiny flat at the top of a steep narrow staircase leading from the street.

When Leo bounded up that staircase one evening and told her about the Coldharbor job, they discussed it for exactly thirty seconds – the time it took to open a bottle of sparkling Spanish wine.

The Cape was a revelation after St Andrews. They arrived in the spring of 1994 and, as Margot wrote home to her mother, it was like opening a long-locked door in a dark and dreary house and discovering a brightly lit room filled with colour, light, sound and new faces.

Leo fell in love with the Coldharbor Institute, its resources, and the rich opportunities for field research. He even claimed to like the Portuguese food in the canteen, a popular local cuisine brought over from Lisbon by fishermen who crossed the Atlantic in search of cod two centuries before. As for Margot, she just loved the American way of doing everything, especially driving slowly in a large car sipping a takeaway latte and eating a sugary doughnut while listening to endless weather reports on the local radio station WXTK.

'And the weather in the summer months is hot, hot, hot,' she wrote home to her mother. 'I spend the summer days on the beach with the kids while Leo does his stuff at the Institute. If heaven has another name, it's Cape Cod.'

Also, both of them loved the passionate commitment of the Cape Codders to the environment and history of this strange corner of the United States. Everyone cared, everyone was an activist, everyone saw it as duty to do something to preserve and where possible improve life on the Cape.

There were endless associations and committees to preserve the wildlife, the wetlands, the woodlands, the dunes, the windmills and the historic homes of the old whaling barons. If a seal was found injured on a beach it would be headline news. The emergency services would rush to the scene and cordon the area off. Veterinary surgeons would be brought in and the press briefed. In Norway they would shoot the creature and throw the carcase into the sea.

But just as Tromsø had deceived them, so, in time, did the Cape. Leo's work engulfed them. Every other weekend he was away at a conference, a seminar, a workshop, attending grandly named events that seemed to Margot little more than an excuse for most of the participants to indulge in a weekend of ego-stroking. They allowed Leo and his colleagues to pursue their favourite hobby: impressing each other with their bountiful store of knowledge. It wasn't much better when he was home: every conversation seemed to be about the Stellwagen Bank, seal culls, Canadian policy on declining fish stocks, the latest Norwegian or Japanese position on whaling, sustainable this and irreplaceable that.

Margot became lonely. It was as simple as that. Her fault? Probably. She had Jenny and the WALL lunches. Of course she had Sam, and Julian who had been born a year after they arrived; but as any parent knows, children put their chubby little fingers on time's fast-forward button and press hard. The years somehow slip past and suddenly that blue-eyed baby, almost edible in its deliciousness, has grown up. And you have grown old, and you ask yourself, 'Is this all there is?'

Margot couldn't teach, so she tried her design business, but that failed, and then Julian died. No, he didn't die, he was killed in an accident, a stupid, silly, seal-watching accident. It was no one's fault, except it wouldn't have happened if his father hadn't taken him out that day. But that wasn't fair. Well, fuck fairness, she thought. It was Leo's fault. He killed our son; as good as, anyway.

They had the funeral in the same church in which Leo was to have his, and because the graveyard was full of mossy old headstones they had cremated Julian and scattered his ashes. Not at sea; she wouldn't allow that, although Leo wanted to.

No, they scattered Julian in the woods behind their house where he used to play with the neighbours' children when he was very little. She, Sam and Leo had tipped the grey ash, the culmination of ten years of life, in drifting clouds below the trees, and watched it settle on the mossy undergrowth and the petals of the small crocuses.

She told Leo and Sam to go, insisting they leave her on her own for a few minutes. She poured some cold wine from her Thermos into the plastic cup lid, raised it high in salute to her lost son, and told him that she loved him, had always loved him and would always love him. Then she drank the wine. It didn't make her feel any better.

Leo commissioned a bench, and placed it with permission from the Falmouth council on the town green with Julian's name and the dates of his brief life carved on it and the Latin words 'Ave Atque Vale'. Hail and farewell. Margot would sit there with Sam some evenings in the summer drinking coffee and waiting for the old Saab to come up the road from Coldharbor.

The first thing visitors to Sandy Rowan's apartment noticed were the books. They marched across the walls in the sitting room on smart wooden shelving; they were piled up high on the floor and were stacked on the dining table, allowing only a small space for a single diner to sit and wield a knife and fork; they climbed the sides of an old desk as if in rebuke to the laptop, voice recorder and other digital equipment on top. There were books in the bathroom, damp and slightly mildewed, and more in the kitchen, spattered with stains of ketchup and gravy. There were books under plastic sheeting on the balcony and lining the stairs in the common parts of the building on rickety shelving, the latter a subject of occasional arguments with the landlord but of no great concern to the other tenants, who actually liked the aura of erudition they bought to an otherwise nondescript block of apartments.

Book-buying, preferably cheap second-hand books, was an addiction from which Sandy had suffered for many years. He couldn't help himself. He could no more imagine a day without a glass of wine at the end of it than he could a week in which he did not spend an hour or so casting an eye over the shelves of one of the Cape's many second-hand bookstores. Occasionally, usually after a little too much wine, he would fall over one of the piles of books, and a few armfuls of volumes would be selected more or less at random, shoved into boxes, loaded into the station wagon and driven away to a dealer. Then the buying would start again.

The only challenge to the hegemony of books in the apartment came from a large, glass-fronted wine cabinet of the kind you find in liquor stores. Illuminated from within and refrigerated so that the tightly packed array of bottles were all suitably beaded with moisture, the cabinet occupied half of one side of a wall, shouldering aside the indignant piles of books that surrounded it.

After his rebuff in the Dark Side, Sandy had returned

to his apartment, swept the books from his desk and begun to write. He knew he should have gone round to see Margot and Sam at home, as any good friend would have done, instead of trying to muscle in on the boat trip. But he could not confront the reality that Leo wouldn't be there. This surprised him. Hardened newsman can't face the fact that his friend has been lost at sea? Strange.

Stranger still, he left the wine in the cabinet, and for two hours he wrote down everything he could remember of his conversations with Leo; every joke they had shared; the ideas they had explored; and the wittily obscene comments they had exchanged about the women in the bar.

He wrote fast, and checked the word count. Fifteen hundred words. Good words too, clear, unadorned short sentences. No frills. 'Just give me the facts, ma'am,' as the detective said in that old TV series. That's what this job of his taught you, to write English. That alone made his career choice worthwhile. To be able to sit down and pour old memories on to paper while your heart was breaking.

Then he opened a bottle, sat on the narrow balcony and drank.

Sandy got up early the next morning and walked the waterline of the estuaries and bays that indent the coast north of Chatham. Pleasant Bay and Little Pleasant Bay, and then Salt Pond Bay, Nauset harbour, anywhere a man might have swum seeking shelter from a sudden storm at sea.

He slashed at reed beds with a long stick, tramped through

back gardens, peered into boathouses, kicked and swore at barking dogs and flashed his press card by way of explanation to irate householders and boatmen.

It didn't make sense, of course, but there was still a chance, a faint chance, that Leo might be there somewhere, half dead on an inland shoreline. Once through the dunes Sandy saw the *Antoine* going slowly up the coast, on the same mission impossible as his own, he thought. After three hours' tramping he gave up. If Leo Kemp was anywhere on the Cape, dead or alive, there had to be a better way of finding him.

The *Cape Herald* occupied a modern two-storey building on the edge of Barnstaple Municipal airport and a five-minute drive from Route 6, which bisects the Cape from Provincetown to the Sagamore Bridge.

The new owner who had bought the paper a few years ago had moved its offices out of Main Street in Falmouth, on the grounds that the journalists spent too much time in bars and cafés talking to each other, and not enough out and about gathering news.

The journalists claimed to have discovered that their new offices were sited in an area that had originally been called ITMON, a corruption of a Native American word meaning 'the place to bury the dead'. One wag even got this put up on the paper's website, and it was some weeks before the editor realised that the name was an acronym for In the Middle of Nowhere.

The paper's new home did have the advantage of the nearby airfield; the disadvantage was that there was never a story big enough to justify hiring a plane, and there was no budget to do so even if there had been.

Sandy's pitch for a two-hour charter to fly along the coast looking for the missing scientist met with a predictable response from his editor. The *Herald* had already covered the fact that Kemp was missing, including an interview with the Institute's chief executive and a brief statement from Kemp's wife praising the rescue effort. The students had been banned by the Institute from talking to the press. They had all been offered counselling, but most had opted to get drunk instead. Buck had refused to talk to anyone. There was not a lot left to say until a body turned up.

'And suppose he's still alive?' asked Sandy. 'Suppose he's out there somewhere, unconscious, injured, and unable to move? He's only been gone twenty-four hours. It's possible. They haven't found a body yet, have they? Why not? The sea brings our bodies in on the next tide – always. You know that. You did enough of those stories when you were a reporter.

The editor tried not to look interested. 'Go on,' he said. 'Think of the story if we find him, if we bring him back.'

The editor knew Sandy was right about the body. In the old days, when there were plenty of summer drownings, the bodies always came back, usually on the next tide. The sea was punctilious about delivering up its dead. There should have been a body by now. Kemp had gone overboard only a few hundred yards from the beach. 'Make sure you don't pay the tourist rate,' the editor growled.

The quoted tourist rate for a Cessna 172 was $325 an

hour. Sandy got it for $250 with the promise of a mention for the charter company in the article.

The trip made no sense to the woman in the office of Fairchild Charters at the airport, and not much to Sandy. He told her instead that he wanted to find concentrations of seals. She had raised an eyebrow at that. 'You'd be better off in a boat,' she said, 'but it's your money.'

They took off and swung south-west to start a run up the coast from Martha's Vineyard. The pilot pointed out the spot where John Kennedy, Jr had gone into the sea with his wife and sister-in-law seven miles from the coast on a misty evening in July 1999.

'Tell you something,' he said. 'It was like a mini 9/11 on the Vineyard the next day. People couldn't believe it had happened again. They walked around in a daze. I know, I was there. I spent the next two days flying over the ocean looking for wreckage, on charter to the coastguard.'

Sandy let him talk, but he wasn't interested. He had written enough about the Kennedys to fill an encyclopaedia. He told the pilot he was doing a feature article on seals and their attraction to tourists. It seemed easier than trying to explain that he hoped to see a missing man on a deserted beach, exhausted, dehydrated, semi-conscious, perhaps lying beside an 'SOS' scrawled in the sand.

That was the hope. A million-to-one miracle that would bring a friend back to life and give him a great story. Sandy peered through the window as the pilot dipped to the lowest permitted level of 500 feet.

They flew up the coast for twenty minutes, and passed

121

low over Monomoy Island. Out to sea Sandy could see the lifeboats and smaller craft belonging to local fishermen still working the grid patterns. The chopper had gone back after a few hours, deemed too expensive when all that anyone expected to find was a body.

The seals were there, clusters of black dots lining the foreshore in several rookeries. 'Rookeries' of seals, thought Sandy. When did the naturalists decide to apply the collective noun for fierce, scrawny, squawking birds to sleek, lovable, blubbery sea mammals? He made a note to check it and slide in a reference in the piece. Except that he wasn't writing a piece, he reminded himself.

The light green water of the shallows shaded into darker colours as the seabed dropped down to the deeper level. John Kennedy's Piper Saratoga had gone down in 116 feet, a relatively shallow depth which enabled the US naval salvage ships to recover 75 per cent of the wreckage and the bodies of Kennedy, his wife Carolyn and her sister Lauren Bessette. They buzzed low over Monomoy twice. Sandy tried his binoculars, but it was impossible to focus in a plane that was beginning to bump a little in the lumpy air as the day warmed up.

'Going to be another warm day,' said the pilot. 'Where to now?'

Good question. Below them the dune grass rolled out for miles like a thick mat, giving way inland to patches of scrub that could hide a body for years.

They flew up over Nauset Beach, past the old Marconi towers at Wellfleet, dipped low over White Crest Beach with its surfers riding the Atlantic rollers, on up along the crescent-shaped coastline over beach after beach, occasionally swooping down over a scattering of seals on the sandbanks.

At the Highland Lighthouse near Truro, Sandy decided they had gone far enough, and the plane made a low sweeping turn over a sea whose white crests lazily chased each other to the shore.

'We could try Atlantic Island if you like,' said the pilot. 'Plenty of seals there. Whole island full of them. Seals and birds is all you'll see on Atlantic.'

'How far?'

'Oh, fifteen miles or so. It's beyond Nantucket.'

Too far. If Kemp was anywhere, it would be here, some-where along the coast. Sandy told the pilot to turn back, and settled into his seat. He closed his eyes, suddenly weary of the bumpy ride and let his mind drift. He's dead, he thought, definitely dead by now. Let's just find the body, and then, in the jargon of the age, we can get closure and move on. Just reveal yourself, Kemp. Throw your corpse up on the nearest beach like a good dead person, fling out your arms and lie on the sand, gazing sightless at the sky . . . and suddenly, there he was, walking on the beach, pale, emaciated, recognisably Kemp, and indisputably dead.

'How about a drink?' said Sandy.

'Dead men don't drink,' said Kemp.

Sandy woke with a start, and saw the runway looming through the cockpit window.

'We're almost there,' said the pilot. 'Didn't want to wake you.'

*   *   *

123

Sam Kemp pushed open the door to Mrs Gulliver's studio just off Falmouth's Main Street. An old cannonball, one of 3,000 fired into the town in January 1814 by the British sloop *Nimrod*, weighted a pulley attached to the handle and swung the door shut behind her. Gloria Gulliver was proud of her door weight. Two Gulliver ancestors had fought at Lexington and Concord, the first battles of the Revolutionary War, in 1775. And a Francis Gulliver had been second in command to the gallant Captain Weston Jenkins, commander of the Falmouth Battalion of Artillery which had successfully defended the town against British attack in 1814. The 18-gun British sloop had fired 32-pound balls from half a mile offshore that day, but Gloria told visitors that the only damage done by the bombardment had been to a pillowcase full of feathers.

In the winter the gallery showed mainly watercolour landscapes of the Cape's low hills and sandy shores. Like many artists, Mrs Gulliver found inspiration in old lighthouses and in the few remaining grey-shingled windmills that were once used to grind corn and pump up sea water to produce salt. Those and the lighthouses populated her paintings. To make ends meet during the winter months she also ran evening classes in watercolours.

She was a good teacher, with the gift of making her students understand the simple technique of moving an image from the mind's eye to the canvas with a few strokes of the brush. Her classes were always oversubscribed.

With the season approaching she had switched to portraits in oil, charging $500, with guaranteed completion in a week. The purists sneered that she was little more than a beach photographer but she didn't mind. Sometimes summer visitors came in for a sitting, paid their deposit and never returned to pick up the portrait. Sam looked at the rows of faces: children, mothers, fathers, family groups; character, mood and emotion captured by the colour and texture of paint.

'Can I help you?'

Mrs Gulliver was dressed in tight jeans and a slim-fit checked shirt, with her hair tied back in a ponytail. Only a woman who knows that her figure and the allure of her earlier years have survived into middle age can dress like that.

'I want to commission a portrait of my dad,' said Sam.

Mrs Gulliver sat down, and motioned Sam to do likewise.

'Aren't you Leo Kemp's girl?'

Sam nodded.

'I'm sorry, really sorry.'

'It's all right. I mean, it's not, but we don't know for sure, and anyway . . .' She fell silent, looked at the floor and sniffed.

'Here, let me get you a coffee.'

'No, thanks. I just want the . . .'

'. . . portrait of your father?'

'Yes.'

Sam handed over an envelope. 'These are recent photos; can you do it from them?'

'Of course I can. But I knew your father, he came for classes here.'

Sam looked down. 'I know you knew him, Mrs Gulliver.'

The addition of her name to that sentence gave it an ominous layer of meaning that Mrs Gulliver suspected she understood all too well.

'Are you trying to tell me something, Sam?'

Sam stared hard at her feet. 'Dad kept a diary. I've seen it.'

Mrs Gulliver coloured and stood up.

Sam got to her feet quickly. 'I'm not here for that, really. I'm sorry I said that. I – we – just want the portrait, and it would be so good because you know him, knew him . . . you can use the photos and paint him as he was from memory.'

Leo had told Gloria he was keeping a diary. Nothing explicit, he reassured her, just jottings about the occasional, far too occasional, times when he would linger behind after the evening class and she would light some candles and get the wine out, and they would just drink and talk and laugh for an hour or so. She was witty, cruelly funny about the pomposity of Cape social life in the winter, and a wise counsellor about his adversarial relationship with the Institute management.

It had begun when he had asked her about the cannon-ball door weight one evening after the other students had gone. She said it was a historical memento, a reminder that her family had fought in the Revolutionary War. After the opening battles one of her ancestors had gone on to lead the storming of the British schooner *Diana* outside Boston harbour, the first naval encounter of the war.

Leo had made the mistake of telling her about the Kemp family's slightly less glamorous antecedents. His great-great-great-great-grandfather had been convicted of sheep-stealing in the Scottish highlands and deported to Australia in the

1820s. So his family had fallen out with the British too. Mrs Gulliver laughed, checked herself, and then could not contain her giggles.

She was still half laughing when she apologised. It was absurd, wasn't it, she said, sending a man to the other side of the world for stealing a sheep. For some reason it irritated Kemp that she found this so funny, and the fact that it irritated him made it all the funnier to her.

'So the Brits shackled your great-great-great-great-grandfather with a ball and chain and sent him to a convict colony, did they? Well, they tried to shackle us with cannon-balls. They fired enough of them into this town that day. And that didn't do them any good either. Anyway, we're both from rebel stock. My ancestors fought them with muskets, while yours stole their sheep.' And she laughed and suddenly kissed him, and that's how it started.

She turned back to Sam. 'I can't do this. I'm sorry. And I'm really sorry about your father.'

'Mrs Gulliver, he loved you. He said you were his harbour, his safe haven.'

Those were the very words he had used to her whenever they met. *You are my harbour, my safe haven.* Gloria Gulliver was shocked. 'How do you know that?' She had lowered her voice almost to whisper.

'I know my father. I'm not here to condemn, or to cause a row, or anything like that. All I want is a portrait of my father, and I'll pay for it.'

'Has your mother seen the diary?'

'No. I love my parents, Mrs Gulliver. I don't want to hurt them.'

'So it's your secret?'

'Yes.'

There was a long pause. Mrs Gulliver turned to look at the portraits on the wall. She could remember the personalities that went with every one: good, bad, grumpy, sad, smiley, sexy. When you spend a few hours in a studio with a sitter the skin peels off and there they are, naked before you. She deliberately kept her back to Sam.

'Your mother doesn't know?'

'No. And she won't, I've told you.'

'I mean does she know you've come here today?'

'No.'

Mrs Gulliver turned and faced Sam. 'OK, I'll do it. But I think we should wait. You've had no news, and it's only been two days.'

'The coastguard say men don't come back from the Atlantic alive after two days.'

'I know.' She put out a hand, but Sam stepped away and turned to leave.

The door swung shut behind her, the felt-padded cannonball clunking softly against the door frame.

Mrs Gulliver sat down, feeling slightly faint, and took a deep breath. The girl had been so calm, so single-minded, and apparently so discreet.

Well, she would have her portrait. Her father was a good man, who cared deeply about his work and who wanted to make a difference, a lonely man who had stumbled into her life, and with whom she had found a little fun and laughter.

That serious face of his when he was explaining the migration of the godwit, the ecosystem of the Stellwagen Bank or the radar capabilities of the harbour seal. Leo Kemp did not do small talk. She'd seen him at parties lost for words in the babble of conversation around him, shifting from foot to foot and nervously drinking too much white wine. She remembered him once repeating his latest lecture in the studio after a class, and her leaning over in mid-sentence and whispering a startling obscenity in his ear. He frowned and said, 'Am I completely and utterly boring you?' She undid one button of his shirt, slid a hand over his chest and pressed against his beating heart and said, 'Not now, you're not.'

That was the irony, she told herself. She had given up a well-paid creative job in a New York ad agency to find peace and solitude here on the Cape. She had made an early, disastrous, marriage to one of the ad agency jerks who mistook line after line of coke for a lifestyle and had difficulty working out which should take pride of place in his trophy case: the wife or the Lamborghini.

It was over too quickly for her to have had children, thank God. She got her revenge on him and his whole tribe with a career that took her to the top of the agency. She moved fast, and deliberately turned her back on the conventional marriage-and-kids route to middle age. Then, as if to punish herself – or reward herself; she could never work out which – she threw in the job, rented out the loft to the boyfriend, a copywriter for an ad agency with a face full of freckles and a passion for the poetry of Dylan Thomas. Then she moved to the Cape to begin again. The one man whose advice she trusted, probably the only man she had ever really loved, had thoroughly approved. 'Do something in life you really enjoy,' her father had said. 'That's the secret.'

And what she really enjoyed, and had always enjoyed, was painting with watercolours. She had always painted. Her father still kept the childish early paintings from her school days framed in his office: dark brown cats with brightly coloured rainbows behind them; horses with outsize bodies and stick-thin legs galloping through fields with more rainbows around them; and flowers, always of course with rainbows in the background. Had she ever thought of just painting the rainbows? her father had asked once.

For a while, her freckled friend flew up at weekends to see her, but it had not felt right; it hadn't fitted the plan, and she told herself she should have moved further away. In fact he stopped after a few visits.

She loved the Cape. She liked the arty crowd up in Provincetown, and for all that she mocked the pretensions of the wealthy year-round residents, the fact was they bought her paintings. A small review in the weekend section of the *New York Times* had started it, and then suddenly everyone wanted her work. Cape Cod's popular art-class teacher had become a successful artist.

And now the peace and quiet had gone. Her sad, mixed-up lover was missing, presumed dead, and she had been asked to paint his portrait by his daughter.

JUNE

FIVE

The search for Leo Kemp was abandoned after three days. Monomoy Island and the surrounding coastline had been scoured by teams from the police and coastguard, aided by Institute students and staff. They had combed every inch of the island in case he had somehow dragged himself through the belt of dunes into the scrub of the interior. The sea search had also proved fruitless.

The coastguard wrote a report for the police, who handed it to the coroner's officer. The file was headed 'Missing at Sea, Presumed Drowned'. The coroner opened and immediately adjourned an inquest, setting a date for a new hearing in a week's time. News of Leo's disappearance and presumed death had made a brief story in the *Boston Globe*, but no more, although the *Scotsman* carried a long obituary by Professor Melrose Stubbs. The *Cape Herald* had not carried an obituary. The paper had published a premature obituary of a prominent Boston lawyer who had retired to the Cape some years before and had been sued for libel as a result. These days the editor wanted to hear a body had been found before publication.

Margot and Sam spent much of their time walking the beaches with Beano, the West Highland terrier Margot's parents had given her two Christmases ago, to remind her of home, they said. Beano had been bought sight unseen from a Boston breeder over the internet, and shipped to the Cape on Christmas Eve in a large wire and wicker basket. Margot was amazed. It was the most original present her parents had ever given her, and also the most expensive.

Most beaches were filling up, although the main vacation period had not started yet, but like all Cape Codders, Margot knew where to find solitude on an out-of-the-way beach. On their walks she and Sam talked endlessly of Leo, and as they discussed the funeral arrangements they slowly allowed themselves to admit the fact that he was dead.

One morning Margot suddenly said, 'If anyone says to me again that Leo has gone to join Julian, I am going to slap them good and hard.'

'Who said that, Mum?'

'That idiot priest who came yesterday. He wanted to talk about the funeral. I gave him a glass of wine and he came out with that bullshit.'

'Mum, do you think you're drinking too much?'

'I'm not drinking enough, darling.'

Sometimes they would sit on Dad's deck, as they called

it, looking out over the sound and talking until the lights around the harbour dimmed at midnight. Sam believed in an afterlife, and one night she said, 'I don't care what you think, Mum, but what I think is that they're all together, Dad and Julian and the seals.'

Margot sighed. 'If you say so, darling.'

It was late. Margot was feeling sleepy and slightly drunk. Sam snuggled into her lap and whispered, 'Can I ask you something, Mum?

'Darling, it's late. Let's sleep.'

'Did you love Dad?'

Margot opened her eyes, suddenly awake. 'Of course I did, darling.'

'Mum, I'm sixteen. I want to know, did you two just stay together for me? I mean, did you both have affairs and stuff?'

It's like this with kids. They always ask awkward questions at the most bloody awful times, thought Margot.

'Your father wasn't interested in that sort of thing, or if he was he never showed it. His world was the Institute – you know that, darling.'

There was a silence, and then Sam said, 'And you?'

'Bedtime,' said Margot, lifting herself from the chair and putting Sam on to her feet.

She watched her daughter as she fell asleep, the eyelids lowering, the breathing deepening. She went upstairs and sat on the deck listening to the faint childish snores coming from the bedroom below. No drink tonight, she told herself. She lit a cigarette and blew a perfect smoke ring up to the star-filled sky.

Her cell rang. She checked her watch. It was 11 p.m. His voice sounded strained and nervous.

'I've got to see you,' he said. 'It's important.'

'Why? What's happened?'

'I can't talk now.'

'Tell me what it's about. Is it your wife?'

'No. I just need to see you.'

'OK. Tomorrow night.'

Tom never called her. It was always the other way round. She decided to have a drink after all.

Margot met Tom at the usual time in the car park of the Squire. He seemed as nervous as he had sounded the previous night, which was not like him. He muttered a barely audible greeting as she got in his car. They drove down to the dunes in silence. She was right: something had gone wrong at home. He wouldn't look at her, but stared straight ahead, driving much faster than was necessary. He parked badly, braking suddenly and throwing her forward against her seatbelt. He rested his head on the steering wheel, knuckles whitening as he gripped the rim.

She stroked his back gently. 'What is it?'

Tom didn't look up. 'There's talk, bad talk.'

'What – about us?'

'No, about him.'

'Him? Who?'

'Your husband.'

'He's dead, Tom.'

'No one ever found the body.'

'What are you trying to say?'

136

'There's talk, that's all.'

She leant over and gently but firmly turned his face towards her.

'What talk? Who's saying what?'

He twisted his head away from her and gazed out of the window.

'They say there's a human out there among the seals off Monomoy. A man swimming with them.'

Margot suddenly felt very cold. She fumbled in her bag for a cigarette, and lit one.

'Go on.'

'Open the window. I can't have the smell of smoke in here.'

She wound the window down and breathed out a plume of smoke.

'Go on.'

'There's nothing more. That's all.'

'What man?'

'It's just that when the boats pass Monomoy there's always seals about, and some of the boys say they've seen it.'

'Oh, for Christ's sake!'

'I'm just telling you what they're . . .'

'Stop! "They"? Who are "they"?'

'Guys down at the harbour . . . fishermen.'

'You've seen this man?'

'No, and I don't want to.'

'What does he look like?'

'No one's certain. It's just that they swear there was a bearded face, a human face out there with the seals.'

Margot lit another cigarette, inhaled deeply and tried to be calm. 'Seals look like humans, don't they? Isn't that why we love them so much? Warm-blooded, cute, cuddly creatures with big brown eyes? If spiders had cute furry faces like humans we'd love them too, wouldn't we?'

Tom looked miserable, and mumbled that she was right; it was nothing to worry about. He was sorry he'd mentioned it, and would she just forget it?

Margot said of course she would forget it. There were always going to be rumours when someone went missing at sea and the body didn't turn up. Leo, her husband, her late husband, was dead, and that was that. She released the catch under her seat to make it recline, and flicked the cigarette out of the window.

Margot had told Jenny Hathaway all about Tom. She worked on the principle that a secret is not really a secret unless it is shared with a trusted friend. When two people share a secret it somehow becomes a real secret, worth keeping. She told Jennifer everything: her decomposing marriage; every detail of her quickie sex sessions with Tom (In the car park in the dunes, said Jennifer, are you sure that's wise?); and the pride she took in her daughter. Jennifer pretended to take Margot's accounts of car-park flings calmly, like a woman of the world who had experienced many such illicit pleasures, but in fact she was riveted and just slightly envious.

Jennifer had never married, a fact that she accepted without self-pity and even with a certain relief. She told herself she was far too selfish to share her life, her cats and her money with anyone. She wasn't lonely, or if she was she would never recognise that as a description of herself. She was a spinster, a word she hated, but what else do you call a single woman of 44? There were no children and right now no boyfriend, although 'right now' was a term that covered a period of several years.

She told herself she was lucky and happy. Lucky that she had the things that made her happy: her job, her two Burmese cats, her horse stabled at Falmouth, a circle of friends that provided her with pleasure, the enjoyment of the bridge table, a shared bottle of good wine and travel with a group of skiing enthusiasts, the book club.

The trouble was she could never convince her circle of friends that a single woman in her forties could be perfectly happy on her own. However much she told them (and she did so partially to convince herself) that she could happily live without someone else in her life, her married friends naturally thought otherwise. Married couples have always wished, and worked, to see their single friends, especially women, paired off. A married woman regards a single member of her own sex, especially one of her own age, as a challenge to her skills as a matchmaker. Is it not a truth universally acknowledged that a single woman in possession of her faculties and her figure must be in need of a husband?

Jenny was aware of the guile, not to say duplicity, with which her friends schemed to introduce her to suitable men. Charming bridge partners would appear who were entirely unfamiliar with the correct response to an opening bid of one no trump. Handsome men would surface at parties and reveal in casual conversation a remarkable knowledge of her love of horses, her annual ski trips to the French Alps and her appreciation of fine wine.

Jenny reasoned that this was the lot of a single middle-aged woman. (Well, perhaps not middle-aged, she told herself, that surely begins at 50?) And the occasional social humiliation was certainly worth the affection of her friends, who cared so much for her that they spent a great deal of their time trying to find her a husband.

That was Margot's great strength as a friend. She was utterly uninterested in Jenny's social life. She was far too focused on her own problems to worry about her friend's matrimonial prospects.

The whole point of Margot was that she was not a kindred spirit but someone who made Jenny laugh and occasionally cry, someone she had grown to care greatly for. Margot reminded her of Mehitabel the cat in Don Marquis's books. 'Toujours gai' was Mehitabel's motto, a philosophy which sustained her through a series of disasters all carefully chronicled by a cockroach called Archy.

Mehitabel believed that life was to be lived, and there was no need to be crushed by the mistakes of the past, or even the memory of who we once had been in the past. Since she believed she had been Cleopatra in a previous life, she managed her transition to a mangy alley cat in this life remarkably well.

Jennifer had given Margot the Archie and Mehitabel books to read, but her friend saw neither the point of them, nor the similarity between Mehitabel and herself.

'Look at me,' Margot would say, raising her glass of Chardonnay. 'I had a brilliant education and a loving family, and I did exactly what they wanted and wound up as a primary-school teacher. Absolute disaster. I should have been a wild child rock singer.'

'It would certainly have suited your sex life better.'

'Thank you very much, Jennifer. A little *jalouse*, are we?'

Margot and Jennifer met for their wine and laughter lunches in the Quarterdeck Bar and Grill on Falmouth's Main Street. They liked it both because the restaurant cleverly recreated the interior of an old sailing ship, and because they usually managed to get a table at the back, which allowed them to observe the comings and goings of the customers while remaining largely unseen

Given the discreet setting and the confidential nature of their lunches, it was natural that Jennifer was the first person to learn that Margot intended to return to Scotland.

'The big question I can't answer,' said Margot, 'is whether it would be fair on Sam. She's sixteen, happy at school, has lots of friends here. I mean, she's American, dammit.'

'That's simple,' said Jennifer. 'No, it's not fair on her, and you should wait a year or two before even considering a move. She hates Scotland, you've told me that.'

'But if we stay here, she'll grow up with the ghosts of her brother and her father,' argued Margot. 'Surely that wouldn't be right? She'll be reminded of them everywhere in this small, crowded place. She needs a new start.'

'No,' said Jennifer. 'You mean *you* need a new start. Have you thought you might be acting a little selfishly here?'

'Of course I'm being bloody selfish! I have a dead son, a missing, presumed dead husband, and no job. I can't work here. My qualifications aren't recognised, you know that. I can pick up a good job in Scotland. I can go straight back into teaching. I can get my life back on track. My family is there! That's got to be more important for Sam than anything else.'

Jennifer bowed to the force of the argument. 'All right, yes. On balance I suppose you're right to go.'

Margot chose her moment carefully. She met Sam in the tea rooms on Falmouth Main Street, and ordered coffee for herself and melted fudge ice cream and hot chocolate for Sam.

Then she explained slowly and carefully that she had some news which would be good for them both in the long run, and would allow them to start afresh and put this terrible time behind them. Sam seemed lost in her ice cream, and nodded distantly. They would be returning to Scotland after the funeral, said Margot.

'To visit?' asked Sam

'No, to live.'

Sam's chair went over backwards with a crash as she got up, causing a woman behind her to spill her tea

'Mum!! That's not good news! I don't want to go back to Scotland. I have my friends here. I'm American. I live here, this is my home.'

'Listen, darling—'

'I don't want to listen. I'm not leaving! You can't make me. I hate Scotland.'

Conversation at the tables around them was coming to a halt.

'Sit down,' hissed Margot. 'You don't know Scotland, darling. Be reasonable.'

Sam sat down, noticing with gratification that she had every ear in the café.

'No, you be reasonable, Mum. I've been there. I don't like it.'

'You only went once, to visit Grandma and Grandpa.'

Margot realised that she had gained the attention of a café full of afternoon tea drinkers, but lost an argument.

'I hated it.'

'I know you did, and I understand. But this is different. We're going to live there in a beautiful house, and your friends can come over.'

'Come over? After school they'll fly over and drop in for a chat? I don't think so, Mum.'

Why are children so bloody difficult? thought Margot. So she explained about her need to work now that Leo was gone, her need to have her family around her. She had two brothers and six nephews and nieces back home. She could not stay here on the Cape. She had lost her son here, and her husband. She would be lonely and miserable, haunted at every turn by an awful past. This was the time for a clean break, time to move back home. 'And I promise,' she heard herself say, 'I promise we'll come back every summer for the whole school holidays, back here to the Cape.'

'Lonely, Mum? You say you'd be lonely here?'

Margot was startled. She looked at her daughter carefully.

Your children always know more about you than you could ever imagine.

Sam knew that her mother sometimes took condoms with her when she went out at night after a few muttered words on the phone.

Sex was a foreign country to Sam, but one she had visited so often in the virtual world all her age group inhabited that it held few mysteries for her. Girls in her class at school talked about it all the time, as if they were discussing a fast-food menu. The way they talked, sex seemed to occupy the same level of importance and pleasure as a takeaway pizza. It wasn't true, of course. Fast food, music downloads, cool clothes and the occasional quick ciggie; they were the real deal. Sam and her friends might talk of sex as if it was a slice of pizza, but it was bravado – and they knew it. And Sam knew too that Mum's visits to the Squire – oh yes, her school friends had told her she'd been seen there – weren't about pizza.

They called a truce, and agreed on a visit to the cinema and supper afterwards. Sam's choice. The film was *Mamma Mia*, two hours of shared pleasure and popcorn that repaired the rift between mother and daughter.

As they were leaving the cinema, Margot saw Tom in the crowd with his young and plumply pregnant wife. Their eyes met with a flicker of recognition, and they quickly looked away. Margot felt a surprising pang of jealousy. Her casual, throwaway lover with his blonde, swollen wife. He hadn't told Margot she was pregnant. Or that she was so young. She stopped, half turned and bent down to adjust her shoe strap.

As she straightened up Sam said 'Who was that?'

'Who was who, darling?'

'That man who looked at you.'

'What man?'

'Mum, stop it. I saw. You looked at him, too.'

'Oh him. Just some fisherman. A friend of Buck's.'

'Oh yeah?'

Margot spun round and grabbed Sam tightly by the arm. 'Don't "Oh yeah" me,' she hissed. 'Skip the sarcasm. I have too much else to worry about.'

'Sorry, Mum.' Sam was visibly shocked by the sudden change in her mother's mood.

Margot relented. 'No, I'm sorry. This is a horrible time for both of us. We must be strong, be together.'

They entwined their arms and walked out of the cinema together.

Tom and his wife had vanished.

Leo Kemp's funeral took place at 10 a.m. at St Barnabas' Anglican Church on Falmouth's Main Street, opposite the green. It was exactly three weeks since he had been swept overboard. The coroner had agreed to issue a death certificate at the request of the family, on the grounds that his disappearance had been witnessed by a number of his students, and that it could reasonably and legally be assumed that he had drowned.

Without a body there could be no coffin, and Margot and Sam had agreed with the rector's suggestion that the service be conducted as a celebration of Leo's life. All the same, everyone had dressed for a funeral, since there was general agreement that it was hardly appropriate to celebrate Leo's life given that its ending had been so sudden, and was still so recent.

Neither Leo nor Margot had been churchgoers, but Sam had discovered a talent for singing at school that had led her into the church choir. As a chorister she attended the two main Sunday services, and responded to the inevitable teasing by her classmates and her younger brother by pointing out that the Christian message of love and forgiveness was actually pretty cool.

She had shut Julian up by telling him to listen to the lyrics of Arcade Fire's album *Funeral*, which he regarded as the coolest album by the coolest group. 'All about love and loss and redemption,' she said, 'which was why Christ was crucified.' Julian replied, 'Yeah, whatever,' which was his standard response to any question or comment; but when he sat down to listen to the lyrics properly he was impressed. And then of course he died, and until now she had never been able to listen to the album again.

There was a good turnout from the Institute. Tallulah Bonner was in the second row, flanked by the vice president in charge of academic programmes, the Dean, and senior members of the marine biology department. Buck, bulging out of the only suit he possessed, was accompanied by Renee, a tiny, birdlike woman who clung to his arm throughout.

To Margot's surprise a small group of older fishermen from Chatham were gathered at the back. Sandy Rowan represented the *Herald*, but Kemp's father, now in his late eighties, was not well enough to make the trip from Australia. Jennifer Hathaway was there, wearing a dark suit and a black beret. Mrs Gulliver sat at the back in a black skirt and T-shirt and a black leather jacket.

Sam chose the music: the old slave spiritual 'Shenandoah', which the choir would sing in church and which would leave her in tears at the end. Then she chose the hymn 'To Be a Pilgrim'. Tallulah Bonner read lines from Tennyson's 'Ulysses', chosen by Margot, and Sandy read from an anonymous Indian prayer chosen by Sam.

'When I am dead cry for me a little.
Think of me sometimes,
But not too much.
Think of me now and again, as I was in life,
At some moment it's pleasant to recall,
But not for long.
Leave me in peace and I shall leave you in peace,
And while you live let your thoughts be with
    the living.'

The closing hymn was 'Dear Lord and Father of Mankind'.

Woven into the service were two tributes. The first was from Leo's postgraduate class, jointly written by all the students and read by Gunbrit: 'Leo Kemp was different from any teacher we have ever met. He liked to surprise us, to make us think a little differently. He wanted us to question everything, to take nothing for granted. I suppose he was a bit of a rebel, and I guess we liked him for that. So look, this is a really dark day for Mrs Kemp and her daughter, and we don't want to go on too long, but we do want to give you this, Mrs Kemp.'

The whole class rose to their feet, leaving the rest of the congregation uncertain as to what to do. Gunbrit walked over to Margot with a framed watercolour painting of a godwit.

'This was Mr Kemp's favourite bird, a godwit. We can tell you why later, if you like.'

Margot thanked her, wondering what on earth a godwit had meant to her husband. He had never mentioned the bird. Just another one of his secrets, she supposed. Secrets always come out at funerals, isn't that what they say? The mistresses, the missing money, unknown children claiming a relationship with the deceased. Trust Leo to have made a secret of a bloody bird called a godwit.

Gunbrit kissed Margot, and spontaneously the students began clapping, and then everyone in the church got to their feet and applauded.

As they all said afterwards, it was an emotional moment.

Margot's address was not a comfortable one for anyone present, especially as Tallulah Bonner was so prominently seated with her senior colleagues around her. Everyone agreed that Margot should not have said what she did, and that it would be best for her to leave as soon as she could, and to take Sam back to Scotland. That was what she wanted, wasn't it?

Margot read from a prepared text, rarely looking up at her audience. She had written it the night before, and had refused to let Sam see it.

Leo's was a good life, she said, devoted to a cause he

believed in: the search to unlock the secrets of our oceans and the mammals that live in them. He always said that if you believed in something deeply and sincerely, you should fight for it. He believed the fishing industry and its lobbyists were working to repeal the Marine Mammal Protection Act of 1972 to allow the slaughter of seals and other sea mammals to start anew. And he believed that the Coldharbor Institute should stand up to the big money behind the industry and expose that campaign for what it was, an attempt to turn the clock back to a barbaric age.

'Leo Kemp was an awkward, challenging individual,' Margot continued. 'But that's what made him a great teacher. And that's why he was not afraid to say that his own field, oceanography and the marine biology that underpins it, is growing fat and lazy on the hundreds of millions of dollars of funds it raises with such skill.

'My husband used to say that if you dropped a baited hook three kilometres down into the ocean – and that is less than the average depth of all our seas – there was an even chance you'd pull up a species of fish unknown to science. I can hear him say this now: "How can it be that we know less about the bottom of the sea than we do about the dark side of the moon?" That's why he thought modern science was failing to ask the right questions.'

And then she came out with it: on the day before his death Leo Kemp had been dismissed from a job he loved, not for talking to the media, but for challenging the status quo, questioning the cosy corporate world into which oceanographic science in general, and by implication of course the Coldharbor Institute and its Board of Governors in particular, had sunk.

Dean Bonner sat tight-lipped and grim-faced as Margot went on to say how Leo had used Hoover the talking seal to poke fun at the pomposity of the science establishment.

'Now, let me tell you, I understand that was not an ideal position for a member of the Institute's teaching staff to take. But Coldharbor is a great, big, grown-up organisation, is it not? It can surely accommodate a few voices of dissent. Anyway, who knows? Maybe Leo was right. All he wanted was for the science establishment to admit that it doesn't know it all yet.'

There was no formal gathering afterwards, although the Institute had offered to lay on a small reception. Margot and Sam stood on the church steps shaking hands with the mourners, or celebrators. Most had a word or two with them, but when Tallulah Bonner came out she offered Margot the briefest of handshakes, kissed Sam gently, and left.

She was furious, and rightfully so, she told herself. To have the Institute publicly pilloried at a service to remember the life of one of its senior staff was intolerable. Margot Kemp had told her she was leaving the Cape: the sooner the better.

For old times' sake Margot asked Buck, Sandy and Jenny Hathaway for a drink at the Dark Side. Buck's wife came too and sat by his side saying nothing. Once everyone had settled into their seats and ordered, she asked if she had gone too far in her address. Buck and Sandy muttered feeble reassurances, but Jenny said, 'Of course it was the wrong time and place to say that, and of course it upset Tallulah Bonner. But there was never going to be a right time to get that off your chest, so what the hell?'

Everyone agreed. Margot looked pleased, and amid general relief the conversation turned to that staple of post-funeral parties, the merits of the various tributes and readings. Buck sank into silence, staring into his drink. His body hunched forward and he began to rock slowly back and forth on the chair, his knuckles whitening as he gripped his glass. Renee began stroking the back of his head murmuring something in his ear. The conversation died around him. Margot suddenly thought that this big man, a lifelong fisherman well used to the casual violence of the sea, was about to cry. Instead Buck straightened up, raised his glass and said in a hoarse voice, 'Here's to the best friend I ever had.'

When Margot had to leave, prompted by a call from Sam, she expected Jenny to come with her. But her friend seemed strangely reluctant. Sandy was at the bar ordering another bottle of wine, she explained, and he had promised to tell her the secrets of his blend of Syrah and Viognier grapes. She smiled and said. 'I'm enjoying myself. You go home to Sam.'

That night Margot and Sam started packing. Margot watched her daughter carefully, but she seemed to have weathered the emotional storm, or its first wave, anyway. The fact that Sam had done so much to organise the service had really helped.

Sam's friend Mona phoned and asked Sam how she was, and whether she would like to chill for an hour over at her house if her mother didn't mind.

'Are you sure, darling?' asked Margot. 'I mean, we only had the service this morning.'

'Mum that was a service to celebrate Dad's life. I loved it. I loved what everyone said, and the music and the readings. I'm fine about Dad. Maybe I won't be tomorrow or the day after, but right now I'm OK, so don't worry about me. But I do worry about you.' Sam gave her a big hug and a kiss. 'Why don't you ask Jenny Hathaway over?' she said, looking positively cheerful as she skipped to the door. 'I'll only be gone for an hour. Take care.'

God, she's looking after me, thought Margot, and suddenly she felt very alone. I'll soon lose her. In a year or two she'll go to university, maybe St Andrews, and I'll be all alone. They will all have gone.

Gloria Gulliver left the service realising how much she missed the man in whose memory it had been held. It had not occurred to her that what had felt like a brief and casual affair was anything other than that, a little warmth blown in on a chance summer wind. She had not taken it seriously. But listening to his students and to Margot's excoriating address, she realised how much Leo's passions and beliefs had touched those around him.

She returned to her studio and threw away the half-finished watercolour portrait. She decided to start again, in oil this time. Gloria loved watercolours because the technique was fast, immediate and unalterable. You just mixed water with a palette of colours and laid the images on paper with swift brush strokes. There was no going back with watercolours. The paint dried almost immediately, and the finished work was there before you. That's why Gloria was a watercolourist. Once you began a painting you had to finish it quickly. There were no second chances with watercolour. She liked that. It suited her.

She had completed the watercolour of the godwit the students had commissioned in just over three hours. She knew the bird all too well. Leo had talked endlessly about the godwit, describing in detail its plumage, the long curved bill and above all its extraordinary strength, the power that lay in its wings. Gunbrit explained that the painting was a gift to Margot Kemp as a tribute from Leo's students. Gloria had refused payment.

But the portrait of Leo was different. The beauty of oil was that you could build the painting over days, changing colours to alter skin tones, light and shade, altering the whole feel of the composition, which allowed you to explore the inner character of the subject. There was a deeper truth to be found and conveyed in oil. She mixed her paint with linseed oil, making the consistency more liquid than usual; the longer the oil took to dry, the more time there was to modify, adapt and strengthen the portrait.

She decided to turn the portrait into a statement about this strange man and the work that so obsessed him. It wasn't that she disagreed with his views on the fishing industry and the science of oceanography. But she wanted to take him out of that world, make him laugh; make him

153

realise that life did not have to be an endless battle with those of opposing convictions.

'Someone should inject you with a joy drug,' she had once told him. 'Look at yourself! Sandwiched for a heart-beat of time between two eternities of darkness, and all you can do is put your fists up every day and fight. How about a little fun in this short life of yours? I'm going to show you how. I'm going to make you see there's more to it than endless angst about those seals of yours.'

He didn't object. In fact he laughed out loud when she made a quick sketch of two seals in copulatory position and gave him a mock lecture on their mating habits with microscopic anatomical detail – a perfect parody of the self-congratulatory pomposity that characterised so much academic teaching: probably including his own, he thought.

She decided early on in the portrait that Leo would be smiling that slow ironic half-smile that very occasion-ally creased his face when she said or did something outrageous. The first time that had happened was when she had placed a finger on his lips during a passionate discourse on Canadian seal-culling policy and told him to get into the bath.

'What, now? Why?'

'Go on, just do it.'

So he had undressed and got into the bath while she lit candles and placed them all around its edge. She put Ravel's 'Bolero' on the tape deck and turned it up loud.

'Remember Dudley Moore in the film *10*?'

'Remind me.'

'Some gorgeous Hollywood actress is trying to seduce

him, but Dudley Moore doesn't want to know. She puts on this piece by Ravel – all men marching off to war with drumbeats and crashing chords, very sexy – and Dudley says, "What is this?" And she just comes out with it: "Music to make love to."'

He smiled and said, 'That wasn't quite what she said, was it?'

'No, but I don't like four letter words.'

That had made him smile.

She finished the painting in three days, using a scalpel to work in new oils and scrape off the old. She put a closed sign on the studio door, turned the answer phone on and worked until her eyes blurred with fatigue. But she got what she was looking for: Leo on a rocky foreshore, binoculars strung around his neck, hands shoved deep in the pockets of an old anorak with a pod of seals scattered among the seaweed covered rocks in the background. He was staring straight out of the frame, the blue-grey eyes looking out at eternity, the mouth creased in a slight smile as if a sudden pleasurable thought had interrupted the melancholic reverie that lay behind those eyes.

Gloria was a fierce self-critic. But she knew she had caught something of Leo and the world that obsessed him: refracted light from a sunlit sea playing on the rough texture of his face; that half-smile below those haunted eyes; the slick, blubbery bodies of the seals; and beyond them a sea churned to waves by a wind that whipped spume from the crests. The painting was an allegory, of course, but she wanted it to look more like one of those works of photorealism beloved by nature artists. She wanted it to smell and taste of the sea that Leo had loved so much.

She wanted to show him with feet planted firmly on land, a survivor of the sea and a violent and destructive marriage. Gloria knew this portrait was for Margot, Sam and the wider family, but it was also for her. She had a stake in Leo as well as they did. He had been hers as much as anyone's. Yes, she told herself, perhaps she really had loved him.

SIX

Leo Kemp spent the day of his funeral twenty miles north of Monomoy Island, on a deserted stretch of coast near the village of Wellfleet. He was with the same pod of seals he had been with for the past three weeks. He had long since given up questioning his existence; whether he was dead, alive or dreaming, he didn't care. If this was life after death, if he had returned to the world of water mammals from which man had struggled so many millions of years ago, then so be it. He felt at peace. His skin almost blackened by sun and wind, his hair a tangled mat, a beard covering much of his face; he had come to resemble the seals around him.

The sea held no terrors for him. He told himself he was a warm-blooded, air-breathing mammal just like the seals, and with a similar lung capacity. He scraped a diet of mussels, crab, clams and seaweed from the rocks, the latter becoming his dietary staple, the bread and butter of his new existence. There was a great variety of seaweed in the intertidal area, but he ate for choice the long, flat, leaf-like strands of kelp and the dark bubble-wrap seaweed. Leo knew that marine algae was rich in vitamins and minerals and easily absorbed by the human digestive system. The ancients called algae sea vegetables, and Leo reckoned he could probably live well on it alone, provided he had plenty of clean water to drink.

Water was more of a problem, because rainfall at night was rare in the summer months. There was plenty of water to be found, but he had to cross the belt of dunes at night to reach one of the almost a thousand freshwater ponds scattered along the Cape. Kettle ponds, the Codders called them, and there were at least twenty of them within reach of the shore around Wellfleet. At night Leo would drink and swim in them, washing off the salt that had encrusted his body during the day. He only went to the ponds at night, and was never seen. Dogs occasionally chased him, but they always backed away growling when they came close enough to smell the rank odour of decaying fish that he exuded.

He adapted to his new diet and lifestyle without regret or any physical reaction. After only a few days he felt healthier and fitter than he ever had done. He could swim further and faster and was soon able to make free dives of thirty to forty feet to search out scallop beds, as he had done as a young boy in Australia.

That's where it had started: long childhood days spent fooling around on the beach with his friends like any other Australian kid. But in truth he had always been more interested in the dolphins to be seen gambolling in the waters of the 'rip' at the south end of Melbourne's Port Phillip Bay, where two headlands of beach create a narrow neck of water leading to Bass Strait. He had got a book on dolphins out of the public library, and had been struck by the title of the first chapter: 'Half Fish, Half Mammal, and Wholly Human'. From then on he had haunted the harbour at Mornington. Some of his strongest childhood memories were of the fishing boats with their silvery, slithery catches of fish in big wire baskets, including the occasional shark.

His father could only afford a dinghy on his teacher's salary at Mornington High School, but the Saturday-morning expedition with a borrowed trailer to the ramp at Fisherman's Beach where the dinghy was launched was a much-loved childhood ritual. Better still, his uncle ran a scallop boat from Mornington pier, and it was the day-long trips to the scallop beds up the coast that first made him realise what a strange and different world lay beneath the sea.

His uncle had encouraged him to free-dive to the shallower beds, using a mask, a snorkel and gloves. To begin with he could spend only a few seconds on the seabed, gathering the bivalves within their corrugated, orb-shaped shells in a small net. Even at only twenty or thirty feet below the surface he saw an array of brilliant sea creatures that seemed so different from the pallid illustrations in the reference books in the Mornington public library. It was the scallop-boat trips that set him on the path to the zoology department of Melbourne University, and a B.Sc. in Marine Biology.

He wondered whether his early experience of free-diving for scallops had expanded his young lungs. He could not submerge as the seals could for up to thirty minutes, diving to 600 feet, but after three weeks living in the wild every time he followed them in their dives he found himself able to go deeper and to stay underwater for longer.

It had taken millions of years for seals to evolve from land-based, dog-like creatures and to adapt to life in the oceans. They began their evolutionary journey later than whales and dolphins, and so had not quite shed their land-based ancestry. Whales made their move to the ocean 100 million years ago, and were now, like dolphins, totally sea-based, although still warm-blooded, air-breathing mammals. Seals still returned to land to mate and to whelp.

As he began to dive deeper with the seals, first thirty, then forty feet and more underwater, the fantastic thought occurred to Kemp that he might have become the beneficiary of fast-track evolution. Maybe twenty-first-century time had compressed the whole evolutionary cycle, and he was turning into a seal, just as apes had turned into early man.

Kemp had written a paper on the apparent acceleration of the evolutionary cycle the previous year that had been widely published and well reviewed in the academic press. Fresh invitations to appear on the conference circuit followed. His thesis had been that evolution is happening at a greater speed than ever before, and that it is happening all around us, in front of our very eyes.

As an example, he cited the polar bear, which has had to adapt to the sudden melting of the Arctic pack ice, and thus the disappearance of its traditional hunting grounds. Polar bears were now swimming more, and hunting in the water more frequently. How do we know that? Where he could, Kemp always worked video clips into his conference presentations, and on this occasion he clicked a link to YouTube. The lights lowered, and on the big conference screen a small white object appeared on the surface of the sea, moving slowly towards an ice floe on which a sleeping seal was lying. The floe was hardly bigger than the seal, and the camera drew back to show that the seal was sleeping safely in calm, open water. The ice floe began to rock slightly as ripples from the approaching object reached it.

'About ten yards from the seal,' said Kemp, 'you will see that white thing – which is actually the tip of a polar bear's snout – vanish beneath the sea. The seal is operating on the basis of knowledge acquired over the millennia. It feels safe from waterborne attack because it knows – or rather it thinks it knows – that it would see a polar bear swimming towards it. But this bear has been swimming almost underwater, and has now dived as it comes in for the kill. The seal is facing a brand-new tactic forced on the bear by the break-up of the pack ice. Polar bears obviously cannot match the speed and skill of a seal in the water. So the seal is half-asleep, one eye cautiously on the sea where normally it would spot an approaching predator. It thinks it is safe.'

The seal was wrong. The polar bear exploded from the water, landed on top of the seal, killed it with dispatch, and swam off with the bloody carcase.

161

'That clip shows', said Leo, 'how these bears are evolving into marine animals just as their prey, the seals, did before them. In evolutionary time it will not be long before polar bears develop webbed feet, shed their fur and learn how to deep dive. One day, perhaps in a few hundred thousand years, they will be hunting seals in the ocean very much as the orca does today.'

The acceleration of the evolutionary cycle had since become a fashionable topic among scientists, although few remembered that it was Leo Kemp and his YouTube clip that had begun that particular academic paper chase.

Leo told himself he did it as a joke, but he actually found himself checking to see whether he had really been propelled on to the evolutionary fast track by feeling the skin between his toes for any sign of webbing. There was none, of course, but there was no doubt that he could dive deeper and stay underwater longer than at any time since he had been a kid diving from the scallop boats.

He had been a great swimmer in those days, a school champion at 16 when he had done the 100 metres freestyle in 50.2 seconds, at a time when the world record stood at 49.36 seconds.

It was free-diving in the clear warm waters off the coast that had taught him just how quickly the human body reaches its limits underwater. Later he had heard of free dives down to 300 feet, but he had scooped scallops off the seabed at thirty feet, and had only been able to remain at that depth for about a minute.

Both man and his distant cousin the seal require oxygen when submerged; they cannot absorb it as a fish can from the water. So both take the oxygen with them when they dive, stored in lungs and bloodstream. Unlike humans, for whom carbon-monoxide build-up means rapid death after two minutes under water, seals can survive at crushing depths of up to 600 feet for thirty minutes.

The secret, Kemp knew, lay in the heartbeat. Over millions of years the hidden hand of evolution had taken the heart of the seal, which was very like the human heart, and recalibrated it so that seals could lower their heartbeat from 120 beats a minute to about ten when diving. This allows the whole vascular system to contract, so that the oxygenated blood is used only for the brain and the vital organs. While humans only store oxygen in their bloodstream, a seal can also keep reserves of this life force in the myoglobin of its muscles, drawing on its reserves sparingly because millions of years of evolution have taught it to tolerate a high carbon-dioxide concentration.

In that time man has learned to crawl, and then to walk, and has acquired the technical skills to become the master species on the planet. So, thought Leo, I'm actually taking a step *back* down the evolutionary road.

He fantasised about compressing a million years into as many minutes, and becoming a true seal, able to swim, dive, and sleep at sea as they did. He would roam the seas of the world and maybe one day appear in human form like the selkies of the old myths. He would emerge from the sea on a lonely Scottish island, shed his skin to become a handsome young visitor seeking long-lost relatives, and sweep a blue-eyed Celtic girl off her feet. He would woo her, bed her, wed her and father fine children with her. Then, on the longest night of the year, in the depths of winter, he would shed his thin, milk-white man skin and slip back into the warm, blubbery cloak of the sea creature he really was, and return to the waves where he belonged.

At night Leo hauled up on beaches, sand spits and rocky promontories, sleeping rough and waking with the sun. Sometimes the pod would sleep close to him, but more often he would wake alone and scan the empty sea knowing that the seals were asleep offshore, just below the waves.

This was usually in calm weather. The seals would lie suspended in the water a few feet below the surface, buoyed by their blubber. Every ten minutes they would make a few strokes with their rear flippers, rise to the surface, breathe in deeply and sink back below the waves – all while sound asleep.

Leo had thought he knew everything about these creatures that he had studied for so long: their mating, eating, birthing habits. But what he had not appreciated was the sheer joy they took in playful behaviour, arching their sleek, glittering bodies out of the water, chasing each other and racing through the waves for no other reason than pure fun. He could not join in, but they accepted him as a spectator and, or so it appeared to him, deliberately swam at his slower speed when moving from one territory to another.

Below water they twisted and turned around him, their grey-black bodies weaving tight circles above and below as he swam. It was a game, he realised. They were playing with him.

When he dived below the waves they did too, and when he broke the surface they arced out of the water and slid back beneath the sea in single semi-circular movements, sleek, glistening sea creatures reminding him that they, not he, were the masters of their marine environment.

They never got closer to him than a foot or so, but they never let him get too far away. Occasionally he imagined himself a prisoner, held against his will in a colony of seals, shepherded from shore to shore, guarded against predators but prevented from returning to his own kind.

He warmed to the idea that he was a human hostage held by mammals that his kind had for centuries slaughtered and turned into fur caps and candles. He tested the thesis two or three times by leaving the area where his pod had hauled up and slipped quietly into the water. His plan was to swim strongly out to sea for several hundred yards and then turn up the coast, seeing if he could put a headland between himself and the seals. But each time, within minutes a whiskered head would break the surface a few feet away, never looking at him, and quickly submerging again. He knew they were there, though, below the surface and around him in the water.

He knew too that seals had superb underwater eyesight, their large, light-sensitive eyes giving them emmetropic vision in the low-light conditions below the surface. On land, especially in the glittering whiteness of the polar pack ice, the pupils of a seal narrow to thin slits, allowing it to filter out the glare and see well, but only at short distances.

The seal's incomplete evolutionary cycle had left it stranded halfway between land and sea, and it was on land that this short-sighted, legless, blubber-rich beast was most vulnerable. It was on the Arctic pack ice that seals had been killed by the million in the last 200 years.

Like the seal pups, which had put on weight and gained a layer of blubber in their first few months of life, Leo was learning the dangers of the warming waters and the new season's northern migration of fish. He could see seals feeding greedily on the bass, herring and flounder in the shallow waters. They would surround a large shoal, charge in to break it up, and then their dark shapes would follow the silver flash of fish through every twist and turn of their flight. He kept still during these hectic chases, treading water, allowing the fleeing fish to flood past him. Helped by his lengthening fingernails, he began to try to catch his first fish by hand.

But with the rich schools of fish came the predators. Leo realised that the pod had moved to Wellfleet for a reason, and he soon realised what it was. The Cape's only surfing beach, aptly named White Crest Beach, presented a panorama of waves rolling in from the Atlantic, breaking thunderously in the shallows before expiring in foam along miles of beach. To the human ear the surf was an attractive background murmur of sound. Below the surface, where noise was magnified and travelled great distances, it created a mad, roaring cacophony. And it was in this uproar of noise that seals found safety when their great marine enemy the orca, the killer whale, sought its favoured prey.

Leo's pod knew that a group of killer whales had arrived in the Wellfleet area. The behaviour of the seals and their refusal to leave the surf told him the same story. There was no other reason why the pod would have left the open sea. He knew too that his seals would be listening to the echo-locating clicks that would bounce back telling the orca the distance, size, speed and direction of the object located. And somehow the seals' computational brains had worked out that these orca were not looking for fish. In the tumble and roar of the incoming waves they sought sanctuary from whales whose only diet was warm-blooded flesh.

Leo could not see the orcas, but he knew they were there. He could sense the seals' fear as they remained amid the spray and spume of the waves, allowing themselves to be pushed shoreward and then swimming back through the rollers before turning again to stay in the sheltering surf.

The beach was empty of surfers and bathers, so Leo swam closer to shore, seeking out an inlet or cove. Whatever ability he had acquired to survive in shallow waters with the seals, he was not going to try his luck with an orca. To a killer whale he would just be another echo bouncing back, signalling food – a smaller meal than a seal maybe, an *hors d'oeuvre* rather than the main course, but food all the same. In theory he could rely on the intelligence of the orca to ignore a blubberless 180-pound human and choose instead the meat-rich and fatty 400-pound option on the menu. But he didn't want to risk it. Even a killer whale can make a mistake.

He had seen what even a small shark bite can do to a human body, and the sight of a white thigh bone showing through a mass of blood and sinew on Mornington beach had become one of those childhood memories that slot into the recesses of the mind and remain there until dementia or death.

Leo crawled on to some flat rocks backing on to high cliffs, and lay on a bed of seaweed. He could see the heads of fifteen or twenty seals in the surf, mostly adults, but with a few pups among them. A solitary walker with a dog appeared at the far end of the beach, forcing him to retreat from the rocks and scoop out a hollow in the soft sand and chalk of the cliff to stay out of sight.

He stared out to sea, knowing the orcas were out there, trying to get a sight of one of their black dorsal fins. Sunlight bounced off the water, creating momentary shapes and shadows as the big swells moved towards the coast. Two miles out, several fishing boats were visible against the horizon.

Then he saw the fins, each a clear two feet above the water. There were five of the killer whales, about ten yards apart, swimming almost in formation, tacking back and forth towards the beach. Moving fast from their position a mile off the coast, they were preparing to attack. It was late afternoon.

Frustrated by the lack of pinpoint direction, but knowing that their prey were somewhere in the surf, the whales switched from their diagonal tacks when some fifty yards from the shore. Almost in line the five orcas charged straight towards the beach and into the breaking waves, thrashing around for victims.

Just as the surf confused the echo system of the whales, so it reduced the ability of the seals' radar whiskers to determine hostile movement in water. In the surf the seals could see nothing but white foam, hear nothing but the roar of pounding waves; they could no longer receive the myriad sounds and signals of the ocean which their brain could normally translate into information vital to their survival.

After the first attack the seals fled for the open sea, and then turned back as the orcas pursued them, racing for the safety of the surf again. The deadly game of blind man's buff ended after only a few minutes, with spreading stains of blood visible on the white surf. In the churn of the waves Leo could see glimpses of the black-and-white upper bodies of the orcas, first one, then two, with seals clamped in their jaws, the great heads shaking back and forth to tighten the grip on their struggling prey while the whales backed into deeper water. He imagined what must have happened below the surface. A terrified seal, knowing the enemy was close, twisting and turning in the white roaring world of the surf. In an instant the curtain of water would have ripped apart as the head and jaws of the orca exploded into view at a speed that made flight impossible.

The whales moved off after the first foray. They had taken three or four seals; not a great victory, but enough to provide food for the pod.

That night the surviving seals moved to a beach up the coast, and hauled up further inland than usual, seeking out a soft incline of sandy beach backing on to dunes which gave way to high cliffs. Leo slept a few yards away among the dune grass. It was a warm night, with a light offshore breeze. The stars were clear in the cloudless sky. He fell asleep dreaming of Gloria Gulliver.

The next morning the seals spent longer than usual hauled up and did not go into the water until well after daybreak. At first only two or three older males swam out about 200 yards from the beach and began diving, flattening out across the ocean bed, staying under for several minutes at a time, working their way into deeper water. They were listening for the tell-tale locator clicks of the orca and using the sensitive antennae of their whiskers to decode the distant vibrations of the sea. On land those whiskers folded back into the head but underwater Leo had seen them standing stiffly out from the seals' faces. He had seen them move their heads back and forth underwater to ensure that no signal from the depths was missed. Whales can communicate with each other across tens, perhaps hundreds of miles of sea and he saw no reason to suppose seals were any different.

He walked into the sea after the first seals and swam with them, always keeping a few feet of distance from the pod scouts. More than ever he felt that this was where he belonged, here in the water with the same animals he had been with since he had been swept overboard. After half an hour the whole pod was in the sea and moving slowly up the coast about 100 yards from the shore. He could see early-morning walkers clearly on the shore and rationally he told himself that they could see him, although at that distance he guessed he would just be another black head of a seal, worth a look but no more.

His species, *Homo sapiens*, was a few score yards away, walking, sometimes running, on two legs, and swinging its arms after a breakfast of coffee, orange juice and maybe a croissant. Here he was amid a different species, using legs and arms to propel himself through the water after scooping up some seaweed and a late-nesting plover's eggs for a meal at the break of day. There the reasoning ended. He perceived no mystery in the life he was leading; saw no contradiction between his physical self, his identity as a human being, and the alliance he had forged with wild sea mammals.

It was simple really, he told himself. He had let himself go, severed every connection with the past and had found a new way to live. His family, Margot, Sam and his father were all there but in the outer orbit of his new existence. Like photographs in a family album he looked at them from time to time, smiled at the memories, and closed the book. The one family portrait he could not find in his book of memories, the face that eluded him, was that of Julian. He needed to find him.

* * *

Memorial Weekend, which turned May into June, had seen the start of the high season, when Cape Cod got down to the serious business of making money. In the next three months the hoteliers, bar owners and shopkeepers would expect to bring in most of their annual takings.

The High Tide Motel in Wellfleet, like every similar establishment on the Cape, had brushed itself down and painted itself up for the summer. The bedrooms, whose big picture windows gave straight on to a boardwalk, were only feet from the sea. 'If this motel was any closer to the ocean we'd be swimming' was the slogan printed on the brochure.

The motel provided a library of leaflets for the enquiring tourist: deep-sea fishing, sailing, whale-watching, hiking, biking, birdwatching, canoeing, guided visits to lighthouses, windmills, carefully preserved life stations and the old salt works that were a source of profit for generations of past Cape Codders. If the excursions failed to interest the visitor there were the secondary attractions: the beauty parlours, antique shops, art galleries, fitness studios, craft shops and one-of-a-kind boutiques.

All this was laid before the half a million visitors who arrived from June onwards, but especially in the high season months of July and August.

For some years the High Tide Motel's owner had concentrated on attracting a particular group of visitors. What he grandly called his marketing strategy involved emailing birdwatching groups affiliated to the American Birding Association, on the grounds that they were mainly elderly people who made no trouble, had money to spend and liked a beer or two at the end of the day.

Groups of birdwatchers were given special rates, and to make them feel welcome the motel stocked a range of books about the birds of the Cape. Handwritten notes about the latest sightings of rare avian visitors were distributed at breakfast.

The motel was perfectly placed for birdwatching, since the dunes and marshland of the Wellfleet nature reserve, one of the largest on the Cape, were in plain view of the breakfast room. What ensured the motel a high level of return business from the birdwatching fraternity was the observation deck built out from the first floor and equipped with powerful telescopes that could scan the shoreline of the sanctuary and a large area of its reed beds and marshes.

The motel made much of the claim that the Cape was the greatest place for birdwatchers on the whole east coast. Some birdwatchers might well have argued this point, not least because the claim emanated from the motel itself, but it is a fact that the Cape has long been a stopover for many migrant bird species travelling the Atlantic flyway from the Caribbean to northern climes. This brought a great variety of seasonal visitors, but it was the rare residents that the birdwatchers most hoped to see. The chief prize was the piping plover, a small, sand-coloured bird that had been placed on the threatened species list after a loss of habitat due to the huge increase in beach developments.

It was on the observation deck of the motel one evening

in the last week of June that an elderly gentleman from Wichita Falls, Texas, turned his binoculars from the foreshore of the Wellfleet sanctuary to a group of seals in the water about fifty yards out to sea.

Mr Terry Krafinski, a retired postal engineer, had spent the afternoon with his wife and a group of twelve fellow enthusiasts tramping the paths through the sanctuary. Burdened with cameras, notebooks and a guide book to the various species of birds that could be seen in the region, and walking much of the time on sand-clogged paths, they had passed an exhausting few hours. The group was relaxing with a few beers and a rare daiquiri for Mrs Krafinski, who felt she deserved it, when her husband, who had been scanning the sea with his binoculars, gave a small exclamation.

Among the seals he thought he saw – no, he was sure he saw – a human head, the bearded face of a man. He almost jumped out of his chair as he thrust his binoculars at his wife and rushed to one of the mounted telescopes. He swung it seaward, focused and swiftly found the seal group. He moved from one grey-whiskered head to another. The face had gone.

'Well, I'll be damned,' he said, as he sat down and scratched his head.

The image had been so strong, the light so clear and the sea so calm that there was no mistaking what he had seen. The group listened sceptically as Mr Krafinski repeated the description: a man with a dark, sunburnt face, a black beard and matted hair swimming in among the seals, very much part of the pod.

Mrs Krafinski had rarely seen her husband so animated, and she told everyone that as a man of very few words, he must have seen something out there to cause his excitement. At this Mr Krafinski almost lost his temper. He had not seen just *something*. He had seen a human being, a man, out there among the seals.

There was an embarrassed silence while the group variously looked deep into their drinks, hard at their shoes or far out to the horizon. Terry Krafinski was clearly getting too old for these trips.

Then Mrs Krafinski came up with an explanation, and everything became clear. It must be some kind of new Cape diversion for tourists. After all, people went whale-watching and dolphin-spotting, and swimming with dolphins was very popular down in Florida, so maybe some tour operator was offering trips to swim with seals up here on the Cape.

The group relaxed. Of course that's what it must be. They probably called it something like the seal experience, hired out wetsuits to adventurous visitors and dropped them off near a rookery when the tide was right. But Terry Krafinski was not happy. He said he was going to call the local paper in the morning and ask if anyone was offering seal-swimming expeditions.

Lewis Chadwick, the trainee reporter on the *Cape Herald* who took the call, said he would check it out, scribbled down a few notes and forgot about it.

Two days later he was scrabbling to find his notes.

Mary Maloney, the large, blustery lady who managed the coin-operated laundry in Hyannis, had appeared at the

Herald's office with a story. She wanted to talk to the chief reporter, and no one else. Her story was of such importance, she implied, that the paper might well wish to pay her for it.

Sandy always took these interviews. Not because they yielded stories – that was rarely the case – but because among the human flotsam and jetsam that drifted into the *Herald*'s ornate front hall with what they supposed to be a front-page news story there was always a character or two. Misfits; underdogs; the lonely, lost and defeated; those done down by the council, the tax man, their spouses, the weather and local pickpockets: they all washed up in the *Herald*'s interview room.

Sandy loved them all. It was, he realised, a very un-American trait, but failure fascinated him. The reason, as he pointed out to himself in moments of stern self-examination, usually after a glass or two in the Dark Side, was that he too was a failure of heroic proportions; a man who had magnificently failed to fulfil both his own ambitions and the expectations of a loving family. How else to describe the career path of a brilliant student who had left NYU with a masters degree in history and a Ph.D. beckoning on the subject of Harry Hopkins's influence on Roosevelt's foreign policy, and wound up twenty-five years later writing stories in a local paper about proposed changes to the summer parking regulations?

In his more masochistic moods Sandy would remind himself that he had once planned an academic career in such detail that he knew the first essay subject he would set his postgraduate students. *On 1 December 1941 President Roosevelt was having lunch in the White House with his special adviser Harry Hopkins when Secretary Knox called to say that the Japanese were bombing Honolulu. His response was to continue lunch with Hopkins: Discuss*

He could have gone on to any of the top Ivy League universities. An academic career would have followed – and respectability, social status and a certain celebrity within learned circles.

Instead, he fell in love with a young woman who thought foreign correspondents were the new rock stars. 'Imagine Mick Jagger doing dangerous stuff,' she had said. So he tore up his career plans and flew to London to join Reuters. 'Come back when you've had some local paper experience,' he was told. He had written to every local paper on the eastern seaboard, and finally landed a traineeship at the *Cape Herald*, where he had been – happily, he had to admit – ever since.

Sandy and Chadwick saw Mrs Maloney in the sparsely furnished interview room which contained just a table, a few chairs, a carafe of water and a large poster of the *Herald*'s masthead over the slogan: 'You Shall Know the Truth and the Truth Shall Set You Free'. He told Mrs Maloney that he would decide whether payment was appropriate after he had heard the story. He always said this. The *Herald* never paid for stories, but Sandy had found that the prospect of payment always helped an interview along.

Mrs Maloney drank from her glass of water, placed her

large forearms on the table, leant forward, looking directly at Sandy with pale watery eyes – dead sea bass eyes, he thought – and began.

Two nights ago, her 17-year-old son had been out at night with his .22 rifle – nothing illegal, you know, he'd gotten his licence. He and a friend had been walking through the dunes of the Wellfleet sanctuary . . .

'With a gun?' interrupted Sandy.

'They weren't hunting, or anything illegal,' said Mrs Maloney. 'They were just walking; you know what boys are like. Anyway, they saw a whole bunch of seals.'

'That's what they were looking for, seals? Perhaps a seal trophy or a bit of target practice?' said Sandy.

'Certainly not,' said Mrs Maloney, who did not like being interrupted, and wanted to get on with the story, so she wouldn't forget her carefully rehearsed narrative. 'Anyway, they crept up through the dune grass to see how close they could get . . . you know what boys are.'

'I do, Mrs Maloney.'

'And . . . well . . .'

'The gun went off?'

'It was an accident, my boy tripped.'

'Anyone hurt?'

'No,' she said. 'What happened was an accident, and would the paper please print the fact that my son has a licence?'

Sandy reminded her that seal-hunting was illegal.

'I know, I know, but you know what boys are.'

'What actually happened, Mrs Maloney?'

'I think a seal was hit; certainly it rolled over.'

'That's the story? Your boy shot a seal?'

'No.' Mrs Maloney took a noisy gulp from her glass, wiped her mouth with the back of her hand and fixed her watery eyes on Sandy again. 'One of the seals got up and ran at the boys, shouting its head off.'

Mrs Maloney sat back, crossed her plump arms and looked at them triumphantly.

'Could you repeat that, Mrs Maloney?'

'What I said. A seal ran at them shouting – actually swearing, swearing real bad – well, that's what they said.'

Be patient, Sandy told himself. She's a disturbed woman, so hear her out and then get her out. He looked at Chadwick, who was writing something down.

'Seals don't have legs, Mrs Maloney,' said Sandy. 'They don't shout and swear.'

Mrs Maloney was unmoved by this observation. Her boy was telling the truth. She knew that, because she knew he wouldn't and couldn't make it up. He didn't have the imagination. Her boy was telling the truth. He'd been chased off a beach in the middle of the night by a seal that got up and ran at him and his friend. And it swore real badly.

'Are you sure the boys didn't make this up to cover up the shooting of a seal?'

'Why would they do that?'

'Because someone heard the shot, didn't they, and called the police?'

'The police came, yes.'

'Thank you, Mrs Maloney.'

'You're not going to do a story?'

'We'll think about it, Mrs Maloney.'

Sandy saw her out, brushed off another suggestion that

179

the *Herald* might care to pay for this information, and went back to the interview room.

He asked Chadwick what he thought. Chadwick looked a little awkward.

'I got a call a couple of days ago from a guy with a group of birdwatchers at Wellfleet. He claimed to have seen a man's head among a pod of seals when he was scanning the foreshore with binocs for birds. He asked whether it was a new tourist thing, swimming with seals.'

'You get his name?'

''Fraid not.'

'Idiot.'

If you look at a large-scale map of the mid Cape, as Sandy did that night, you will see that the distance from the point where Leo Kemp disappeared off Monomoy Island to the Wellfleet sanctuary is twenty-five miles as the crow flies. An easy distance to cover for a seal, and not entirely impossible for a human being to swim.

Except, as Sandy told himself, it was completely impossible, because Kemp had been missing for twenty-seven days. He was dead.

On the other hand, as his late friend had advised him so often, take nothing for granted.

Nothing.

Sandy began at the Squire in Chatham, and worked his way down the coast. He knew where the fishermen drank, although he didn't often choose to drink with them. He was well known on the Cape, though, and that made his task much easier. He would buy a few drinks, commiserate with them on the state of the fishing industry, maybe offer to pay good money to be taken out on an overnight trip, and then let the booze do the talking. The fishermen drank beer mainly, with Jack Daniel's chasers. Sandy stuck to wine. He had managed to persuade most bars he frequented to stock what he liked to call his own creation, the blended Viognier, and he reckoned he must have drunk a good bottle of the stuff by the time he got to the fourth bar in Hyannisport. Aware that he was well over the limit, he drove carefully.

It was in the Dawn Trader down by the harbour that he heard the first rumour. He found the fishermen in a corner of the bar, playing cards. They didn't welcome the intrusion, but he told them he was writing a piece about old sea myths, the stories about seals in human form and how they came ashore in remote islands shedding their skin to become beautiful women who trapped fishermen into marriage.

In the other bars he had been told with varying degrees of civility to get lost, beat it, lie down in a darkened room and – the one he liked best – buy us all a drink and then beat it.

His reception in the Dawn Trader was different. The men looked shy, uneasy, and asked to see his press card. Then one nodded to another.

'Jack, you seen something, right?'

And so it turned out. Nothing substantial, just a blur among the seals in the sea off Wellfleet a few days ago. The blur of a face, a human face that ducked under the water quickly and then resurfaced; a strong, bearded, dark brown face framed by a mat of long straggly hair.

'Could it have been a seal?'

'Could have been, but it wasn't.'

'Must have been a fucking mermaid,' said one of the other fishermen, and they all laughed and Sandy bought another round of drinks.

They were embarrassed, yet seemed pleased by the attention they were getting from this persistent reporter. Sandy had deliberately not produced a notebook or tape recorder. But when he laid a map on the table and asked the man to pinpoint the spot where he had made the sighting, he suddenly became reluctant.

'You say you're from the *Herald*?'

'You saw my press card.'

'Why all the questions?'

'I told you, I'm doing a feature.'

'What else have you heard? You said you talked to others up the coast.'

'Just rumours,' said Sandy. But he had lost them. They bunched up at the far end of the table and began whispering among themselves. In the end he gave them his card and asked them to call him. He knew they wouldn't.

The late spring run of herring and an abundance of bass and mackerel made feeding easy for the seals off the Cape coast that June. But it was cod that had made the Cape famous, and had shaped its history as much as the whale. The Cape had been given its name in 1602 by the English explorer Bartholomew Gosnold, who had been amazed by the shoals of cod that surrounded his ship, the *Concord*, so thickly that, as he wrote in his diary, 'I could well have walked across the sea upon their backs.'

But there were no cod in the waters off the Cape that June. As he moved with his pod up the coast, Leo saw the seals feed off mackerel, herring and squid, swallowing the smaller fish whole and crunching their bones with strong, sharp teeth. With larger fish such as hake and halibut they simply ripped out the stomach and left the rest. Fishermen hated them for the waste, but in practice they did exactly the same.

Leo knew that the seals would not find cod here in the offshore waters of the Cape where they had once been so plentiful. The deep-water fishermen had given up on cod for almost ten years and sought other fish.

The collapse of cod stocks actually posed a greater danger to the seal population than the occasional forays by killer whales. At least with the orcas there was a balance of power, a test of skill on either side, a chance for the hunted to outwit the hunter. But there would be no escaping the cull that was successfully being urged on the Canadian Department of Fisheries by the fishing lobby. This year, 2008, it would be 275,000 harp seals, 12,000 greys and 8,000 hooded seals, a slaughter perpetrated in the name of restoring cod stocks.

Various reasons had been advanced for the disappearance of the once-abundant cod, but the only conclusion that was backed by impeccable science and supported by independently audited statistics tied it purely and simply to over-fishing.

Man the predator had eaten too many fish suppers.

Leo's pod of seals, now twenty strong, took their food as they found it while moving slowly up the coast pausing only to investigate a line of lobster pots on the seabed or the remnants of an old wreck. These creatures were driven by curiosity rather than hunger, Leo realised, as he watched them dive down and circle the well-filled pots, pushing their faces close to the wire mesh and rattling the cages of the trapped crustaceans inside.

But the seals' favourite playgrounds were the hundreds of wrecks that lay scattered over the sea floor from just beyond the low-tide line to the deep waters off the coastal shelf. Whalers, cargo vessels, tramp steamers, the yachts of the rich and famous of their day: they had all found their way to the bottom of the seas around the Cape.

The wooden ships had almost all crumbled away, although occasionally the cross mast of an old whaler would appear from the preserving sands after a storm.

But the big cargo vessels were still there at eighty feet and deeper, sunk by shifting cargo or collisions in fog, or swamped by rogue waves.

Through the ghostly interiors of these old ships the seals would chase each other, breaking off to pursue the plentiful shoals of fish. Leo could not follow them on the deeper dives, but down to forty or fifty feet he was now able to hold his breath for ninety seconds or more.

At those depths and with that endurance the daily search for food became easier. He picked up scallops, clams and oysters from the Wellfleet beds and smashed them open at night on the rocks, slurping back the flesh and salty liquid in single gulps.

Running his hands over the scallop shells took him straight back to his teenage days working on the boats out of Mornington. But the memories, although clear, were carefully preserved like the butterflies he had collected as a child and pinned into display cabinets. As with the photographs in the family album, the rule was look, but don't touch. His past was another world.

The search for food was continuous. Leo found most of it in the shallows or among the tidal pools at night. Crabs were the best and easiest food. He found the smaller ones hidden beneath seaweed in the tidal pools and caught them easily, breaking their hard shells on rocks and scooping out the raw white and brown meat. The larger king crabs lurked in cracks and crevices beyond the tide line, and were always to be found around the wrecks. If he was lucky he could spot the tell-tale tracks on the seabed that led to their hiding places and catch them as they scuttled for safety.

And there were lobsters, the Cape's most famous seafood, down there in hundreds of pots up and down the coast, tethered to their marker buoys. They lay between thirty and fifty feet below the surface, within easy reach of his diving abilities, but he didn't dare risk putting an arm into the narrow aperture of the traps. Lobsters could move with surprising speed in the confines of their cage, and faced an intruder with claws strong enough to break a wrist or finger.

So he left the lobsters alone, as he did the remnants of picnics that he found along the beach and in the dunes where he would hunt for birds' eggs. There were sandwiches, half-eaten apples, discarded hamburgers by still smouldering barbecues, and candy bars left carelessly in the sand waiting for the army of volunteers who would arrive in the morning to clean up with their shiny waste sacks and pointed sticks.

He could have gorged himself on the leftovers, but the thought revolted him. The one exception was bananas. If there was so much as an old banana skin to be found Leo would seize it with delight and strip off the remaining shreds of fruit. Then he would chew the skin into a pulp, sucking the moisture out and reducing it to a fibrous pellet which he would spit out with great satisfaction.

His mother had always told him that bananas were the one food that man could survive on for years, packed as they were with the right balance of vitamins and minerals.

'Never mind that apple-a-day nonsense,' she would say. 'Eat a banana a day and you'll live longer.'

Otherwise he lived off mussels, clams, and seaweed. It was some time before, after many failed attempts, he caught his first fish. It was in the evening, and he had watched a flock of seagulls swooping into the sea with loud cries about 100 yards from shore. Thirty or forty birds repeatedly dived into the churning water and emerged with small sprats and young herring in their beaks, swallowed them whole in flight and then plunged back to renew the feast. Leo swam out and dived beneath the crowded shoal, surfacing to find fish everywhere around him. He immediately caught a herring, digging long fingernails into its squirming flesh. He eviscerated it there and then, ripping out the backbone and eating the flesh while treading water.

JULY

SEVEN

A couple of weeks after the funeral, with what her neighbours and friends thought indecent haste, Margot Kemp had begun her preparations to leave Cape Cod and start a new life back in Scotland. The realty agent had told her she could expect a reasonable price for the house, probably from someone who worked at the Institute. She had made arrangements to take a house near her parents in Perth. The next step was to apply for a primary-teacher's job.

Sam watched her mother go through the process of divorce from the Cape, cancelling membership of the gym, placing small ads in the *Herald* for pieces of unloved furniture, parcelling up old clothing for the local Salvation Army shop.

Margot seemed happy. 'We're slowly lifting the anchor, darling. Then we'll raise the mainsail and sail home across the sea. You do understand, don't you? We can't stay here, not after all this.'

'I know, Mum.'

But she didn't know. She wanted to stay with her school friends, in the only place she had ever known. Anyway, what about Beano? There were strict quarantine regulations about dogs. How long would he have to spend in a cage somewhere before he could join them? How was an American dog like Beano going to like it in Scotland? Come to that, would she like it there? The one time she had visited her grandparents, she found the food horrible. At around five in the afternoon they served a huge meal of cakes, waffles, sandwiches, sometimes fried sausages and a large pot of tea, and that was it – no supper. And Grandma smelt of stale talcum powder and Grandpa farted all the time.

The curtains had been taken down in the front rooms, Sandy noticed as he walked through the garden gate and up the path to the front door. He hesitated before ringing the bell. He felt nervous. Inside, he found Margot in the midst of packing. There were open suitcases in every room and boxes strewn across the floors. She had what looked like a yellow duster tied as a bandana around her head.

She told him that she and Sam were leaving in a week's time, taking the direct Boston–Edinburgh flight. She didn't look him in the eye as she said this, but threw the remark over her shoulder while bent over a packing case. She said it as if it was the most normal thing in the world for a widow to leave home for a new life without waiting for her husband's body to be found.

Margot knew what Sandy was thinking. She knew what

they were all thinking, even that nosey priest who kept coming round and asking how she was.

'I'll be bloody glad to shake the sand of this place off my feet, that's how I am, Father,' she had told him. It wasn't quite true, of course. Despite the social snobbery and the stultifying boredom of the off season, she loved the violence of nature that gripped the Cape every winter. The summer landscape of beach, dunes and foreshore disappeared as the wind swung to the north-east and drove in the storms that clawed at the base of the wide summer beaches and the dunes beyond.

That was what she would really miss. Here in this north-eastern corner of America they had real weather: three-foot-deep snowfalls; storms that roared in off the Atlantic out of nowhere and just tore away a whole beach, shifting it up or down the coast. In Scotland, the tides just went in and out four times a day, and nothing ever changed.

Sandy sat down on a packing case and waited for a break in Margot's frantic activity. Eventually he coughed politely.

'This may not be my business, Margot . . .'

She straightened up, stretched, arched her back and grimaced, but didn't look at him. Whatever it was he had to say, she didn't want to hear it.

'Sandy, if you've come to tell me I can't leave right now, then join the queue. But I can't stay. I've had enough. This place is full of ghosts for me. I've had good times, maybe, but there are bad memories, very bad memories.'

Sandy couldn't think of another way to do this. He had

thought about a letter, a phone call, even using his column to write a parable, but none of them seemed right. Knowing Margot, it wouldn't work this way either, but what the hell.

So he went straight in, and told her there was talk among the fishermen down in the harbour bars about a bearded human face among the seals.

She stopped packing, and looked at him for the first time since he had arrived.

'Come on, Sandy. Give me a break.'

'I just think you should know, that's all.'

She sat down and lit a cigarette, breaking her Number 1 house rule. No smoking in the house. Ever. Except now. Sandy was the second person to have told her this crazy story.

'Know what, Sandy?' she said. 'Telling me that my husband, my late husband, is somewhere out there in the ocean, does that help me? Is that what friends are for?'

She was right, of course. It was crazy to have mentioned it. The whole thing was crazy.

Margot was angry.

'You ask those fishermen, and they'll tell you there are mermaids out there. They'll tell you the sea can swallow a ship at night before the captain has time to get out of his bunk. They'll tell you about squid the size of a house grabbing men off the deck with tentacles as thick as tree trunks. Fishermen have been telling these bullshit stories for centuries, because it glamorises their job, makes them heroes battling the dark forces of the unknown. We all know it's nonsense, so why come here to my house now repeating that crap?'

'I'm sorry,' said Sandy. 'I just thought you should hear it from me rather than from someone else. People are talking about it. Sam will hear the stories, and I thought it best you knew.'

Margot stood with her hands on her hips, cheeks flushed, breathing hard.

'It's OK. I understand. It's just that I don't need this right now. I'm trying hard to keep everything together, but it's tough. Sam doesn't want to go, and I'm desperate to get out of here. Half the Cape thinks I'm a wicked witch for sounding off like that at the service, and now you come in with a story about some merman, if that's the right word.'

She sighed, kicked a suitcase shut and unwound the yellow bandana.

'Why don't you get us a drink? There's a bottle in the fridge.'

They sat down on the deck, a bottle of wine in a cooler between them. It was a warm evening, and Margot was wearing shorts and a v-necked T-shirt without a bra, he noticed.

'You think I was wrong to say that stuff about Leo at the service?'

It was the second time she had asked him this.

'Like I said, I'm with Jenny. You spoke your mind. Leo would have approved.'

'That's not quite a straight answer, is it?' She laughed. 'You're too diplomatic, Sandy, too nice. Look, I had to say it. What other chance was I going to have? Anyway, that stuck-up Bonner woman deserved it. Fancy firing a man for giving a few interviews and making a few speeches. And he always praised the Institute. You know he loved the place.'

Of course Sandy knew that. He knew that Leo Kemp had been an exceptional scientist whose weakness was always to view conventional wisdom as part of the problem, not the solution. He also knew that Leo was dead. He wished he hadn't mentioned those ridiculous rumours.

'What are your plans when you get to Scotland?' he asked.

'The first thing I'll have to do is get Sam into a school for the autumn term. In St Andrews maybe.'

'Where you met Leo?'

'Yeah. My good-looking Australian scientist, giving interviews about talking seals, and there was I, a little primary-school teacher.'

'Love at first sight?'

'Bollocks. He saw me in the bar of the Cross Keys with a crowd of other teachers and thought I had great boobs. That's what he told me.'

'So it was love at first sight.'

They laughed, and she poured another glass.

'Maybe I'm mad. It's cold, grey and rainy back there. Half the year you live in darkness, or it feels like it. In the winter you get about four hours of real daylight.'

'So why are you going back?'

'It's family, isn't it? Sam and I need to put some roots

down. She's sixteen. In two years she'll be at university. And it may sound very practical and unfeeling, but I really am not up to doing the grieving widow act here on the Cape.'

The doorbell rang. Margot sighed and got up to answer it.

A group of Leo's students, headed by Gunbrit Nielsen, stood in the doorway carrying a large bunch of lilies. They had come to say goodbye. They filed in and sat self-consciously amid the packing cases, saying how sorry they were and how much they would like to keep in touch.

Margot thanked them as she busied herself cutting the stems and putting the flowers in a vase. Behind the platitudes and the awkward pauses there was a sadness among the class that left Margot feeling strangely elated after they had gone.

'He really touched their lives, didn't he?' she said.

Sandy drove home wishing once again that his friend had not said quite so often: think the unthinkable, embrace the impossible.

Weeks before every birthday and Christmas Sam would draw up a long list of wished-for presents, in careful order of priority. Now she had drawn up a list of conditions for her departure, and presented it to her mother for signature.

Beano's quarantine was to be as short as legally permitted; Mum had to keep her promise that they would come back every summer; wherever they lived in Scotland there had to be a garden for at least two of those big floppy-eared rabbits she planned to keep as pets; she wanted a brand-new bike; and finally Sam insisted that they say goodbye to some of the places on the Cape that they had enjoyed together as a family.

They rented bikes and cycled the sea path from Falmouth to Coldharbor; they took the ferry to Martha's Vineyard and biked over to Oak Bluffs, a honky-tonk town that likes to think of itself as the hippy answer to the stuffy villages of Edgartown and Vineyard Haven.

In Oak Bluffs they took photos of each other standing in front of one of Leo's favourite places on the Cape, the memorial statue of a Union soldier erected in 1891 as an act of redemption and forgiveness by a Confederate soldier, one Charles T. Strachan of the First Virginia Regiment. Leo always said that anyone with even a vague knowledge of American history would understand what a powerful statement that was at that time, and how much better one felt about the human race having looked at it for a few minutes.

They ate the classic Cape Cod lunch at a little restaurant overlooking the harbour: a bowl of chowder and a grilled lobster, with a Budweiser for Margot and a Coke for Sam.

The final day of their farewell tour was spent in Provincetown, looking at the art galleries and ending with an argument about whether or not to make the long climb up the 252-foot Pilgrim Monument tower. Margot protested that she was tired, and that 116 steps were a hell of climb for a view of what, exactly?

But it was a clear day, and Sam insisted. She had come here with her class when they were doing a project on the Pilgrims, and this, the tallest granite tower in America, was a reminder that it was here in Provincetown that they had first landed in 1620. They spent five weeks anchored in a sheltering bay off what is now the harbour, and it was here that history was made with the publication of the *Mayflower* compact, drawn up to quell the rumbling dissent among indentured servants on board who, having survived the sixty-five-day crossing, now wanted their liberty and full rights. This they were granted in a document that was a forerunner to the US constitution. Therefore Provincetown could claim a more important stake in US history than Plymouth, to which the Pilgrims sailed having failed to find fresh water on the Cape.

At least, said Sam, that was the way they told it in Provincetown. Plymouth probably had a different view.

Margot listened to her daughter's breathless history lesson and hoped that the Scottish school system was going to give her as good an education as she had clearly received at High School in Falmouth.

'Come on, Mum. There's a great view of the town, the beaches and the whole outer Cape, plus you can see Boston on a clear day, thirty miles across the bay.' Sam was reading from the information chart at the bottom of the tower.

'Who wants to see Boston on any day?' Margot grumbled as they began the long climb.

But it was worth it. The view was panoramic, and you could peer through telescopes down at the ant-like figures in town and on the beaches. Beachcombers, dog-walkers, joggers and sunbathers populated the sands that stretched away into the hazy distance. On a small spit of sand running out several hundred yards to sea, probably flung up by some recent storm, were a score or more seals, some in the water, some hauled up dozing in the sun.

Margot swung the telescope lazily over them. They were mainly harbour seals, with a few greys among them. As they rode the waves together they would occasionally vanish beneath the surface, having sensed the presence of fish beneath them; Buck had told her that the average seal ate forty pounds of fish a day. Maybe the fishermen were right, thought Margot. Maybe they did need to be culled.

A patch of sea mist rolled, in shrouding the seals and leaving visible only their faint outlines. Margot tightened her grip on the telescope, focusing on the blurred shapes shifting gently in the swell about thirty yards away. A seal in the water in those conditions and at this distance might easily be mistaken for a human, she thought. As the mist cleared and they came back into clear view she realised how easy it would be for a fisherman to make that mistake.

There were no human heads or bearded faces anywhere out there . . . except for Leo, of course. He was there some-where, floating on the tides, pulled hither and thither by the currents and the wind. What would his body be like now? Bloated, blackened flesh, unrecognisable as the husband she had known, peeling off in chunks and being eaten by sea creatures? Eyes scooped out by the waves leaving sightless sockets staring at the sky? She shivered at the thought.

Suddenly Sam was jumping up and down with excitement.

'Hey, Mum! Look at this! Quick!'

Margot grabbed her telescope from her, almost pushing her aside.

'Mum!'

Margot apologised. She didn't know what she had been expecting, but Sam had only been looking at a riderless horse on the beach.

'Must have thrown him off,' said Sam. 'Mum, will you buy me a horse in Scotland?'

'No.' Margot swung the telescope back to the sand spit. A speedboat carved through the water just beyond it.

The seals had gone.

On the way back down the steps, Margot let Sam go ahead, and paused on the landing about halfway down. The image of Leo's body rolling in the waves would not leave her. She looked out over the beaches to the sea beyond. He was out there somewhere, and sooner or later they would find him, a body on the beach brought in by the tide like a piece of driftwood. An early-morning jogger running along the tide line would see the corpse and swerve away, fumbling in his Lycra shorts for a mobile phone.

Downstairs in the café, Margot took a deep breath and told Sam she had changed her mind. She had been very stupid. They could not possibly go back to Scotland yet. 'The thing is, darling, people are right. Your dad's out there somewhere, or his body is, and we have to wait until they find him. We have to bury him properly here on the Cape.'

Sam jumped from her seat, her face lit up with pleasure. She clapped the palms of her hands.

'That's wicked, Mum, really cool, thank you!' she said, and hugged her mother. Margot brushed away a tear and ordered a glass of wine.

This is the time, thought Sam. The time for my surprise. She had waited, uncertain of the timing and fearful of her mother's reaction. Now she knew the time was right.

'I've got a surprise for you,' she said on the way home.

'Do tell,' said Margot.

'Not now. When we're home. It's a big surprise.'

'A nice surprise?'

'Of course,' said Sam, leaning over and giving her mother a noisy kiss on the cheek.

'Good, I like nice surprises.'

At home Sam made Margot take Leo's usual seat in the sitting room, and told her to close her eyes. She left the room and shuffled in backwards, holding, as Margot could see through half-closed eyelids, a square object covered by a sheet.

'You're cheating,' said Sam. Margot screwed up her eyes. Sam turned and whipped off the sheet.

'OK, open wide.'

And there Leo was, beautifully caught in an oil painting. But . . . Margot gasped: that half-smile on his face, that cold, hard stare, those seals in the background and that angry sea, was that her husband?

'How extraordinary,' said Margot. 'Who did this?

'Mrs Gulliver. You know, the art teacher he used to go to. She did the godwit painting for the students.'

'Yes, of course. But who chose the setting? I mean, with those seals in the background?'

Sam looked at her mother. She had said 'those seals' as if they were vermin. Maybe they were to her, she thought. No wonder she and Dad used to argue all the time.

'I didn't ask her for that, but I think it's great, don't you? I mean, she knew Dad worked at the Institute and did all that stuff on seals, so that's the way she did it. She said she thought it was a great way to remember him.'

'Well, she was right,' said Margot, getting up to examine the painting with care. It was technically excellent. For once that stern face of his was creased in a half-smile. When did I last see him smile, she thought? When did I last see my husband happy? He looked happy here, and of course that was where he was happy. Standing on the rocks in front of his bloody seals.

She ran her fingers over the layered oil paint, feeling the texture of his skin, the rough early-morning feel of an unshaven face.

'Clever Mrs Gulliver,' she said. 'She's really got him. When did you ask her to do this?'

Sam explained that she had gone to ask for the portrait when she knew her father wasn't coming back. Something special to remember him by.

'And how much did it cost?' asked Margot, coming back to earth.

Sam looked embarrassed.

'She wouldn't take anything for it. She said it was a gift in remembrance of a good man.'

201

'In remembrance of a good man? Well, how sweet of her. Lovely. We'll put it up over the mantelpiece.'

'You don't like it, do you, Mum? I can tell.'

Margot hugged her daughter, holding her in a long embrace. Playing for time, thought Sam.

'I love it, darling. I think it was a wonderful thing to do, a marvellous idea, and it's been done so well. It's just a bit of a surprise, that's all.'

They both knew she was lying.

In truth Margot thought the portrait was mawkish, sentimental chocolate-box art; but far worse, it was an unwelcome reminder of a husband she had lost long ago, and who would now stare down at her wherever she went, in whatever house she lived in. This was not a painting she was going to be able to shuffle off to the attic. For Sam's sake she was going to have to put up with the bloody thing.

Almost four weeks after Leo Kemp disappeared, the *Cape Herald* had published an investigation into his death and an appreciation of his life and work written by Sandy Rowan. The analysis of the events surrounding the accident involving the *Antoine* concluded that extraordinary weather conditions had led to a drowning for which no one was to blame. Buck's seamanship was commended and he was specifically exempted from responsibility.

Even so, Buck had refused to cooperate with the investigation and had slammed the phone down when Sandy had called him. He spent his days aimlessly at sea on his

44–foot boat and his nights in the bars around Chatham. And every night he would awake from the same nightmare, bathed in whisky sweat and shouting out orders to a crew.

The second and longer article contained a large cut-out picture of Leo standing on the transom of the *Antoine*, with the text artfully cut around it under the headline 'A Man for all Mysteries'. The article laid great emphasis on Leo's fascination with the mysteries of the ocean's deeps. Passages from his recent speeches were quoted, including one in which he said that while twelve men had walked on the moon, no one had set foot on the ocean floor at its greatest depths and only two people had ever seen it with their own eyes through the pressurised windows of a deep-sea submersible. 'Huge creatures live at that depth,' Leo was quoted as saying. 'What they are, and how they live, we do not know. Why don't we know? Because we are not looking.'

Sandy wrote that the late scientist would have been amazed that, more than a month after his death, the ocean had still not surrendered his body. The head of the coastguard in Coldharbor was quoted as saying that never in his experience – and he had been in the job for forty years – had a body that had gone missing within sight of shore failed to beach up in a few days.

Sandy had ended the article with the thought that, morbid though it might seem to some readers, Leo would have enjoyed the mystery surrounding his missing corpse.

The editor cut the paragraph on the grounds of taste.

* * *

Tallulah Bonner read the article over breakfast coffee on the deck of her Penzance Point house.

'He doesn't go away, does he?' she said to her husband, who was steering his hand towards a glass of fresh orange juice while reading his own newspaper. She put the glass into his hand and watched him raise it to his lips without taking his eyes off the paper – the *Wall Street Journal*, of course.

'Who?' he said, not bothering to look up.

Tallulah had once attended a management-training course in California, on the first day of which the twenty attendees had been asked to write down the three biggest mistakes they had made in their lives. The anonymous lists were printed out and circulated for general discussion. Twelve people had said that marrying the wrong person was one of the mistakes. They were all women. Tallulah was one of them.

Leo Kemp's replacement in the marine biology department took his first class soon after Kemp's funeral. Adam Swift came from an old Cape family, and could claim direct descent from Elijah Swift, who in 1820 had been one of the first men on the Cape to realise the wealth to be made from the whaling industry. Generations of Swifts ever since had been brought up to uphold the maritime traditions that had enriched the family.

With that reverence for the Cape's history came respect for the institutions that had developed from the seafaring lives of the local people. Chief among these was the Coldharbor Institute for Marine Studies. Adam Swift was therefore naturally anxious to shield the Institute from the perceived criticisms of the late Leo Kemp.

Leo's sacking had become public knowledge soon after the funeral, much to the embarrassment of the Institute. There had been a difficult board meeting, at which the chief executive was questioned closely about the handling of Leo's case. When she protested that it was they, the Board, who had sanctioned his dismissal, an elderly Board member said quietly: 'We did indeed, but perhaps we did not have the full facts.'

Tallulah Bonner was forced to bite her tongue. There were no 'full facts' to disclose, as every Board member knew. Kemp had indirectly criticised the strategy of the Institute, and had held it up to ridicule by reviving the whole ludicrous story of Hoover the talking seal. On top of that, he had attacked government policy towards the Stellwagen Bank marine reserve. And if you really wanted to make a case that Leo Kemp was a rogue academic, look at the way he attacked the Canadian government's entire fisheries policy. Tallulah Bonner had made the Board aware of all these factors. Now that Leo was dead they were getting snippy with her.

Adam Swift began his first lecture on what he hoped was a conciliatory note. He paid tribute to Leo Kemp as a colleague of great ability whose memory would live on in his published work and in the future careers of the students he had taught. He then proceeded, as far as the students were concerned, to attempt to demolish the intellectual basis on which Kemp had approached the entire subject of marine biology. Communication between sea mammals, he argued, was of secondary interest compared to the crucial question facing marine scientists: the effect on the oceans of climate change. The density, salinity, temperature and current flow of the waters of the seven seas were the real issues; the mammals who inhabited that universe could not be the prime focus of research, nor could they be the main intellectual consideration of the students.

Above all, he said, the notion that space exploration should take second place to the study of the oceans was at the least arguable. 'He never said that,' said a woman from the back but her soft voice did not carry and few people heard.

When Adam Swift advanced these views he did so from genuine belief, not in order to be provocative. Intellectual life was the endless pursuit of truth, and that required complete honesty. In Swift's opinion Leo Kemp was a hopeless romantic who had misled his classes through his emotional commitment to a cause.

Leo's problem, as Swift saw it, was that he had arrived at Coldharbor as a teacher and had turned into a preacher. In Swift's view, preachers had their place, and while Leo's cause may well have been just, indeed honourable, it had nothing to do with the teaching of marine biology.

Adam Swift was not stupid. He did not expect students who had so clearly loved their previous teacher to be swayed immediately by his new, more intellectually rigorous approach to their chosen subject. They would come round in time, he believed, because he was right, and those well-developed postgraduate minds would see the strength of his arguments. He had heard it said that

Leo Kemp had the courage of his convictions, the strength of purpose to speak out for what he believed in. Well, so did he.

Swift acknowledged to the students that his views were different from those of his predecessor, and encouraged the class to discuss the differences. The debate changed direction when Jacob Sylvester stood up awkwardly and pushed his spectacles up his nose.

'Look,' he said, 'for Mr Kemp, seals were the centre of a belief system. They were the intellectual beginning of a journey that led him to question the way modern marine science works.'

'I understand that,' said Swift, a little too obviously impatient with the patronising tone of his student.

'No you don't!' shouted Jacob. The whole class went quiet, even the usual gossiping crowd at the back. The activity that goes on in the background of any academic class, the chatter, the fidgeting, note-passing and nose-picking came to a halt.

'The point', said Jacob, 'is that here we are studying, researching, working up computer models, while just fifty miles away one of this country's great marine reserves, Stellwagen, is being comprehensively destroyed. Mr Kemp thought we should do something about it.'

'Universities are not centres for direct action,' said Swift smoothly. 'They—'

'Universities should use the power of reason to allow reasonable force to be seen as a moral option,' said Sylvester, his voicing rising with anger.

'You mean we should advocate violence?'

'No, I mean that Leo Kemp was trying to make us understand a reality out there, and trying to persuade us to go out and campaign. Not force. I never said that.'

'That's exactly what you just said, Mr . . .'

'Sylvester. And that's not what I said, not what I meant anyway. You're twisting my words.'

The class had grown restless, and was on the verge of open anger. Swift realised that his idea for a debate had been a failure. He ended the session early.

Gunbrit Nielsen and several classmates met regularly in the Coffee Obsession – 'a coffee house with character', it called itself – in Coldharbor. After Adam Swift's disastrous lecture they assembled there to decide on a strategy to rid themselves of their new teacher.

The first step was a letter to the *Herald*, which the editor obligingly placed in a prominent front-page position. 'Late Lecturer's Work Attacked', ran the headline, and the accompanying story noted that Leo Kemp had been a bitter critic of the annual Canadian seal cull, and had warned that the commercial fishing lobby was working to overturn the 1972 Marine Mammals Protection Act.

Sandy Rowan had just taken a long call from Mrs Fiona Chadwick, and had endured a twenty-minute lecture on the iniquity of the paper's treatment of her trainee reporter son Lewis, when a knock on the glass door of his office and a gesture of alarm from a subeditor holding a phone away from his ear told him there was more trouble on the line.

Tallulah Bonner came swiftly to the point. She did not

normally talk to junior editorial staff, but since the editor was out, Mr Bowen or Rowan or whatever his name was would have to do. The Coldharbor Institute had never been subjected to such one-sided, innuendo-driven drivel in her whole experience as chief executive. The worst aspect of the case was that no attempt had been made to obtain the Institute's side of the story. The Institute's lawyers would be in touch, seeking redress, and not just an apology but serious damages for reputational harm.

She was about to put the phone down when Sandy said, 'No need, Mrs Bonner. We'll give you equal space to reply.'

'You should have thought of that before,' snapped Tallulah.

Sandy never understood why supposedly intelligent people like Mrs Bonner could behave so idiotically.

'We did, Mrs Bonner. We offered Adam Swift the right of reply, and faxed the entire article to him before publication. He never came back to us.'

There was a silence at the end of the line.

'Nice talking to you,' said Sandy.

Lewis Chadwick had been congratulated by his colleagues on his good luck when the news editor chose him to undertake a survival mission on a desolate beach south of Provincetown. 'Reality journalism', the news editor called it. Sandy Rowan was put in charge of the project. The idea was to follow up the disappearance and likely death of Leo Kemp by showing whether or not it was possible to survive for a few days on the foreshore and among the dunes without help or resources. At first Lewis thought he was indeed the lucky one, guaranteed a big feature spread with a photo byline and perhaps a page-one cross reference. 'Reporter Survives Week in the Wilderness' was the headline he had in mind. But he did not feel quite so fortunate as he watched Sandy get back into the pick-up truck that had dropped him off on the remote beach.

For a start, he was four miles across country from the nearest road. Secondly, Sandy had made him dress in shorts and a T-shirt and had given him only a 125-millilitre bottle of water for use in emergency. His equipment was a Swiss army knife. When he complained, Sandy told him he was lucky not to have been made to begin the exercise by swimming ashore and starting off soaking wet. They had at least spared him that.

The story was that he was the only survivor of a ship that had gone down, and he had to fend for himself until he was rescued. But he was not told when the rescue would take place. The only instruction was to use his initiative.

'This is all a bit over the top, isn't it?' said Lewis as Sandy prepared to leave him.

'You've got it,' said Sandy. 'It's completely over the top. But if you stick it you will get a great piece out of it.'

EIGHT

Leo Kemp had never understood the fashion for expensive watches that can tell you the time on the other side of the world or work at 300 feet underwater. His own cheap plastic digital watch had long since expired, but in his new, timeless world, where he rose with the sun and slept under the stars, and where life was determined by wind, waves and the food he could find, this hardly mattered. He swam close to the pod, moving only a few hundred yards a day, from one beach to another. The seals were more wary after the shooting, and spent most nights sleeping at sea. Leo slept in the dunes, moving back into the water at daybreak.

The hot summer and the movement of the tides over the warmed shallows and sand shoals made the sea a welcome relief after his chilly nights on shore. He spent his days swimming and resting up after food hunts along the shoreline before dawn. He combed the dunes at first light looking for the one picnic leftover he still craved, a banana. Naturally and unquestioningly he hid from human sight, ducking beneath the waves and swimming away when fishing boats came in sight, and moving swiftly offshore when bathers or walkers appeared.

The sea had become his world. By day he would swim out half a mile or more and dive as deep as he dared, seeking old wrecks in channels around the sandbanks where fish gathered in glittering shoals.

In the murky half-light below water the shifting currents around the wrecks would swirl sand from the sea floor into ghostly shapes so that it was perfectly possible to believe that long-departed sailors still haunted the ships on which they had once sailed. The bones of the dead had long since crumbled into the sandy detritus of the seabed, making all the more real the human forms created by current and tide.

Maybe, thought Leo, there was some logic behind the old myth of Davy Jones's locker, whoever Davy Jones was. Sailors from medieval times had mentioned him in hushed whispers – a satanic spirit roaming the seas welcoming those who slid through the waves to a watery grave.

More and more he took to the water at night, revelling in the liquid silver world created by moonlight. When the moon was down and the skies clear he would lie back, arms outstretched, and float, looking up at all those stars and trying to remember which formations made up Orion's Belt or the Bear.

Only 3,000 stars are visible to the naked eye, he had learnt at school, but from the sea at night there seemed a billion of them clustered overhead, casting a luminous glow on the water. He avoided storms, learning quickly how to decode the signals in the waters around him: it was easy by day because the sky always gave warning, but at night a storm could blow up around the Cape in minutes.

Leo could tell from a change of current and a strengthening tidal pull that bad weather was brewing well before the waves heightened and the winds began to blow harder. He was always ashore bedded down in a shallow scoop among the dunes when the storm broke. However, he would stay in the water for the occasional night rainstorms that spattered long silver needles into the calm dark sea. Then he would float on his back with his mouth wide open and drink the best water he had ever tasted.

It wasn't just the ghosts of past mariners that haunted the seabed. The ocean was a noisy place. Leo could clearly hear the hum of the big underwater power and communication cables that snaked along the ocean's floor, some to cross the Atlantic, others turning south and north to link with communications centres and power plants up and down the coast.

Worst of all was the sonar, long bursts of sound that rippled through the water, usually in the hours before dawn, from a US Navy ship trialling submarine-detection devices, sometimes over 100 miles away.

Inaudible to the human ear, the sonar was torture to the whales and seals, whose acute auditory senses were thrown into painful disarray by the acoustic attack. Seals would flee the area of any sonar activity, and would often make straight for land even if there were humans close by. The whales had no such option. Caught in a web of hydro sonic sound beamed on frequencies that penetrated the very core of their being, a pod of whales would be driven into a frenzy, diving down to the ocean floor and cannoning off the seabed to the surface, then diving again.

In his second week at sea Leo watched from 200 yards offshore as three whales beached themselves north of Wellfleet in a desperate attempt to flee the noise that was destroying their auditory sense and their means of navigation. Two floundered in the shallows while the third drove himself with huge exertion up on to the beach and lay there quivering.

It was not long before teams of yellow-jacketed emergency services personnel had taped off the beach and covered the whale in wet blankets. A tractor was brought in to tow all three mammals back into the water. Those in the shallows were gently pulled back to sea, towed by the tractor on a bed of rubber blankets. No sooner had the rescue teams regained the beach than they turned to see the whales once again in the shallows, flailing their tails to lever themselves towards the shore.

By now the falling tide meant a four-hour wait before a second effort could be made to return the beached whales to the ocean. It was a pointless exercise, as many among the rescue teams knew. All three whales expired of shock and exhaustion before the tide turned, and were trucked away that night to be delivered to the incinerator.

The only time Leo ever felt in any danger was once when returning from a long and exhausting swim a mile offshore following a flock of seagulls in the hope of finding fish. He got caught close to the beach in a rip tide, one of the well-known and widely feared currents along the Cape coast that can take an inexperienced swimmer from the warm shallows and drag him to his death in deeper, colder water.

Almost every week in the summer season the *Cape Herald* carried a report of a rip-tide fatality, always involving a visitor, usually a middle-aged male. As the safety leaflets distributed to every hotel and guest house pointed out, the way to survive a rip current was to swim across it, never against it.

By then Leo was a much stronger swimmer than most summer visitors to the Cape. But he was tired when he was caught, and found himself unable to break out of the current. Usually the powerful flow of water, created by shifting sandbars in the shallows, was no more than thirty yards wide, but he found himself in a far broader current which was moving much faster than the falling tide in the surrounding water.

He surrendered to the rip and lay on his back, floating out to sea. For the first time since he had been washed overboard from the *Antoine* he felt afraid. Death had lost almost all meaning in his new existence, because in his rational moments he believed himself to be trapped in a dream after death. But the fear of drowning as the rip sucked him into the deep water came as a powerful reminder of his mortality. The bone-numbing cold and his exhaustion had drained him of the energy to swim. But he was alive, and he wanted to live.

Then a familiar head broke the surface close by, followed by another. The seals vanished as quickly as they had appeared, but when Leo finally staggered ashore an hour later he felt they had given him the will to survive.

A few days later, through what he admitted was his own stupidity, he found himself in even more deadly danger. He was free diving on an old wooden gillnet boat that had gone down about 100 yards beyond the tide line in thirty feet of water twenty years previously. The boat was half sunk into the sand and much of it had rotted away, leaving the rusting frame of the cabin and a hatchway to a cavernous hold above the seabed. It was a bright day, and sunlight illuminated a portion of the hold, revealing a wealth of marine life among the tangle of rotten timbers and the long trailing fronds of seaweed. Big king crabs scuttled across the sandy floor and darted into bushes of weed, their long antennae poking through the greenery to reveal their hiding places. Leo had twice dived into the hold, spending about thirty seconds inside each time. He swam down the ladders of light to what had once been the bottom of the ship's hull, circled the sunlit area of the old hold and then kicked for the surface. On his second dive he had surprised and caught a large king crab, using the remnants of a wooden spar to pin it to the sea floor.

Swimming with one arm and carefully carrying the crab by the rear of its shell, he had taken it to a deserted spot among the rocks and smashed it open. Even after the strong ridged claws had been ripped from the body they continued to snap open and shut for almost a minute before the nervous system finally closed down. Leo wrapped what would be his meal that night in one of the many plastic bags that washed around the shallows and hid it under a tangle of seaweed.

Emboldened by this success, he returned for a third dive. The sun was setting, and there was little light left underwater. He had just entered the hold when a conger eel twelve feet long appeared from the gloom and circled him in a fast flash of silver, closing to within a yard of him as the circle tightened.

Leo told himself not to worry. He was being circled by a fish that was simply a long tube of muscle attached to strong jaws. But conger eels are shy, nocturnal creatures, emerging from their hiding places in old wrecks to feed on fish and squid. Only rarely will they attack swimmers or divers, preferring to flee at the sight or sound of underwater intruders.

As Leo turned, thrashing his legs to scare off the beast and make a speedy retreat to the surface, it came straight for him, mouth agape, rows of sharp teeth gleaming in the half-light, razor sharp and ready to rip and tear.

Leo was all too aware of the one exception to the rule about congers' usually timorous behaviour. They will always attack anything that they feel threatens their young. This had happened to a diver eight miles off the coast of St Andrews in 2004, not long after the Kemps had left Scotland. The 42-year-old scuba diver had been exploring a trawler wreck at a depth of 80 feet when a 250-pound conger clamped its jaws on to his arm and dragged him deep into the hold of the vessel. He was slammed against the side of the ship, and could have been pinned there until he suffocated or bled to death, but with great skill and strength he managed to force the eel to release its grip by squeezing its back with his free hand.

The eel seized Leo by the ankle, dragging him back towards the depths of the hold but leaving both his arms free. The fight that followed was over very quickly. Leo twisted down and punched the creature hard on its snout, then pushed his thumbs roughly where he thought its eyes would be, and the fish released its grip.

Leo felt no pain as he surfaced, but he knew he would be bleeding. He had been under for just over a minute, but it had felt like a year. He regained the shore in the twilight, limped to the cover of the rocks and wrapped the deep lacerations on his ankle in seaweed. He removed the dead crab from the plastic bag and used that to bind the seaweed to the ring of lacerations on his foot. With its high iodine content seaweed was an excellent medical dressing. He had once read a paper by a marine scientist at Swansea University in Wales that claimed traditional harvesters of seaweed along the coast never bothered to dress their cuts or grazes, as they healed quickly without treatment.

Leo knew had been lucky. Had the conger clamped on to his leg higher up it could have severed veins or even a main artery. The shock and immediate loss of blood would probably have killed him. At the very least the beast would have torn off a chunk of his calf muscle. As it was, the pain kept him awake that night and left him limping the next day as he scavenged as usual along the foreshore at dawn, scooping up molluscs revealed by the retreating tide before the arrival of flocks of waders.

He took great care on these shoreline food hunts to keep as far from human presence as possible. If anyone on the beach happened to see him at sea, he would be just another black dot amid the waves, another seal head. And if illegal overnight campers emerged from their sleeping bags among the dunes in the first glimmerings of dawn, all they would see was a mad naturist treasure-hunting along the shoreline in the distance.

When he was ashore during the day he hid deep in the dunes or among seaweed-covered rocks close to the water. He kept clear of all boat traffic but the frequent flash of sunlight on binoculars aboard fishing boats told him that the local fishermen were still looking for something or someone in the coastal waters. Once or twice he thought he saw Buck's gillnet boat working up the coast, but the possible sighting of someone he had known so well standing on the rear deck was like an abstract image, unattached to any emotion. Not so the dreamlike visions of Julian swimming among the waves and underwater, his long hair streaming behind him. The dreams wove their way through Leo's mind whether he was asleep or awake. Julian never talked to him, never looked at him, but he was there in the sea around him and on the shore at night. He was with him when he awoke and began hunting for breakfast of birds' eggs or mussels, and still with him when he fell asleep exhausted in the dune grass at night. He had found Julian. With that knowledge came a feeling of inner content that Leo had not known for years, maybe ever.

*　　*　　*

The strength of the big storm that hit the Cape in the fifth week of his new existence took Leo by surprise. He had watched the weather worsening for thirty-six hours as the wind shifted to the north-east. It grew colder and he could sense the falling barometric pressure as the low system moved in. To his surprise his pod of twenty seals seemed more agitated than usual by the changing weather, and had moved from Wellfleet down to Monomoy Island the evening before the storm broke. They joined several hundred grey and harbour seals who sought shelter overnight in one of the many lagoons formed by shifting sandbars. The next morning, as charcoal clouds scudded across a dark sky, the whole group began swimming from the calm waters of the lagoon into the steepening waves of a slate-grey sea.

They had left the lagoon almost as a unit, seemingly acting on some secret order, moving through the water with military precision and a clear sense of purpose. Leo was puzzled; usually seals would seek the shelter of a rocky foreshore in rough weather. Now they were heading out to sea, clearly with a distant destination in mind. He followed, struggling to keep up with the rearmost seals, diving into the waves and sliding through them as they did, never raising his head to plot a direction. Every time he fell behind he would find seal heads around him, seemingly pointing the way forward.

Then he lost them in the mist of spindrift and spume. Exhaustion rather than the cold slowed him down. Feeling his strength failing, he turned on his back and let the sea carry him. He felt like another piece of driftwood being

220

tossed around on the waves. Metal drums, wooden fruit boxes, lobster-pot marker buoys, assorted planks and waterlogged bales of what looked like hempen rope floated briefly into his path before being snatched away by the wind and tide.

As he grew weaker, he lost the energy to do anything more than kick his legs out in vague imitation of a frog. He tried to reason with himself. He was not mad, and still had the remnants of a rational mind. It was tempting to succumb to the belief that he had died and was in purgatory, cast upon the oceans to expiate his sins through suffering before entering the afterlife cleansed of his worldly vices. But he was not a Christian; still less did he subscribe to medieval theology. So answer the question, he said to himself: what are you doing trying to swim through a storm with a group of seals, who have in any case vanished into the vastness of the ocean around you?

Answer came there none. He didn't know why he had left the safety of the island. He had been impelled by a strange desire to do as the seals did and since they had chosen to move from what would soon be a storm-battered coast he had simply followed. That would have to do.

Leo was shaken from his semi-conscious state by the thump of a heavy object slamming into his side. He doubled up with pain and reached out to fend off his attacker, only to find himself clinging to a substantial panelled wooden door, complete with a brass knob and knocker. It was large enough for Leo to lever himself up on to it and use it as a makeshift raft.

Of all the flotsam in the ocean, he thought, I find a front door, presumably from a container full of furnishings swept off the deck of a cargo vessel and broken open by the waves. It was made of teak, he guessed, like the trunk that had ended Julian's life.

Whether he slept or lost consciousness he did not know, but he became aware of a brilliant night sky and a calmer sea. The door was no longer climbing the waves and slamming into the troughs, shaking every bone in his body, but was rising and falling rhythmically in a long, sweeping swell. He had survived. Famished and thirsty, he drifted back to sleep.

The sound of a motor engine close by woke him. He was still sprawled across his front-door raft, clinging to the door knob and knocker. He raised himself on to an elbow and craned to see over the wave tops. A trawler had heaved to 400 yards away, its bow anchor taut in the strong swell left behind in the storm's wake.

Beyond the trawler Leo could see a coastline a mile distant. A boat was coming towards him: a small launch. A man in the bow was looking through binoculars in his direction. The other crew members were shouting something and pointing towards him.

Leo levered himself up into a crouching position. The men in the launch were wearing lifejackets and oilskins – they were probably crewmen from a trawler based at Chatham or Falmouth. The man in the bow had exchanged his binoculars for a coiled rope attached to a buoyancy ring. He waved at Leo and shouted something unintelligible.

This was Leo's chance: he could be on board that boat in minutes. They would wrap him in a blanket and give him a steaming mug of chocolate laced with rum. He would be back in harbour in an hour, back on land, back home. Back with Margot and Sam. Back in the Dark Side drinking his vodka-laced health drinks with Sandy. Back fighting for his job at the Institute. Back with Gloria.

He rolled off the raft, hearing a faint shout as he hit the water. He duck-dived and swam as strongly as could, down and away from the approaching launch. He swam till his lungs felt as if they were on fire, and then, digging deep into the reserves of endurance built up over the past five weeks gave two more hard strokes before breaking the surface. Between the rise and fall of the waves he could see the launch circling the wooden door. They were looking for him, but the big rolling swell made it difficult for them to see him. And he didn't want them to. He didn't want to go back. He didn't want to surrender the freedom he had found in the twilight world he now inhabited, half man, half sea creature.

Finally he had realised his childhood fantasy, the secret and impossible ambition that had haunted and driven him at every step of his life. How he had longed when walking the beaches near Mornington to run into the sea and shed the skin of humanity that clothed him, to turn his back on the species into which he had been born and become something else, a breathing sea creature, a seal, whale or dolphin, anything that gave him the freedom to escape and find a gypsy life at sea.

While he was growing up he had fallen asleep at night

with that dream in his head. He imagined himself in that magical place where the sky met the ocean, an Elysium in which the sea would free him from the drudgery of school, the endless sibling bickering at home, the angst of teenage life.

He had felt the same longing when teaching at St Andrews, where the sea constantly pounded the two shores lying north and south of the craggy outcrop on which the town stood. To be able to walk into that sea and vanish into a new world, to find truth in the old selkie myths about seals becoming human and then returning to their own world, leaving broken hearts behind in revenge for the slaughter inflicted on them by man since the dawn of time. That had always been his dream. It was the theme of a school essay he had written when he was 14. The subject was: *My ambition in life.*

Every other boy in the class had chosen to become someone important or famous: scientists, fighter pilots, astronauts or test cricketers. The teacher had read out the list and commended them all for their high-flying ambitions. Then, to Leo's acute embarrassment, he said, 'But Kemp wants to become a seal!'

The class had laughed, but the teacher had stopped them. Leo's was the best essay, he said, because it was so different and so imaginatively argued. Anyway, what was so wrong with wanting to be a seal? The sniggering continued at the back, but the teacher quelled it with a stony stare.

He asked Leo to come up in front of the class and read the essay out. Leo had refused, shaking his head, remaining stubbornly at his desk. So the teacher read it out himself. After a while Leo looked around shyly, and was surprised to find that the class was actually listening with interest.

After he had finished reading, the teacher had asked him a question. 'You want to walk into the sea and live the life of a mammal, a seal or dolphin. That's wonderful. But you don't tell us whether you want to come back. Do you?'

'No,' mumbled Leo, staring down at his desk: he wanted to stay out there, at sea, for ever, he said

'But won't that be rather sad? What about your family? They would miss you, and wouldn't you miss them?'

Leo nodded his head, still looking down. 'I'd miss my mum and dad, yes, but I'd be a different person in a different life: I'd be free. I wouldn't have to worry about anybody. I'd be gone.' He looked up at his teacher. 'You don't understand, do you?'

'I think I do' said the teacher quietly.

His essay won a prize. It was after that that his father arranged for him to go out with his uncle on the Saturday scallop-fishing expeditions.

The launch was now widening its circles around the door, and Leo could clearly see the faces of the fisherman looking in every direction. He sank low into the water, breathed in deeply and dived again, this time swimming strongly in the direction of the shore. When he surfaced he saw the launch returning to the mother boat. There were half a dozen crewmen lined along the side of the vessel, all scanning the sea with binoculars. He dived again, deeper this time, and stayed under longer.

When he surfaced for the third time the boat was heading out to sea. Fishing is about time and money, but had the captain thought there was a chance of picking up a survivor from the water, he would have stayed. Unlike his crew, he must have been convinced that if they had seen anything at all, it had been a corpse. And he was not going to waste valuable time looking for a drowned swimmer who had been carried away by a rip tide.

He would report the possible sighting of a body on a piece of wreckage to the coastguard. If there were any vessels available the sea would be searched; and nothing would be found. The coastguard would conclude that the fishermen had been mistaken. Conditions in the heavy swell that had followed the storm made it easy to mistake a tangle of flotsam for a body. Anyway, they would know that nobody had been reported missing recently.

Nobody except Leo Kemp, of course. But he had been officially declared dead, and his file had been closed.

By the time Leo crawled ashore the fishing vessel had vanished over the horizon. He had no idea where he was. He walked unsteadily across a broad beach into thick dune grass, and collapsed.

Buck had never lost a man in more than fifty years at sea. Since Leo's disappearance he had shunned company, and had cancelled his contract with the Institute. He planned to put the *Antoine* up for sale, but in the Chatham boatyard they had told him he would be lucky to find a buyer at any price for an old, fuel-hungry tub at a time when gas prices were beginning to climb.

If he could not sell the boat, he would have it broken up for scrap. There would be a few hundred dollars in that. And then, come the fall, he would leave for Hawaii, and settle for good on his smallholding. At 72 it was time to move on. He knew he wasn't responsible for Leo's death. But he had been the captain. Leo had been in his care, and that was enough for him. He felt guilty as hell, and as the weeks passed the feeling didn't get any better. Could he, should he, have turned the *Antoine* faster? Should he have seen the wave earlier? The questions never stopped.

Renee had told him over and again that it wasn't his fault, but it didn't help, nor did the rum, nor did the sleeping pills. He wanted to cut loose from the Cape, with its dying fishing industry and its daily reminders of Leo, and bury his memories in the warmth of the Pacific.

So Buck was not pleased when he found Sandy Rowan waiting for him on board the *Antoine* at Chatham harbour. The interviews he had given after his successful conference speech to the Scripps Institute had softened his views on journalists, but not by much. And he didn't like anyone on his boat without an invitation.

'Want a coffee?' asked Sandy, holding up a new jar of Nescafé.

'Nope.'

'Got a minute?'

'Nope.'

'Buck, I just need a quick word – and not "nope". Three nopes in a row would depress me.'

Buck looked at him and said, 'Nice piece you wrote.'

'Thanks.'

'OK, I'll take a coffee.'

Sandy made the instant coffee in the tiny galley while Buck worked on his nets.

'Another good warm morning,' said Sandy as they sat on the rear deck.

Buck fished a flask from his pocket and poured a generous slug into both their mugs.

'Thanks. You've been fishing these waters for a long time.'

'Yup.'

'You know them as well as any man alive, I guess.'

'What do you want, Mr Rowan?'

Sandy gave a sigh, swigged his coffee and grimaced.

'How long could a man survive out there if he was stranded on some beach?'

'Depends. Why?'

'You know why.'

'No, I don't know why.'

'"Take nothing for granted", remember. That was what he always said.'

'Sure, but that doesn't tell me why you're asking these questions.'

Sandy stood up and drained the remains of his coffee. He didn't know whether he was more irritated by Buck's play-it-dumb routine or by his own stupidity in pursuing a dead-end conversation.

'Because you must have heard the rumours going round the fishermen's bars.'

'Maybe.'

'Well, maybe you haven't heard that a birdwatcher says he saw a man swimming among the seals off Wellfleet. And that same night two kids with a gun out to shoot themselves a seal got the fright of their lives when they were chased by one; a seal with two legs. They swear it. I've talked to them.'

'Anything else?'

'That's enough, isn't it? Enough to make you think?'

Maybe it was the rum, or his guilt, or both, but Buck began to talk.

'A man might live out there for weeks if he put his mind to it and the weather was warm. There's plenty of food if you look: crab, mussels, clams, certain types of seaweed, fish if you can catch them, and birds' eggs in the dunes. There are plenty of freshwater ponds just across the dune line and showers at sea, mostly at night.'

'So he could be alive?'

'Look, the sun's going to go down tonight, and it will be up again tomorrow morning. Beyond that, I don't know.'

'You've been wrecked, haven't you, Buck?'

'That was in winter, and we were picked up real quick. Sure, strange things happen out at sea. Men have survived on pieces of driftwood for days, far longer than you'd think possible. We've had a warm couple of months – in the shallows the water temperature won't be bad.'

'OK,' said Sandy. 'Just one last question, and then I'll leave you in peace. Where is the biggest gathering of seals around here? Is there someplace they all go at this time of year?'

Buck sighed. 'Right now they're on Atlantic Island. There was a storm two days ago, the wind shifted north-east and a lot of them will have gone with the wind and the tide rather than swim against them. It's about ten miles beyond Nantucket, big bird sanctuary, birdwatchers go there sometimes.' He got up, threw his coffee dregs into the harbour and walked up the steps to the cabin. 'I've got work to do,' he said, throwing the words over his shoulder to close the conversation.

Margot called Buck that evening to charter the *Antoine*. She wanted him to work out the currents, tides and wind directions since Leo had gone overboard, and try to plot an area where his body might have washed up. She knew the coastguard had searched the shoreline, but she had to try again, she said. Leaving him in the sea to rot was not an option. If she left the Cape without finding him at least she wanted to do so feeling justified, feeling that she had tried everything.

Buck spent the evening poring over charts, occasionally tapping information into a laptop. After a while he rolled the charts up and put the laptop away. He knew where they would go in the morning. Three hours there, four hours onshore and three hours back. A full day's trip.

The *Antoine* left Coldharbor soon after eight o'clock the next morning. Margot had not had breakfast, but she did not feel like the sausages Buck produced from the small galley. The smell of fried food made her queasy, and the feeling grew worse as the first swell lifted the *Antoine* and it settled into the long, rolling ride out to Atlantic Island.

She had left Sam asleep at home. They had agreed that there was little point in her coming on what Margot had been careful to describe as just a sea trip to clear her head and blow away the cobwebs. Sam was happy to let her go. If she was eventually going to be hauled off to Scotland, the land of darkness and horrible haggis as she called it, she didn't want to waste time chugging around the Cape in a tug.

Atlantic Island is a crescent-shaped sandbar ten miles long and a mile wide at its greatest width. Emerging from the continental shelf twenty miles north-east of Cape Cod, it sits on a north-east–south-west axis astride the shipping lanes from North America to Europe. Sailors have cursed it over the centuries, and 350 wrecks recorded since the early nineteenth century provide the grim reason why. Surrounded by shifting sandbars, treacherous currents and thick, swirling fog, which descends without warning when tentacles of the cold Labrador current meet those of the Gulf Stream in the surrounding sea, the island has all too often proved a trap for ships blown off course or making small navigational errors.

Atlantic Island is not a place that any sailor would choose to go. There are no reliable charts, because even more than the Cape, shifting shoals and sandbars create fresh navigational hazards every year.

When they reached the island Buck steered cautiously towards the old stone pier which was the only landing point. The early French settlers had shipped the stones

231

over from the mainland, piled them up between iron pilings and then poured a cement mix over them to create a crude L-shaped harbour wall.

Buck and Margot had not talked much on the crossing. Buck busied himself with charts and checking the weather reports on the radio. Margot felt seasick, and was beginning to think she should never have changed her mind and extended her stay on the Cape.

On the face of it, it was a crazy journey. Atlantic Island was fifteen miles from where Leo had been washed overboard. Even allowing for the vagaries of tide and current, there was no reason why his body should have been washed up there. Buck told himself he was doing this as much for Leo as for Margot. Leo had never made it to Atlantic Island. He had always wanted to do a seal count there, but time and again trips had been cancelled because the weather had closed in. Eventually he said there must be a jinx on the idea, and dropped it. And since Leo was the only person who had ever wanted to go to the island, Buck had never been either. Still, at least it would give Margot a chance to exorcise whatever demons had driven her there, he thought.

He gave her the wheel as the *Antoine* nosed up to the old pier, and jumped ashore to secure a line to a rusting bollard. The tug's draft of nine feet just cleared the bottom, but the tide had begun to turn, and he would have to push out in a matter of minutes.

He had given Margot a map of the island, and marked the footpath running along the central ridge, which forked after three miles, with the left-hand path turning down into a broad bay about a mile long.

'That's where the seals mostly are,' he told her. 'There are about 250,000 on the island so you won't miss them.'

Then he told her about the horses. There was a herd of 300 feral ponies on the island, which ranged wild, feeding on grassland and watering at several freshwater ponds. The herd had grown from a few animals brought to the island in the late eighteenth century by a community of French-speaking farmers who had been exiled there by the British after the conquest of Canada. Although the horses were completely wild, they were considered harmless by the birdwatching parties and naturalists who made occasional visits to the island.

Here I am, thought Margot, on an island in the middle of the Atlantic with a quarter of a million seals and a herd of wild horses for company. I must be mad. She watched as Buck traced her route along the path with his index finger. As for a body, he said, it could have washed up anywhere. Trying to plot the tide and the wind direction was hopeless in this lonely place. Too many currents swirled around the island, creating skerries where none had existed for years, shifting sand and rock to carve out new bays in a matter of weeks.

Buck squinted at the sky, gauging the weather as Margot hitched on a backpack. As agreed, he would pick her up on the next tide, at 3 p.m. If for any reason either of them missed the pick-up, he would be back on the next daylight tide, at six o'clock the following morning.

'What are you going to do for the next four hours?' she asked.

'I won't be far away.' He pointed out to sea. 'Out there, this side of the horizon.'

'You'll stay in sight, won't you?'

'Sure. I'll be watching you.' He tapped his binoculars.

'There's no one living on the island, is there?'

It was a silly question, because she knew the island had been deserted for years, but now she was actually there, and about to step off into bleak and unknown territory, she felt a need for reassurance.

He laughed. No, there hadn't been anyone living there for years.

'And the horses? Where are they?'

'God knows. They're wild, but they shouldn't bother you,' he said.

She unhitched her backpack and checked it again. Binoculars, flask of coffee, bottle of water, packet of sandwiches, chocolate bar and a banana. Feels like I'm back in a Girl Guides' camp, she thought. She smiled, but he knew she was nervous.

'See ya soon,' she said, jumped down on to the pier and began to walk along what looked like an old sheep path through gorse and scrub. She turned back to see Buck reversing the tug out of the bay and into open sea. She wanted to keep him in view. The *Antoine*, with its familiar top-heavy superstructure, was a comforting sight. Buck blew a couple of blasts on the siren and waved through the cabin window.

The path meandered along the spine of the island. On

either side the ground sloped away to small cliffs which broke into bays, tidal pools and long stretches of sand. There was a strong breeze which bent the grasses, but the day was warm. Margot told herself she was there because her husband was missing at sea, believed drowned, and that because his body had never been found there was a chance, just a chance, that it might have been washed up in this desolate place.

But she was also there because in that small corner of her mind where imagination made the fantastic possible, she thought, or rather dreamt, that maybe he had migrated to another life, and had become one of those mythical creatures of Celtic legend whose stories he had woven so elegantly into his lectures.

'Oh, what bloody nonsense,' she said out loud.

She looked at the miles of low-lying scrub ahead of her and the endless tidal beaches that framed the crescent of land. Feeling ridiculous and a little ashamed, she turned to go back, and then remembered that Buck would not be able to bring the boat in until the tide had risen again. She looked at her watch. It was noon. She had been on the island an hour. Another three hours. On a bay down to her right she saw a couple of semi-derelict buildings with brick walls and rusting corrugated-iron roofs, probably the remnants of the old weather station. She walked down an overgrown path to take a look. Inside were signs of human habitation: a table, chairs, some old newspapers and a paraffin stove. The glass had long gone from the windows. She looked at the papers, browning copies of the *Boston Herald* dated five years previously.

She ate her sandwiches looking out over the sea, with her back to a sun-warmed brick wall. The tide had pulled back to reveal a hard white beach. A few birds hung in the wind over the low cliffs at either end of the bay, seemingly motionless as they slid from one updraft to the next. Otherwise she seemed to have the island to herself. Buck's map told her it was still about twenty minutes' walk to the seal beach.

She walked back to the ridge top, and saw the *Antoine* slowly making its way up the coast parallel to her own route. The path dropped away on the other side of the ridge, and she left the comforting sight of Buck and his tug and walked quickly until she came to the summit of a small hillock. Breathless, and thinking that if nothing else this was a good day's exercise, she stopped. There, several hundreds yards away in a long bay, thousands of seals were beached up on rocks, along the sand and among the dunes. She had never seen so many seals. They covered every square yard of the beach, a sleek, black-grey, almost motionless mass. In the calm shallows there were more seals, their heads moving through the water, swimming without apparent purpose.

It may have been July, but the pups were still distinguishable as that season's offspring. Like the adults they snoozed in the sun, occasionally moving position but always careful to keep a certain space, only a foot or two, between them.

Margot walked slowly towards the colony, closing the distance to about fifty yards. They paid not the slightest attention to her. She had never involved herself in Leo's work, but she had attended enough of his lectures in the early days to know that these were all grey and harbour seals. On their seal-watching trips to the Farne Islands Leo had taught her to look at the nose. The grey seal's nostrils run in two almost parallel lines, while the harbour seal's are set in a long V that almost touch at the point.

Margot sat down on a springy bed of heather and wild grass and began to scan the rookery with her binoculars. She started at the front, sweeping slowly through the attractive, well-whiskered faces. Sleek creatures, she thought, well fed on the fat of the oceans, so easy to hunt and kill, so vital to the survival of early man and so much a victim of his later greed. Christ, I'm beginning to think like Leo, she thought, and looked around, half expecting him to be there and to say it out loud.

It took her half an hour to work her way through the rookery, tracking seals as they slipped into the water, watching others haul up, clumsily shuffling on to the beach on their clawed front flippers. She could hear no sounds above the soft breeze in the grass and heather, but Leo would have told her that the seals had seen her, and were talking to each other. Seals know all about man, and stored deep in their collective memory is an abiding fear of him.

Two blasts of the *Antoine*'s siren had her scrambling to her feet. It was 1.30, much too early for the pick-up. She walked rapidly to the top of the ridge as the siren sounded again. Cresting the ridge, she looked out to sea on the far side of the island and saw the fog rolling in. She could just make out the blurred outline of the *Antoine*, about 400 yards from shore. She knew the fog moved fast, but it was still weird and frightening to see the blanket of grey, swirling mist steadily shrouding the island, darkening and dampening the contours of the land and the air around her. It was like something soldiers must have seen in the First World War, clouds of spreading gas slowly rolling towards them

Except this was just fog, she told herself. It was wet and cold and a nuisance, but no more. She turned back to retrace her footsteps to the huts. In a few minutes the path petered out, and she stood uncertainly seeking the way ahead. The fog had thickened. She put her hand out in front of her. In the half-light, wisps of grey and yellow curled around her fingers.

The huts had been built on a gentle slope leading to that beautiful beach on the far side of the island. She listened for the waves, hoping that at least she could find the shore-line and work her way round, but the fog muffled all sound. She could see nothing around her, and heard nothing but the soft squelch underfoot as she walked uncertainly down the slope.

It should have taken her ten minutes to reach the shore-line, but half an hour later Margot was still stumbling through wet, clingy grass and gorse. She had lost all sense of direction. Feeling increasingly panicky, she decided to stop and do nothing until the fog lifted. She peered at her watch using her sleeve to wipe beads of moisture from its face: 2.30 p.m. It had been an hour since she last saw the tug.

When they came, the horses did so without sound,

galloping out of the fog as if on muffled hoofs, their blurred outlines assuming recognisable shape as they emerged from the smoky gloom three or four abreast. Margot froze, clutching her Thermos flask to her chest. The horses streamed towards her, suddenly in clear view, plumes of breath flaring from their nostrils, manes flailing from side to side.

Something must have frightened them, she thought – something, or someone? The thud of hooves on the coarse grass was now audible, the delayed soundtrack of a nightmare. She stood still and closed her eyes, remembering that the horses had been wild for over 200 years, and would be more afraid of her than she should be of them.

She realised later that she had been standing on a narrow pathway through deep grass, the path the horses would naturally have taken on their headlong flight from whatever had frightened them. That was why they had literally brushed past her, rocking her body from side to side with the flick of a mane or a tail. The sweaty reek of horse told her just how close those hoofs had come to trampling her.

The herd vanished into the fog as quickly as they had come, the last of their streaming tails silently disappearing into the gloom. Cold and frightened, Margot steadied herself with a long gulp of coffee from the Thermos and wished she had not declined Buck's offer to liven it up with a shot of rum.

The fog had lifted slightly when she finally stumbled into the old huts some hours later. The light was fading outside and inside the hut was cold, dark and smelt faintly of urine. She shivered, feeling both foolish and frightened at finding herself alone at night with only basic shelter on a wild island in the middle of the Atlantic. Fear gave way to anger at her own stupidity as she ate the last of her chocolate. She had missed the appointed time for meeting Buck, and he would not be back until morning. What a bloody fool she had been. Exhausted, she went to sleep on a bed of old newspapers, dreaming of feral horses rearing up from the sea, galloping over the waves towards her, wild-eyed and silver-hoofed.

Margot awoke the next morning to bright, warm sunshine that cast a dazzling light over the beach. The fog could have been part of a dream. She was chilled and hungry, and looking at her watch she saw that there was an hour to go before pick-up. She walked to the ridge top, and there, a mile out in the bay was the tug. She waved, but there was no sign of Buck.

She walked back along the ridge looking for the horses. It would be good to see them in daylight, peacefully grazing with their heads down, their tails swishing at flies, and to take that image back with her, rather than that of the wild-eyed demons of her dreams. But there was no sign of the horses, nor of the seals on the long beach. Only birds seemed to inhabit the island, black-headed gulls borne aloft on the Atlantic wind and cormorants skidding over the waves.

It was just after 6 a.m. when she wearily climbed aboard the tug. She had been on the island for just nineteen hours but it felt like a year. Buck didn't say much, beyond asking if she was all right. She mumbled an affirmative, left it at that and curled up to try to sleep on the ripped plastic covering of the banquette at the back of the cabin. Buck didn't look at her, but addressed the wide ocean as if he was talking to himself. He had been worried by the fog, he said, but he knew there would be shelter on the island.

She closed her eyes and tried not to feel queasy as the *Antoine* slid into the three-hour journey back to the Cape. Once he had set her course Buck made coffee for them both, laced as usual with rum. Warmed by the drink, and suddenly feeling alive, she told him about the seals and the horses.

He nodded, and told her the horses were said to be very skittish in fog. Birdwatchers had reported that even a small thing could set them off – the flutter of a bird's wings, or the aggressive advance of a seal with pups on the beach. But it must have been scary, he ventured.

'Very,' she said.

The rum made her dozy and, despite the heaving, pitching ride back to Coldharbor, Margot fell asleep, slumped sideways across the seat.

As they docked, Buck apologised for her wasted journey. She had been seasick most of the way out, and on the island the fog had rolled in, those horses had appeared and she had been trapped for the night. All in all a disastrous trip.

'Don't be sorry,' she said. 'It's not your fault. But will you do something for me? A favour?'

'Sure,' he said, not thinking.

Margot had been thinking about how to say this, and decided the best thing was just to come straight out with it.

'I'd like to go back tomorrow.'

'You're crazy. What's the point?' Buck said.

'There's no point, and I'm crazy if you like. But I want to go back. I want you to take me. Will you?'

Buck shrugged and shook his head.

'I'll pay you.'

'It's not the money. You know that.'

'Well?'

'Take a look in the mirror. You're all in. You haven't eaten for a whole day. Why not think it over?'

'Tomorrow, Buck. Will you take me?'

He looked at her. She was a mess. Her hair was plastered to her skull; there were hollows below her exhausted green eyes. Her face had a ghostly pallor.

Buck suddenly became irritated. He had made two long trips out to the island and back in memory of a man whom he admired – not a great friend, he didn't have any really – but someone he cared for. Now the man's widow was turning grief into a gothic fantasy, trying to pretend she could exorcise her ghosts on a godforsaken island fifteen miles out in the Atlantic.

'Give me one good reason.' He had raised his voice, and she jumped slightly, startled by his vehemence.

'Because!' she shouted back

'Because what?'

'Just because!' She thrust out her face, looking him straight in the eye.

'Who's looking after your daughter?'

'Never you mind – Sam's fine.'

Margot walked up to him and put one arm on his shoulder making Buck step back in surprise.

'What . . .' he began

'Look me in the eye, Buck, and tell me you're going to take me out to the island tomorrow. I don't care if you think I'm mad. I just have to do it.'

'That's not good enough,' he said. 'No way am I going back there. It's pointless. I'm not doing it.'

She dropped her arm and stepped back.

'I know it's a day out of your life, but for me it's the rest of my life,' she said. 'It's really important. I can't explain it. But if you want a real, real reason, here it is. I hardly saw the bloody island. I didn't have a chance to take a proper look at it. I know I can't walk every foot of the place but I need to do more out there. I am trying to find my husband's body. I have to go back. I need to. Badly, very badly.'

Buck stamped away from her across the lower deck. He breathed in deeply, looked out across the harbour to the ferry terminal, and then turned round.

'Damn,' he said. 'Damn, damn, damn.'

NINE

The *Antoine* left the next day at 8 a.m. under a silver-grey sky and with the barometer showing fair weather.

Buck and Margot did not speak once on the three-hour journey. Margot hunched up behind her dark glasses staring at the infinite waves ahead while Buck busied himself as usual with the radio and his charts; displacement activity, Margot said to herself. He doesn't need a chart for this trip. He just doesn't want to talk to me.

The tug slipped and rolled through a slight swell at just under its maximum speed of fifteen knots. To save fuel Buck should have been going more slowly, but he was fed up and wanted to get the whole thing over. He never should have got involved, never should have said yes. It wasn't even as if he was being paid for it. OK, she offered, but she knew he wouldn't take it.

He consoled himself with a stronger wozza than usual. The rum blunted his irritation. A lonely, lost woman looking for a dead man who wasn't going to be there. It was a shame, and he should be glad to be able to help someone in such distress.

He was about to point out the various sea birds that had attached themselves to the bubbling wake, but one look at the hunched figure in the cabin told him it would be a waste of time.

Just get me to this island, Margot was thinking. Let me have one good look around, and that's it, I'm out of here, out of the Cape, gone.

They reached the island at 11 a.m., and went through the same procedure as before. He'd be back on the next tide, at three. This time she was better prepared, with a strong waterproof coat, a torch and a whistle in her backpack. She let Buck pour a little rum into the Thermos. 'Good for the soul,' he said.

'And the fog? What do you think?'

They were almost the first words she had spoken to him that day.

'Don't know. Doubt it, though.' He sniffed loudly. 'Doesn't smell like fog to me, not cold enough.'

Margot had worked out her plan for the day. She would walk for two hours. That would take her past the seal beach she had seen and on to other larger beaches further along the island. She must have seen several thousand seals the day before yesterday, but that was only a fraction of the 250,000 supposedly on the island.

For an island that rises only thirty feet above sea level at it highest point and is only half a mile wide, Atlantic does not give itself easily to a visitor. Hidden hollows screened by gorse concealed small pools, the freshwater ponds the horses drank from, Margot guessed. Deep crevasses opened into gullies choked with wildflowers and brambles. The land rose and fell like a rumpled rug, much more so than was apparent from the sea. The changing contours and a succession of small ridges meant she rarely had a clear view to the end of the island. Distances were hard to calculate. As she walked she kept an eye out for the horses, still hoping to see those creatures of the fog under more normal circumstances.

She passed the beach where she had seen so many thousands of seals two days before. The sand was empty. There was not a seal in sight.

She stopped for lunch, sitting on her waterproof, eating tuna and sweetcorn sandwiches, swigging coffee straight from the Thermos and remembering how her father had insisted on taking a small primus stove on their family picnics to the beach at St Andrews. He could never be persuaded to take a Thermos, claiming that the tea tasted better when brewed on the spot. But actually the family knew he just loved messing around with the little stove and watching the kettle slowly come to the boil.

After walking for half an hour, Margot saw, half a mile away on the Atlantic side of the island, a deep bay between two headlands with a broad crescent-shaped beach covered in what looked like black sand. As she approached she saw that the dark sand was in fact seals, a huge rookery covering the entire beach, tens and tens of thousands of them, many more than she had seen on her previous visit.

Harbour and grey, as before. She walked quietly and slowly, working her way to a vantage point on one of the small headlands. She knew a seal rookery this size would have lookouts, but she could see none. Across the far side of the bay she could see some of the horses grazing, heads down, small, wiry animals, peaceful enough now.

The ground was damp but she decided to crawl the last 100 yards to a point on the slope below the headland leading to the beach. As she struggled through the heather and grass, she cursed herself for an act of stupid, emotional madness, a purely selfish desire to assuage grief, a melodramatic gesture to deep freeze the tangled emotions of misery and loss that she could not shed.

Grief, she thought. Grief for Leo? She lost Leo long ago. So what was she doing, crawling through the undergrowth on an island in the middle of the Atlantic just to peer at a million seals?

She stopped, fished the binoculars out of her backpack and leant forward on her elbows to scan the rookery.

As she moved the binoculars from one face to the next, she found the seals all looked exactly the same. She could tell the difference between young and old. She knew a harbour seal from a grey, and she could describe a harp seal in detail, but after twenty minutes working through half a mile of seals she found herself looking at one identikit whiskered face after another. Apart from the sheer numbers, this was very much a repeat of the previous fruitless exercise. And the fast-growing seal cubs really did look identical. How, Margot wondered, does a mother seal on the Arctic ice sheet recognise its pup among 5,000 others when returning with food from a hunt?

She could see the lookouts now. There were several on either headland and a few positioned among the gorse at the edge of the beach. They were older males, their coats scarred from long-ago battles, watching for predators. The wind was freshening and the sea growing choppier, turning wave tops into white horses that rolled in towards the beach. She spent another half an hour moving her binoculars from face to face, then rolled on to her back, cushioned her head on her waterproof and snoozed in the sun.

When she woke her face was hot, and probably burnt by the sun. She checked her watch: 2.30, time to go. She got to her feet and took one last look at the rookery.

And then she saw him.

With her own eyes she saw him.

He was partially concealed from view by the seals around him. Disbelief turned to shock. Lightheaded and giddy, she knelt down in the grass and fumbled for her binoculars.

He was burnt dark brown by the sun, his hair was matted and he had a thick beard. He was lying on his side, resting on one elbow, doing nothing, like the thousands of seals on the beach. He seemed naked, although it was hard to tell in the throng of seals; his eyes were half closed against the sun, and like the creatures around him he appeared asleep. She held the binoculars on him, twisting the lenses to focus more clearly. He was thin, almost emaciated, and there seemed to be cuts, some fresh, some healed, on his deeply sunburnt torso.

Still kneeling, she put the glasses aside and looked at him with her naked eyes. It was definitely him. She looked out to sea to make sure she wasn't dreaming, and then back again. Yes and yes. He was there. This was not an apparition, not a spectre conjured up by a demented widow's imagination, but the living and very obviously breathing person of her husband, the late Leo Kemp, now not so late, now alive among many thousands of seals.

She felt a surge of elation as she crawled forward, confirmation that buried deep in her subconscious had been the hope, or maybe the fear, that Leo had survived after all.

Margot was twenty yards from the outer line of seals and about seventy-five yards from Leo when she could bear it no longer. She stood up abruptly and shouted his name again and again. There was a ripple throughout the rookery as thousands of seals shifted to identify the source of the noise and assess the danger. Leo's head turned. For a second their gazes locked, his deep-set eyes holding hers, and then he looked away, seemingly uninterested. Then he turned again to look at her, his mind flipping through the photo album in his head. He knew who she was. Margot, the mother of Julian and Sam. She had stepped out of that compartment in his mind where he had carefully placed her and the children. She was no longer that photograph in the book.

The seals began to flop urgently towards the water, a mass of moving animals, folds of fat rippling along their shiny bodies as they levered themselves forward with their front flippers, using their strong claws to get traction on the sand.

Margot started to run towards the throng, her eyes fixed

on Leo. She threw off her backpack and ran skipping and jumping over the grass, heather and gorse, shouting his name, waving her arms.

He had got to his haunches and was looking at her, transfixed, as the beach and the rocks around him emptied of seals. She opened her arms as she ran, shouting, screaming his name.

Suddenly he moved in a low stooping run towards the water. Around him the seals were splashing into the sea and sliding in from the rocky outcrops at either end of the beach, their bodies, so sluggish on land, moving with balletic grace once they were in the water. Now Leo was in the sea with them. A flurry of spray, a splash of brown legs and he was gone, swimming strongly away from the shore, moving with ease through the waves.

Margot reached the water's edge and shouted after him: 'Sam loves you, she needs you. Come back!'

Leo turned in the water, his dark, shaggy head almost merging with the seals around and beyond him. The whole rookery was now in the water and heading out to sea. Leo broke away from the main body and swam parallel with the shore, twenty yards out. Margot ran to the first of the rocks, scrambled up it, and jumped and slithered from one to another to keep up with him.

She missed her footing and slipped, sliding down a sharply inclining slab of rock feet first into the sea, hands scrabbling at the seaweed in an attempt to stop going all the way in. Her shins were skinned and she was winded. She whimpered with pain as she dragged herself out of the water, heaving herself half upright and turning to look seaward. She was crying, tears running down her face. And then she began screaming, long, wordless screams of helpless rage.

After all this, he was leaving her again.

She never knew why, what instinct or memory had arisen within him, but Leo turned and began to swim towards her.

She shouted again: 'Sam needs you! Come back!'

Now the images were becoming clearer in his head. Sam, mouth full of pizza, face full of smiles, always teasing him for being *so* serious. 'If I was a seal, Dad, do you think you'd talk to me more?' Sam on the beach doing cartwheels into the sea, collapsing in the waves with a shriek; Sam with her hours of homework, head down over the kitchen table, asking endless questions: 'Dad, what exactly is a logarithm?'

Leo emerged from the water and stood upright, a lean, brown, naked figure with scars and scratches on his legs and upper body. He took long strides up the sloping rock towards her. When he reached her side he bent down and helped her up.

He stank. His whole body exuded the smell of raw, rotten fish. She recoiled involuntarily, putting a hand to her mouth and nose, and then flung herself at him, holding him as tight as she could. His arms remained fixed at his side, pinioned by her embrace. He wriggled free, and gently held her away from him.

'Come home,' she said looking into his unknowing, dark brown eyes sunk deep into their sockets.

Leo said nothing, but let her take him by the hand.

*   *   *

252

The *Antoine* docked at Coldharbor at six o'clock that evening. Nothing in his near seventy years at sea had prepared Buck for the moment when Margot led Leo up the gangplank. In shock he had become an automaton, backing the boat away from the small pier and turning her to head back to the Cape. The moment the *Antoine* was on course he had tried to talk to Leo. His friend's hollow eyes, the thousand-yard stare and the mute incomprehension of the world around him made communication impossible. It was as if Leo had stepped out of his nightmares and into his life, thought Buck.

Margot had begged Buck not to radio the news to the coastguard, and he had agreed. God knows what the coastguard would have said. He found it hard enough to come to terms with Leo's return after being missing at sea for six weeks and kept turning to look at the figure hunched in a blanket at the back of the cabin. It was Leo all right. At least, Buck thought, he wouldn't be carrying the guilt of his friend's death to his grave.

There was no one around to watch the *Antoine* nose into its mooring place at the Coldharbor pier and tie up that evening. Buck let down the boarding plank and watched as Leo emerged from the upper deck and climbed down the steps. He was shoeless and wearing Buck's sea jacket and a faded pair of beach shorts. An old baseball cap was jammed down over his matted hair. Buck put out a hand, and Leo took it to steady himself as he stepped ashore. The two men looked at each other wordlessly. Buck turned to Margot to say something, but she tapped a finger against her lips and shook her head. He pulled her aside anyway.

'You should take him to hospital. And you need to tell the coastguard.'

'He's coming home, and I'm telling no one till I get him there. Do me one last big favour, Buck. This is the last time I'll ask anything of you. Don't say a word just yet. I want to get him back home, and then we'll see.'

Buck grunted.

Leo walked to the Saab with an awkward, drunken gait. Buck waved as Margot drove off, and then crossed the road to the Dark Side. There was no more appropriate place to have a drink, a lot of drink, that night.

The story of Leo Kemp's survival after being missing for almost six weeks made headlines around the world. Sandy had broken the story on the *Herald*'s website, and had persuaded the editor to follow up with a special edition of the paper, which sold out across the Cape the following morning.

He had gone reluctantly to the Kemps' house the previous night, fearing that Margot had been drinking again. Her cryptic message had said: 'He's back, and I want you to handle the story.'

As he entered the house, Sandy smelt Leo before he saw him. The sight of his friend in a dressing gown, looking like the old man of the sea, was shocking. Leo half raised his hand, and Sandy noticed the long, curling fingernails. But it was the cloying, oily smell of old fish that confirmed where he had been for the past few weeks. Margot had warned him that Leo had yet to say anything, not one word. He refused to talk, shaking his head when

Margot pleaded with him for an explanation of where he had been and what he had been doing.

They looked at each other, and Sandy sat down. What do you say to a friend who has come back from the dead, and who sits there looking at you mute and apparently unconcerned about what has happened to him?

'You need a shave,' Sandy said. Leo smiled and nodded.

With a presence of mind for which he would later be profoundly grateful, Sandy borrowed Margot's small digital camera and took a quick couple of snaps of Leo before he was led away uncomplainingly to have a shower and what proved a long and difficult shave. He even allowed Margot to cut his hair.

Sandy went into the kitchen, poured himself a glass of white wine and sat down to work on the intro to his piece. He was never going to get a better story than this. Nobody was ever going to get a better story than this.

Six weeks after he was swept overboard in a sudden storm and presumed drowned, the well-known marine scientist Leo Kemp has been found alive and well on a remote island in the Atlantic.

When Leo emerged he did so as the old Leo, beardless, his hair cut, nails trimmed and a shy look of surprise on his face. The dank fish smell lingered on over the soap and aftershave, but the old man of the sea had gone.

He sat with Sandy, drinking coffee and listening politely to the repeated questions. But he didn't speak a word, merely shook his head and smiled. Sandy read him the opening paragraph of his story and looked at him for some reaction. There was none.

'Show us at least that you can make a noise,' he said. 'Make a sound.'

But Leo just shook his head, hunched his shoulders and sank back into himself.

The flashlight photograph of Kemp's dark, bearded face, his deep-set eyes gazing out from beneath a mass of tangled hair, was the image that went round the world. Sandy's story had gone with it, tagged 'world exclusive'. The photograph was to make him rich, a quick shot with a cheap borrowed camera of a man whose survival was widely proclaimed as miraculous. But there were no interviews, not so much as a quote, from the man at the centre of what quickly became a medical mystery story.

To Margot's relief Sam had been out with friends when she had brought Leo home that night. She could think of no better way of preparing her daughter for the biggest and best surprise of her life than by leaving a voice message on her cell phone telling her exactly that. So when Sam came bounding through the door she knew her father had come home, and accepted that fact with unquestioning joy.

'I knew you'd come back! I knew you'd come back!' was all she could say. In the teenage world where dreams merge with video games and TV sitcoms everything becomes possible, Margot reflected. She on the other hand had needed several glasses of wine when she had got Leo home even to begin to understand what had happened.

Over the next two days Sam attached herself to her father like a koala bear to a branch, hugging him constantly, sitting on his lap whenever she could, standing beside his chair as he read the papers and drank endless cups of coffee.

The doctors gave Leo extensive check-ups and reported that his physical health was fine, except for a dramatic weight loss of several stone. Blood tests were clear, and the function of the vital organs – heart, lungs, liver and kidneys – was excellent for a man in his early forties. But they told Margot that he was suffering from severe PTSD, post-traumatic stress disorder, and should on no account be questioned about his ordeal. She was warned that he would exhibit the classic symptoms of someone recovering from the trauma of a near-death experience: sudden and repeated night waking, panic attacks and flashbacks.

'And the treatment?' she asked.

No drugs could be prescribed. PTSD was usually treated by intensive one-to-one psychotherapy followed by group therapy sessions.

So that they could avoid the scrum of journalists camped outside the house the Institute arranged for the Kemps to move into accommodation within the Coldharbor campus, which could be closed off to outsiders. A visitors' apartment was made available with two bedrooms, a large open-plan kitchen-lounge area and a deck overlooking the sound.

Sam and her father spent their days on the deck playing Scrabble, reading and watching the boat traffic on the sound between Coldharbor and Martha's Vineyard. She hoped to awaken his memories by getting him to look at the fishing and tourist boats ploughing up and down. Leo happily spent hours looking at the boats on the water through binoculars. He smiled and hugged his daughter a lot, but still said nothing.

'Ordeal?' snorted Margot as she sat down with Jennifer at a hastily arranged WALL lunch. 'I don't think it was an ordeal. I think the whole thing was a mind trip, something he did subconsciously to deal with his dismissal. Don't tell me he got washed off that boat by accident. I'm sure Buck doesn't think so either.'

She and Jennifer were meeting as usual at the Quarterdeck, a rare occasion, as Jennifer said, on which the WALL club had actually managed a lunch.

'Trouble is,' Margot continued, 'I say that and immediately feel guilty. So it's double jeopardy. I have a husband who won't talk to me about his near-death experience, but who guilt-trips me when I wonder what was really going on in his head before he went off that boat. I can't win; I get it coming and going. I think I'm the one who's going through an ordeal.'

Jennifer suggested they share a bottle of wine, as it was her day off, but Margot insisted that they start with a kir, a glass of decent white with a splash of cassis which adds an alcoholic kick and turns the drink light pink. When drunk on an empty stomach a kir is a mood-altering experience that greatly enhances the meal that follows. At least that was Margot's theory.

Jennifer relaxed as she listened to her friend pour out her troubles. Margot was beginning to think that the man she had rescued was an impostor. She felt the real Leo was still out there with the seals. Her husband had become a stranger, someone who was perfectly pleasant but who remained mute, refusing all entreaties to discuss the one topic she and Sam and the rest of the world wanted to talk about. He spent his days reading, watching TV and drinking coffee. He seemed to regard the extensive press coverage about his reappearance as something that was happening to someone else.

Jennifer repeated what she had heard from the doctors at the Institute and the specialist who had come down from Boston. Post-traumatic stress can take many forms, and Leo was actually suffering from a relatively benign version. He was in denial about what had happened to him, and could not come to terms with it. That was quite normal.

'I don't do normal any more,' said Margot. 'Life isn't normal. Even Leo's symptoms aren't normal. He's supposed to suffer from screaming panic attacks at night, but he sleeps like a baby. There haven't been any signs of the flashbacks the doctors talked about. He just sits on the deck all day with Sam and says nothing.'

'Exactly,' said Jenny. 'He's internalising his emotions, refusing to communicate and rejecting the reality of what he's been through. A classic case of post-traumatic stress disorder.'

'You know what my problem is?' Margot said. 'I think I was happier when I thought he was dead. I'm not sure I can cope with him coming back like this. Isn't that awful?'

She began to cry, brushing the tears away with the back of her hand and then dabbing at her eyes with a napkin as the waitress brought their coffee.

Jennifer took Margot's hand in hers. 'As both your doctor and your friend, I'm telling you it's perfectly normal to feel like that. Leo is suffering a form of nervous breakdown, and you need to come to terms with that, just as you need to recognise that you've been deeply traumatised as well. Remember, you both have Sam, so hold her in your head and your heart, and work this out for her.'

Margot laughed. 'You should take a drink more often, doctor,' she said, fishing out a handkerchief and blowing her nose loudly.

In a slow news period the speculation about what had actually happened to the missing scientist filled feature pages and news websites, and inspired bloggers around the world.

The media collectively threw cold water on the assumption that Leo Kemp, the marine biologist who had passionately defended seals' cause against the fishing lobby, had gone overboard accidentally. All the evidence suggested that he had staged his disappearance as cover for a mission of which his Institute had disapproved. He had spent weeks on the ultimate research trip, living rough among the seal colonies of Cape Cod and Nantucket. The mission had lasted longer than planned; Leo had had a nervous breakdown in the wild, and had been rescued against all the odds by a faithful wife long after the rest of the world had assumed him dead. And now he was on the road to recovery.

This made good copy, but except for the nervous breakdown it was all nonsense, as Sandy Rowan tried to explain.

But due to Kemp's refusal to talk, there were very few verifiable facts. So the questions and the theories multiplied. No one could explain how Kemp had made the fifteen-mile journey across the sea to Atlantic Island. And how had he survived in the open for so long? Had he really been able to sustain himself on a diet foraged from the seashore? On the latter point the journalists and experts were on safe ground. Nutritionists agreed that it was perfectly possible to live on a diet of seaweed, shellfish and birds' eggs for months, provided there was access to fresh water.

When this question was discussed at the *Herald*'s daily conference, the editor suddenly remembered the trainee reporter who had been sent to try to survive on the beaches south of Provincetown. It had been his idea, and a very good one it was too. Readers loved reality journalism like that. So where was Lewis Chadwick? The editor threw the question out, and looked around to find his executives apparently engrossed in the agenda sheet.

There was a general silence. Sandy Rowan coughed and looked a little embarrassed. Apparently, he said, Lewis Chadwick had been seen in a McDonald's in Provincetown having a Big Mac and fries the day after he had been dropped off on the shoreline. When finally tracked down to his parents' home he explained that he had been told to use his initiative and he had done just that. Furthermore, he did not think that freezing to death on a Cape beach and trying to eat rock mussels for breakfast was any way to become a journalist. So he had resigned as a trainee. He had also said that his mother had written a sharp letter

261

to the owner of the *Herald* complaining about the treatment of her son.

'Brilliant. Anything else?' asked the editor irritably.

'Yes. He's going to enrol in drama school and become
an actor, apparently.'

The case of Lewis Chadwick did not prevent the *Herald*
from concluding that the experts were right. Providing
Leo had found access to water and had taken cover in
the long grass of the dunes during the chill nights, there
was no reason why he could not have survived for the six
weeks he had been missing.

Denied access to any member of the Kemp family, and
with the Coldharbor Institute refusing to comment, the
international media turned gratefully to Sandy Rowan for
interviews and background. He worked out that he had
given over a hundred radio, television and press interviews
in the week after Kemp had returned. He had tried to see
his old friend again, but Margot and the Institute were
adamant. Leo was seeing no one until he had recovered
sufficiently to begin talking about his experiences to his
doctors or within the family circle.

The story was given a further twist when the correspondent of a British television news channel revisited all the
statements about Leo's ability to survive for six weeks on
the Cape foreshore, and produced a new set of medical
experts who disputed the earlier conclusions. No one, they
said, could survive without assistance or supplies for such
a length of time, even in the summer. The television report
included an interview with Lewis Chadwick, in which the

former trainee reporter claimed to have been on the edge of collapse after only a day scouring remote beaches for food and water. Chadwick said that survival would be impossible in such circumstances, and added that he would be suing his former employers for placing him in such jeopardy. His performance convinced Sandy that he had been right to choose an acting career.

The British reporter concluded with considerable fanfare that the entire disappearance had been staged by Mr Kemp in order to draw attention to his crusade about the culling of seals and the overfishing on the Stellwagen Bank. He had been secretly supplied with provisions by 'friends' – for legal reasons the programme was careful to exempt Margot from collusion in the conspiracy – and had been conveniently found alive and well when his publicity aims had been achieved.

Sandy put out a statement from the Kemp family denouncing the story as media fabrication and threatening legal action. In any case, the caravan of journalists camped out around the Cape had moved on. Leo Kemp's inability to give any indication of what had happened to him – or his wilful refusal to do so, no one could work out which – and the family's firm 'No comment' to all questions left them with little else to do but repeat themselves. Gradually, other stories drew them away.

TEN

The doctors had told Margot that Sam was the key with which to unlock Leo's frozen mind. And so it proved. Two weeks after his return, Sam offered him some more coffee while they were sitting on the deck as usual after breakfast. She stroked the side of his face and, putting her face close to his, whispered: 'Dad, I want to show you something.'

The painting of Leo and the seals had been placed above the mantelpiece in the sitting room, but he had shown no interest in it and Margot had decided not to point it out to him. He would surely notice it and remark upon it in his own good time. As for the godwit painting, that might raise the awkward subject of the funeral, so Margot had hidden it in a bedroom wardrobe.

Sam had other ideas. She fetched the portrait and set it against the wooden railing of the deck.

'Look, Dad,' she said, stepping away to allow him a clear view.

Leo frowned and peered at the painting. If he recognised his image in the half-smiling man standing on a rocky foreshore with a scatter of seals behind him, he did not show it.

'Look, Dad. That's you there, and the seals. You remember the seals? You studied them; you talked about them all the time . . .'

Sam startled her father by jumping across the deck and sinking to a kneeling position at his feet. She took his hands in hers.

'In fact, Dad, you became a bit of a seal bore. Do you know that? In a nice way, of course. A nice seal bore. You remember, don't you? The seals? I'll bet you remember everything, really? You remember taking me to that pizza parlour when the little girl at the next table was sick all over the place? You remember taking me to the aquarium at Coldharbor and telling me about that talking seal? You do remember, Dad, I know you do.'

She was pleading with him now, looking into those sunken, unknowing eyes. He shifted his gaze back to the painting and began to look at it more closely. She laid a hand on his arm, and could almost feel his memory stirring. It was like watching a deep covering of snow slowly sliding off a roof in spring as a thaw weakened the grip of a long hard winter. And she was the sun, breaking through the frozen darkness of his mind.

'Dad,' she said. 'Look at the painting and tell me you remember. I know you do.'

He got up and knelt down in front of the painting, frowning as he looked at his own likeness with that quirky half-smile and then at the finely detailed painting of the seals; even in the background their whiskers could be seen sparkling with water droplets. He stood up and stepped back, staring at the whole composition: a man, some seals and wind-ruffled water.

He made as if to speak, and then shook his head.

But Sam knew he had remembered. She knew it wouldn't be long.

That afternoon the two of them went for a long walk down Surf Drive Beach to Falmouth's inner harbour, and then circled back along Main Street past the fire station, Betsey's Diner and the book store. At the village green they paused to rest on Julian's bench, where Sam talked of the longing she felt for her lost brother.

They finished up in the Coffee Obsession on the corner of Route 28. Sam handed Leo the menu and watched as he studied it. He looked up at the sound of a familiar voice. Gunbrit Nielson, Jacob Sylvester and Rachael Ginsberg had just come in and were settling down two tables away.

Gunbrit saw them, and rose to her feet, looking slightly shocked at the sight of her old lecturer. She hesitated, but Sam motioned her over.

'Dad, this is one of your students. You remember . . .'

'Gunbrit Nielsen, Mr Kemp. It's good to see you again. How are you?'

Leo stood up, looked at her, nodded his head and said slowly: 'It's good to see you again, Gunbrit. We must talk soon.' He turned to Sam, smiled, and said, 'Let's go home, darling.'

That evening father and daughter sat and talked for hours. It was if a spell had been broken, Sam said later. Leo began by saying how sorry he was to have caused everyone such distress. Margot joined them, quietly taking a seat on the deck, anxious not to break into their conversation.

Leo knew where he had been and how he had survived. He had lost track of time, he said, although otherwise he felt fine and mentally fit. But he would not explain how he had survived, or why had he not simply walked across the dunes to safety, to his home and his family.

This was the question that Sam would return to again and again. Did he not realise what pain they had been through? How could he have done that to them?

The psychiatrists had told Sam and Margot that when Leo finally started talking they would feel angry with him, and that it was right to express that anger – up to a point. Once he understood their pain, they were told, he would begin to go back in his mind and unlock the secrets of where he went, what he did – and why.

Faced with Sam's questioning and her occasional flashes of irritation at his refusal to clarify the details of what he had been through, Leo responded by putting his arms around her and holding her tightly in long, silent hugs.

'I can't tell you how sorry I am that you've suffered,' he said. 'But I can't explain it. I didn't mean this to happen. I didn't want it to happen. But when it did, it felt the most natural thing on earth. It felt like the right thing to do. Forgive me, but I can't tell you any more.'

And that was how they left it. Leo refused to talk to anyone else, and he would say no more about his missing weeks.

A week after he had regained his speech and his memory, Leo received a hand-delivered letter from Tallulah Bonner. He was spending the morning, as he did every day, drinking coffee and reading the papers on the deck. He opened the letter, scanned it briefly and handed it to Margot.

'Bonner. She'd like to see me. Congratulates me on my survival, and all that.'

Margot read the letter and sat down beside him. She put an arm around him, and felt him stiffen slightly.

'Well, I think you should see her, shouldn't you? There's no harm in hearing what she has to say.'

'She'll probably offer me my job back.'

'Really?' The thought surprised and slightly alarmed Margot. 'And would you take it?'

'No. I've been dismissed. I'm going to stay dismissed.'

'Not even for the students?'

'Not even for them.'

'They call every day, you know. Gunbrit seems to be their spokeswoman.'

'Gunbrit Nielsen. I met her in the café last week. I remember her.'

'They remember you, too. You know they commissioned a painting for you?'

'A painting?'

'Yes, they gave it to me at the service. The service to celebrate your life.'

She watched as he registered the remark. He had accepted the fact that his funeral had taken place, and had signed the letters Margot had written to apologise for the distress the occasion might have caused to those who had attended. But he had never returned to the subject, and the doctors had advised her not to raise it again. Concentrate on his past life, they said. Now that he's talking, help him build his memory back to the present by reawakening memories of his childhood and his early teaching days.

They told her to treat him like a patient who was slowly emerging from the anaesthetic after a major operation. His faculties were returning gradually after Sam had managed to jolt his memory into life, but his biggest challenge still lay ahead: to make sense of what had happened to him. He had to explain that to himself, and it might take years.

That was all very well, thought Margot, but the time had come to try to get Leo to understand what had happened to him. Sam had shown the way.

She brought the painting out to show him: a watercolour of a godwit on a foreshore, with a flock of other waders in the background.

'This was from the students?'

'Yes.'

'It's done well. The plumage is just right. Who did it?'

'They got Mrs Gulliver to do it, the same woman who did the other painting.'

He peered at the signature and said, 'Good for Gloria.'

'Gloria'? thought Margot. Mrs Gulliver was 'Gloria'? And then she caught the expression on his face, the remembrance and reflection of sensuous pleasure.

And suddenly she knew: those late nights at the art classes. That's why he had come back, tired and happy for a change, flecked with paint and smelling of wine. That's why he had always gone straight to the shower – to wash off her lipstick traces, her smell, the scent of her bed, her sex. That's why.

All the old anger returned as she looked at him, this damaged husband of hers, half man, half what: seal?, who even before he had thrown himself into the sea – oh, sure, that's what he did – was betraying her with Gloria fucking Gulliver.

She walked inside without saying a word, fished a cigarette from her handbag and returned to the deck smoking. He hated her smoking anywhere near the house. Tough luck.

Stay calm, she told herself. After all, you can hardly complain, can you? Think about it.

Leo was watching her calmly, seemingly unaware of the turmoil he had caused by the use of Gloria's first name.

'So will you see her?' said Margot, her voice hard and angry.

'Who?' Leo had lost track of the conversation, and was staring at the distant outline of Martha's Vineyard.

'Tallulah Bonner.'

'Sure. Why not?'

*　　*　　*

271

Margot had refused to allow any photographers near her husband, and had not given out any family pictures. Apart from Sandy's snapshot, the photographs the press had used of Leo were all issued by the Institute. They showed him at various stages of his career, the most recent having been taken a year ago with staff colleagues outside the aquarium. Sandy's photograph of Leo's bearded face with a vacant, haunted stare made a perfect before and after contrast with the images of the neat, well-dressed academic.

When Tallulah Bonner sat down across the dining table from Kemp, she was shocked by the change in him. He must have lost three stone or more, she thought.

'How do you feel, Leo?'

'Fine, but I'm having to work a few things out.'

'Good. I'm here to help if I can, and I want you to know that your colleagues all send their best wishes.'

'Thank you.'

'When you're better, we'd like you back, if you'll come.'

'Why, Mrs Bonner?'

'Tallulah, please, Leo. Why? There's a long story and a short story. The long story is management waffle about you being a great teacher who's been through a hell of an experience, and we'd like to get you back doing what you do so well. Oh yes, and the Institute was too zealous about protecting its own image and reputation.'

'And the short story?'

She looked down at the table and clasped her hands as if to say grace.

'It was a stupid mistake. I made it, the Board agreed with it, and I'm sorry.'

There was a faint smile on Leo's face. Margot stood up, went into the kitchen and put on the kettle.

Tallulah raised her head and looked at Leo.

'Big places like Coldharbor need to be tested, questioned, held to account,' she said. 'That's why we need people like you.'

'You mean awkward bastards?'

'If you like, Leo.' She laughed and he smiled.

He thanked her for the offer, but pointed out that he had become something of a celebrity, at the centre of a big news story. A Coldharbor scientist gets fired from the job he loves, goes missing at sea, is presumed dead, comes back from the grave and gets his old job back. That was quite a story for Coldharbor, wasn't it?

She knew what he was trying to say. Was this just another brand-burnishing stunt to build the Coldharbor profile? Bring the prodigal son back into the fold and reap the PR rewards?

'It's not the story we're interested in. It's you.'

'I'm famous, you know. My story's made headlines all around the world. Some people think I'm a conman – that seems to be the general view among the media. That would hardly help the Institute, would it? Or would it?'

Tallulah felt a flash of irritation. Kemp's arrogance had obviously survived his ordeal.

'I'm sure we would cope. These things die down. And one day you'll write a book and it will all begin again. We'll cope with that, too.'

'I doubt it. About the book, I mean.'

Leo paused. He couldn't but feel a sneaking liking for Tallulah. There was something of the ante-bellum Southern belle about that voice, the fading good looks, the determined jut of her jaw.

'OK,' he said. 'I'm not coming back, although I thank you for the offer. But I'd like to see my students again. I put them though a lot.'

The Institute announced the next day that Leo Kemp had declined to resume his teaching position in order to spend time recovering with his family. The choice had been his, the statement was careful to make clear. However, the Institute was very pleased to announce that he would give a farewell lecture.

Tallulah Bonner and the Institute management went to great lengths to keep the date and time of the lecture a secret. There were to be no journalists at the event. Tallulah had personally told the students that the occasion must not be turned into the kind of media circus they had witnessed over the past few weeks. The important thing was for Leo to get well. The students dutifully agreed, but inevitably the story leaked out.

The day before the lecture, the *Cape Herald* carried the story under the headline 'Will the Mystery Be Solved?' with the sub-deck, 'Kemp breaks silence in last lecture to class'.

The night before the lecture, every one of the thirty postgraduate students in Kemp's class received emails and text messages offering cash incentives for an immediate account of what he said. The amount of cash was not spelt out but the reporters told the students they could meet them at various bars and cafés in Falmouth and Coldharbor.

They all declined.

The main lecture hall of the marine biology department at Coldharbor holds 180 people. There had been an argument about whether Leo should address only his class, or a wider community of his colleagues and other students. In the end, he was left to decide.

'Sure, let them all come,' he said to Tallulah Bonner. 'What have I got to hide?'

She laughed, and then he laughed, for the first time in a long time.

The tiered seats, which had mostly been empty the last time Leo took the podium, were now full. Margot and Sam sat in the front row, flanked by Tallulah Bonner and other members of the faculty. There was no problem getting the audience's attention this time. Every eye was on him. He started with a joke, Sandy Rowan's idea.

'Great to see you all here. I should get swept away more often.'

There was nervous laughter.

'Firstly, I want to thank my students for the painting of the godwit. It's nice to know you listened to something I said in class.'

His students laughed.

'Of course, I'm embarrassed by it, because it was given under false pretences. But I hope you'll let me keep it.'

Gunbrit, who was sitting near the front, mouthed the words '*of course*' at him and gave him a thumbs-up. He gave a small wave of thanks.

'When I last spoke in this lecture theatre I began by saying that we humans are defined not by what we know, but by what we don't know. I said that science has no final frontiers, and it never will have. Beyond the known world, which we understand because science can explain it to us, lies another world, a mysterious world, which science cannot explain.

'Where I have been recently is in that strange place beyond science, beyond our immediate comprehension. I am not going to explain to you, or to anyone, what happened to me there. You will have read many stories and heard many theories. I am not going to comment on any of them. Those weeks have been described as a mystery. They are a mystery to me as well. I know exactly what happened, and what I did, and what I saw, but I cannot rationally explain those things. That does not mean that they did not happen or cannot be explained. They can and will be, as we move into the next age of knowledge.

'I will just repeat – and forgive me, those of you who have heard this before – in your studies, wherever they may take you, as in your life, take nothing for granted. Be humbled by what you don't know. Work hard to increase your knowledge. And remember Galileo. He took the sword of science to the obvious, the conventional, the accepted wisdom of his day. It was considered self-evident when he was a young man in sixteenth-century Tuscany that man was at the centre of the universe, and that the sun circled the earth. Galileo challenged that certainty, and in so doing he challenged a belief system that had underpinned human existence for centuries. He used science to overturn the wisdom of the day on astronomy, mathematics and engineering. He redefined man's place in the universe.

'Remember that if you do that – and I hope I can say *when* you do that – they'll get you, just as they got Galileo. He was hauled before the Inquisition and forced under threat of torture to recant. Therefore, be very careful before you use your science, the body of knowledge that we have acquired over millennia, to dismiss the unknown.'

Leo told them that more than 95 per cent of the ocean floor was only beginning to be charted. Scientists had discovered huge and powerful submarine flows, currents that were reshaping the world down there and could power the world up here. They were discovering holes in the ocean floor the size of Yankee Stadium, evidence of giant underwater avalanches that were still going on, creating mountains and sending us tsunamis, storms and sudden waves of the kind that had swept him away.

Why was he telling them this? Because mankind needed to be reminded that this was a water planet. There were six billion people in the world, and soon there would be nine billion. They couldn't all fly to Mars and find a new life. They had to survive here on this earth, and to do that they would need the oceans around and below us.

Water, power and food flowed from our seas. If we didn't understand that, we might soon be retracing our evolutionary footsteps back to the slime from which we emerged.

He stopped. As usual he felt he had said too much, gone on too long. He looked at the faces in the audience. Tallulah Bonner, the Board and the Dean all looked as if they had sat through one of those overlong, embarrassing wedding speeches by a drunken best man. But his students looked rapt. They couldn't take their eyes off him.

He'd settle for that.

There was a loud pop as he turned to leave the podium. Margot and Sam appeared at his side with an overflowing bottle of champagne and three glasses. They both kissed him.

A voice from the audience, a voice he recognised as that of Jacob Sylvester, shouted: 'Mr Kemp! Mr Kemp! If you're not going to tell us what happened to you, are you going to tell someone? Or write a book about it?'

'I don't know.'

Another voice, this time Gunbrit Nielsen. 'You could call it *My Life as a Seal*!'

'Maybe.' He laughed and waved in a half-salute. 'Goodbye, and good luck.'

He was about to leave the podium, but he stopped and turned back.

'One thing I forgot to say. I won't be teaching here any more, but I would like to say to my students, wherever you go, and whatever you do, I want to hear about the huge mistakes you make and the triumphs you achieve. Trust me, you will do both.'

There was applause as he headed for the door with Margot and Sam. Gunbrit caught up with him, holding out a notebook for him to sign. He thanked her for taking so much trouble over the painting.

Tallulah Bonner would not let him go without a final word. They shook hands, and for the first time in their acquaintance he thought she looked embarrassed as she thanked him and said goodbye.

Margot, Leo and Sam collected Beano and drove to Surf Drive Beach, an old family favourite because it lacked the amenities that brought the crowds and could be reached by a good cycle track, the Shining Path, from Falmouth. They left their shoes in the car and walked barefoot on the sand, Beano bounding ahead of them.

Leo bent down and picked up a piece of dark brown driftwood with an almost perfect crescent shape. 'Just like a boomerang,' he said. 'We were always chucking these things around as kids.'

'And did they come back?' asked Margot.

'Sure. Watch.'

He ran a few steps to the edge of the water and flung the piece of wood as far as he could. It scythed through the air, made as if to turn, then dropped into the sea. He walked back to Margot and Sam as Beano bounded into the waves after it.

Just beyond the wave line, about twenty-five yards from the shore, a pod of seals broke the surface, their heads pointing enquiringly in all directions. Leo stopped and watched them.

They were harbour seals, which had probably chased a shoal of sand eels towards the shore. People on the beach had noticed them, and were pointing them out to each other.

'Dad, can I swim out there?' a boy asked his father.

'No,' came the firm reply.

Beano bounded out of the water and ran up to them, showering droplets everywhere as he shook himself. Margot and Sam protested, but Leo ignored him and started walking towards the sea.

Margot took a few steps after him, but then noticed the seals and stood still. Leo walked straight into the sea as she watched, mesmerised. Sam was chasing Beano around her but stopped as she noticed her mother staring out to sea. Around them beach life went on as usual, some kids with a ball, a couple sitting on a rug and beginning a picnic, sunbathers, walkers and a few people splashing in the shallows.

The water was now almost up to Leo's waist. Margot shaded her eyes against the sun, watching him and the group of seals beyond.

The seals were quite close to Leo now. He bent down, and when he straightened up the boomerang was in his hand. He threw it forcefully towards the pod. They vanished from sight as it splashed into the water a few feet away from them.

He came out of the sea in quick strides, took Margot's outstretched hand, curled his arm around Sam's waist and walked up the beach.

EPILOGUE

Leo Kemp never resumed his teaching post at Coldharbor. Just before Christmas that year, he, Margot and Sam moved back to Scotland, where he had been offered a senior lectureship in his old department, the Sea Mammal Research Unit at St Andrews University.

He consistently refused all media interviews and offers from publishers to write a book about his experiences.

Margot returned to teaching, taking a job at a school in Dundee. Six months after their return to Scotland she and Leo began divorce proceedings, citing irreconcilable differences.

Sam settled in at her mother's school. The following year she would do well in her Advanced Higher exams, which secured her a place studying marine biology at St Andrews University.

That spring Leo, Margot and Sam returned to Cape Cod for the wedding of Sandy Rowan and Jenny Hathaway.

The ceremony took place in Sandy's vineyard, by special dispensation.

Sandy gave a speech in which he said that the only man happier than he that day was the bookseller in Orleans to whom he had sold over 50,000 second-hand books for a ridiculously low price. A man could make no greater sacrifice, he said, than to lay down his library for his bride.

In June that year Leo led an expedition to North Ronaldsay in the Orkneys to study the many seal colonies on the northern tip of the island. He took three senior students from the marine biology department with him. They were equipped with the latest hydrophones and recording equipment, and they camped beside a small bay at Dennis Head, near the Old Beacon lighthouse. A number of harbour and grey seal rookeries were close by. Unusually for those remote islands in the North Sea, the weather that year was very good. On the long summer evenings there were only a few hours of twilight around midnight. In those hours the night sky was lit up as the Aurora Borealis threw long phosphorescent sheets of pink, blue and green light over the northern horizon.

Leo spent most days with his team on the water, working from two rigid inflatable rubber dinghies. Technical advances now meant that small hydrophones, each carrying a large number of sensors, enabled communications between seals to be recorded over greater distances and at greater depths than had previously been possible. The Orkneys were prime territory for this kind of research. The water was clear and clean and the local seal population was frequently increased by visitors.

Leo and his team were able to plot the underwater positions of seals and listen in to communications between them at a depth of 80 to 100 feet. The calm seas and long sunlit days meant that they were able to gather an unusually large amount of data. In the evenings they analysed that day's recordings and mapped the movement of the seals. Leo told them the story of the war-winning intelligence that Roosevelt and Churchill derived from the code-breakers at Bletchley Park in Buckinghamshire during the Second World War, and said that this was the Bletchley Park moment of his career.

After three weeks he wrote a detailed handwritten report claiming a breakthrough in understanding the nature and meaning of seal communication. The long, rumbling underwater signals that flowed between the seals at the northern tip of Ronaldsay and other rookeries many miles distant were beginning to reveal their secrets.

The Aurora Borealis, or 'Merry Dancers' as the lights were called by the islanders, was unusually brilliant on the final night of the expedition. Leo told his team they were a celestial celebration in tribute to their research. The four of them lay back on the heather, watching the heavenly fireworks, drinking Orkney's Highland Park malt whisky and working out what they would do after they won the Nobel Prize. One of the students said later that he had never seen Leo Kemp looking so happy.

As the light faded after midnight Leo left the camp,

telling the students he was going to make a short boat trip around the headland to check the position of some hydrophone marker buoys. The sea was calm, and shimmered in a ghostly half-light. He took a two-way radio with him.

At around 12.30 a.m. Leo radioed back to say he had retrieved two sets of hydrophones, and was approaching a crowded seal colony about a mile from the lighthouse. It was the last signal his colleagues received from him. He never returned to camp. Radio calls the next morning went unanswered. The empty dinghy was found that afternoon floating on a calm sea.

Despite extensive searches on sea and land, Leo Kemp's body was never found.

ACKNOWLEDGEMENTS

I would like to thank the following for the help and support they have given me in the making of this book. Needless to say I take full responsibility for the facts drawn from my research into marine science which forms the backdrop to much of the narrative.

Peter Tyack, senior scientist at the Woods Hole Oceanographic Institute, Cape Cod.

Mike Fedak, Professor at the Marine Mammal Research Unit, St Andrews University.

Dr Susan Whiten, senior lecturer in the Bute Medical School, St Andrews University, where she spends much of her spare time diving in the chilly waters of the Firth of Forth in the company of seals.

Tecumseh Fitch, Professor of Cognitive Biology, University of Vienna.

Peter Corkeron, Visiting Fellow at the Bioacoustics

James MacManus

Research Program, Cornell Laboratory of Ornithology and Sophie van Parijs, leader of the Large Whale Group at the North East Fisheries Science Centre, Woods Hole. Peter and Sophie are a husband and wife team who live in Woods Hole, Cape Cod, and who very generously shared their time and knowledge with me during my research there in the spring of 2007.

Dr Martin Scurr of London, who helped me to understand how Leo Kemp survived for such a long period on the fruits of the Cape Cod foreshore.

David and Susan Balderstone, who are both old friends from my days as a Middle East correspondent based in Beirut and who now live in Melbourne. They gave me invaluable background into Leo Kemp's life as a young boy growing up in Mornington.

The Editor of the *Cape Cod Times*, Paul Pronovost, who patiently answered by seemingly endless queries about life and times on the Cape today.

Jo Fitzbak, who took me out to view the seal population off Chatham harbour and talked with great insight into the problems of the fishing industry.

Robert Lacey of HarperCollins kindly read the manuscript first and suggested many changes which were hugely helpful.

Clare Hey, who as my editor at HarperCollins came up with all the right ideas and patiently dealt with my occasional objections to them.

Caroline Johnston, who helped as ever with tea and sympathy when the darkness descended.

Above all to my agent Sophie Hicks, who loved this

286

book from the start and made sure that I finished it. I could not have written it without her help and encouragement.

Finally heartfelt thanks to my wife Amanda without whom this book would not have been written and to Emily, Elizabeth and Nicholas for urging me to tell them endless bedtime stories all those years ago.

AUTHOR NOTE

This book arose from a fantasy that has entertained me from childhood, a dream of escape into the sea that remains with me to this day. The dream took shape when I was a young boy in the early 1950s. Very few people in Britain went abroad for holidays at that time and, like almost everyone we knew, our family would spend three weeks of the summer in a series of delightful but all too often chilly and rainy seaside resorts – Thorpeness and Aldeburgh in Suffolk, Bembridge in the Isle of Wight and West Wittering in Sussex being the favourites.

The things that delighted my brothers and I when small – crabbing, sandcastles and eating sugary clouds of candyfloss – did not really appeal as we grew into teenagers. We could not follow our father into the pub where he spent much of his time nor did we share his passion for sailing. Dad was frankly dangerous in a dinghy and we always seemed to end up in the water. At least twice I can recall being hauled from Bosham Harbour by the lifeboat.

As the annual seaside holiday lost its magic, and teenage angst took the form of rebellion against everything my parents stood for, I began to dream of escape. I would walk into the waves, swim towards the rim of the sea and magically become a seal, ever more to roam the oceans, sliding through the waves, impervious to storms and a playful spectator of passing ships.

Always in that dream I would look back at the distant shore to see my parents and brothers on the beach and feel no sense of loss at all. Indeed, it was an essential part of the fantasy to turn my back on the world I had known and swim over the horizon to whatever awaited me there.

We never saw seals on our summer holidays but visits to London Zoo had shown me sea lions, extraordinary creatures with whiskery faces, sleek wet-leather skin and big dark eyes. Above all it was the way they moved that appealed to a young imagination. They had bodies like Plasticine, bending, twisting and turning as they dived for the keeper's fish and swam back to the large rock that former the centrepiece of the old seal enclosure. The sea lions were from California, naturally enough, and much in demand in zoos and circuses because of their ability to perform tricks such balancing balls on their snouts. Sea lions and seals are from related, but different, species but that didn't matter to me. The sea lions of London Zoo imprinted themselves on my mind and from an early age they became my means of escape. I clung to that dream as some children to a favourite blanket or soft toy.

When I decided to turn this childhood dream into a story and create fiction from fantasy, the obvious starting point for the research was St Andrews in Scotland, which hosts the Sea Mammal Research Unit, a major centre in Britain for the study of seals and other marine creatures. It also happens to be my old university. At St Andrews, Professor Mike Fedak and Dr Tecumseh Fitch, both experts in the behaviour and history of seals (among much else I should say), gave me three crucial pieces of intelligence which shaped this book:

Firstly the high intelligence of seals has enabled them to develop a language of trills, clicks, grunts and bell like tones by which they communicate underwater with their own species across many miles of ocean. Seals are highly vocal creatures and their jaw structure is such that in at least one famous case they can mimic human speech.

Secondly, Professor Fedak explained how the history of these creatures is interwoven with that of homo-sapiens in a long, cruel relationship from which mankind benefited enormously. When early man moved north from the African landmass into the colder climes of what is now northern Europe 60,000 years ago, it was seals that made the migration possible. They were easy prey for the club-wielding hunters and provided blubber from which to make candles, skins for clothing, and musky flesh for high protein food. This is why seals figure prominently on cave drawings that can still be seen today in Scandinavia. From that time the killing of seals never stopped and by the nineteenth century it had become a major industry in Europe and America. The killing goes on today carried out by the Canadians and various Scandinavians countries driven by commerce and with the dubious justification of conserving fish stocks.

Finally, I learnt that evolution is not something that happened a long time ago. It continues to transform our own racial characteristics and those of the animals around us. Brown bears scooping salmon from the estuaries and rivers of North America are following the same path to the sea that seals took millions of years ago. The ancestors of seals roamed the land as small dog like creatures some 30 million years ago before man had evolved from his ancestors, the chimpanzee and orang-utan. They sought their food from the rich stocks of fish along river banks and coastal waters and over millions of years evolved into aquatic creatures like small otters, equally at home in land or water. Then a mere six million years ago, evolution led to them to became sea marine mammals with webbed feet and a thick coat of blubber. Seals had become the sea animals we know today about the same time that early man descended from tree life in the forests and stood upright on the African savannah. But unlike the whales, whose ancestors left land 100 million years ago, seals never fully became marine mammals. They still had to bear their young on land or, more usually, the icepack. That incomplete evolutionary cycle proved a bounteous gift to homo-sapiens as he moved north from the savannah.

What struck me most about my research in Scotland

was the evidence that seals were highly complicated and intelligent creatures with almost human characteristics. Tecumseh Fitch, whose first names derives from his great, great, great grandfather, the celebrated American Civil War General, William Tecumseh Sherman (who himself was named after a famous Indian chief), believes the language of seals creates music much as humpback whales do with their singing. As with whales, the challenge is to decode the lyrical submarine conversations with which seal colonies communicate deep under the ocean.

Mike Fedak, with whom I had lunch after his final lecture before retirement, and who was suitably buoyed by celebratory champagne, talked of seals as stylish, playful and curious creatures, very much determined to do things their way. One example he gave was the way seals deal with their enemies according to circumstance: in the Galapagos islands, when in great numbers, seals will mob and confuse shark predators; but in northern waters they will defend themselves from killer whales, by hiding in the roar and tumble of the surf thus jamming the echo locating sonar of their ancient foe. That was incredible to me. The clown-like characters in the London Zoo suddenly had become the highly intelligent citizens of the oceans, survivors of a continuing slaughter that had been, and is now, driven by commercial greed.

In the mid-nineteenth century, before the invention of kerosene, the lamps of Europe and North America were lit by oil from seal blubber. About that time, the first bicycle riders rested their bottoms on saddles covered in rubbery sealskin. As the bone-jarring two-wheelers became hugely popular around the world, so the demand for seal saddle covers soared.

As I write this in the summer of 2009 Reuters News Agency reports from Toronto that hundreds of villages in Atlantic Canada are feeling a sharp economic downturn from the European Union's ban in July on the import of seal products. Depressed prices for pelts meant that many hunters didn't bother to take part in the annual seal cull this year so that only 72,156 harp seals were killed against a quota of 280,000 animals. What caught my eye was not the large numbers involved but a complaint by a lobbyist for the seal industry. Canada, he said, would no longer be able to meet growing European demand for Omega 3 fish oil of which seals provided a rich source. The oil that once lit the lamps of Europe was now being used as a health supplement for heart disease.

My research at St Andrews led me inevitably to Cape Cod where the Woods Hole Institute of Oceanography is one of the world-leading centres for marine research. From Dr Peter Tyack, a senior scientist at the Institute, I learnt just how much we don't know about the oceans that cover four-fifths of the world's surface and the marine mammals that live in them. We are only scratching the surface of our knowledge about the behaviour of the animals with which we share this planet. Whether it be the extraordinary dance of the honey bees, the melodic singing of humpback whales or the rattle and clickety-click of seal talk, the science of animal behaviour is far from reaching any frontiers.

Finally it was my good fortune to meet Sophie Van Parijs and her husband Peter Corkeron who proved such enthusiastic guides to my research. Both are marine scientists and it was through them that I came to appreciate the extraordinary passion with which men and women study the behaviour of our marine mammals, seals, dolphins and whales, and the oceans in which they live.

The book is, of course, a novel but I have tried to ensure that the marine science in the story is accurate. I should say again that none of those who I have talked to is responsible for the inevitable inaccuracies or arguable interpretations of facts. Nor indeed have I drawn on any of them for the characters who were well formed in my mind before I began the book. I have, after all, had long enough to think about them.

What's next?

Tell us the name of an author you love

| James MacManus | Go ▶ |

and we'll find your next great book.